Gregory Matthews, the head of the family, is found dead – apparently from nicotine poisoning. He was not a likeable personality, then neither are the other members of the family circle – his two sisters, Harriet parsimonious and domineering, and Gertrude an incurable busybody; the maudlin Zoë, his sister-in-law, with her children, Guy and Stella, and his nephew and heir, Randall, who is the smoothest of smooth young men. Superintendent Hannasyde has to fight his way through a *double* lot of trouble before he can provide a solution to the mystery.

By the same author

April Lady
Arabella
Bath Tangle
Beauvallet
Black Moth
Black Sheep
A Blunt Instrument
Charity Girl
Civil Contract
The Conqueror
Convenient Marriage
The Corinthian
Cotillion
Cousin Kate
Death in the Stocks
Detection Unlimited
Devil's Club
Duplicate Death
Envious Casca
False Colours
Faro's Daughter
Footsteps in the Dark
The Foundling
Frederica
Friday's Child

Grand Sophy
Infamous Army
Lady of Quality
The Masqueraders
No Wind of Blame
The Nonesuch
Penhallow
Pistols for Two
Powder and Patch
Quiet Gentleman
Regency Buck
Reluctant Widow
Royal Escape
Spanish Bride
Sprig Muslin
Sylvester (The Wicked
    Uncle)
Talisman Ring
These Old Shades
They Found Him Dead
Toll-gate
The Unfinished Clue
Unknown Ajax
Venetia
Why Shoot a Butler?

GEORGETTE HEYER

Behold, Here's Poison

GRAFTON BOOKS

A Division of the Collins Publishing Group

LONDON GLASGOW
TORONTO SYDNEY AUCKLAND

Grafton Books
A Division of the Collins Publishing Group
8 Grafton Street, London W1X 3LA

Published by Grafton Books 1963
Reprinted nine times
9 8 7

First published in Great Britain by
Hodder & Stoughton Ltd 1936
New edition published by
William Heinemann Ltd 1954

ISBN 0-586-02723-8

Printed and bound in Great Britain by
Collins, Glasgow

Set in Times

To
Doctor F. C. Ford
Affectionately

1

It was going to be a fine day. There was a white mist
curling away in wreaths over the Heath that told Mary,
standing on the half-landing with the dustpan in her hand,
and gazing out through the tall window, that it would be
sunny and really warm by lunchtime. She would be able
to wear the blue voile after all, in spite of Rose's gloomy
forebodings. Rose said that it always rained on anybody's
half-day. Well, it wasn't going to rain today, not if Mary
knew the signs.

She leaned up against the window, watching the mist,
approving the heavy dew that lay like a grey sheet over
the lawn in front of the house.

It was early. The Heath, which later on would be
scattered over with children, and nurses pushing peram-
bulators, seemed quite deserted, nor was there any traffic
upon the road that lay between the iron gates of the
Poplars and the edge of the Heath. Craning her neck,
Mary could obtain a glimpse of the next-door house
through a gap in the trees. Curtains still drawn on the
backstairs, she noted. Well, she didn't blame the girls at
Holly Lodge, she was sure. If your master and mistress
went away to the seaside you were entitled to take your
ease. Not but what those girls were a lazy lot of sluts,
come to think of it. Common, too. Like mistress like
maid, said Rose, and that was true enough. She wasn't
any class, Mrs Rumbold.

Mary turned her head, transferring her gaze from Holly
Lodge to the house on the other side of the Poplars. It
was a smaller house, and she could not see much of it,
but she noticed that the garage doors were open. That

meant that the doctor had been called out early. It was a shame the way people sent for the doctor at all hours, and half the time for nothing more serious than an attack of indigestion, so Miss Stella said. A real gentleman he was, too, and ever so handsome! She didn't wonder at Miss Stella being sweet on him. It was a pity the Master had taken such a dislike to him. For they all knew in the servants' hall that he had, just as they knew about the trouble with Mr Guy, who wanted money for that queer business he ran with that Mr Brooke, and whom the Master wanted to send off to South America. You'd have to be a pretty fool if you didn't know most of what was going on in this house, what with the Master going in off the deep end and the doctor being called in for his Blood Pressure; and Miss Harriet coming out with bits of talk to anybody, even the kitchen-maid; Mrs Matthews taking to her bed because of all the worry about poor Mr Guy; and Mr Guy himself talking it all over with Miss Stella without so much as bothering to see if anyone was listening. Oh no, there were precious few secrets at the Poplars! Too many people cooped up together, thought Mary, vigorously sweeping the last six stairs. It never did to have two families under the same roof: there was bound to be a lot of squabbling, especially when you got an old girl, like Miss Harriet behaving sometimes as though she was downright simple, and at other times showing you she was as sharp as a needle, and as mean as – Mary couldn't think of anything as mean as Miss Harriet. Potty, that's what she was. You'd only got to see her collecting all the little bits of soap left over, and using them up herself, just as though she hadn't a penny to bless herself with. Regular old magpie, she was. Now, Mrs Matthews wasn't like that, give her her due. She was a nuisance all right, what with her glasses of hot water, and trays up to her room, but she wasn't one to go poking her nose into store-cupboards. You didn't really mind running round after Mrs Matthews, waiting on her hand and foot like she expected, because she always spoke nicely, and behaved like a lady. Nor you didn't mind Miss Stella, neither, in spite of the way she never put anything away, and was always wanting you to do things for her which weren't your work at all, properly speaking. And Mr Guy was that handsome it was a pleasure to wait on him. But when it came to Miss Harriet and the Master things were different. It was queer them being brother and sister, thought Mary, going slowly upstairs again to collect all the shoes which had been put out to be cleaned. Not a bit alike, they weren't. Mrs Lupton, now, from Fairview, over the other side of the Heath, you'd know anywhere for the Master's sister. She had the same domineering ways, though you weren't scared of her like you were scared of the Master. With the Master things had to be just as he wanted them, or there was trouble, and when the Master was angry you felt as though your knees were stuffed with cotton-wool. They were all of them scared of him, reflected Mary, picking up his shoes from outside his bedroom-door; even Mrs Matthews, though if anyone could get round him she could.

Mrs Matthews' shoes were the next to be collected, high-heeled, expensive shoes with Bond Street written all over them, thought Mary, pausing to admire them. The money Mrs Matthews must spend on her clothes! That was a sure sign she knew how to manage the Master, because it was common knowledge that her husband (him as was the Master's youngest brother) had left her pretty badly off. Good job for her she was so nice-looking and attractive, because though you couldn't ever call the Master mean you wouldn't catch him providing for a sister-in-law he didn't like, having her and her children to live with him, and all.

Yes, and didn't it get under Miss Harriet's skin, them being in the house and behaving as though money was no object like they did, thought Mary, picking up Mrs Matthews' low-heeled, trodden-over shoes of black glacé, and tucking them under her arm. There wasn't much love lost between her and Mrs Matthews, though to do her justice the old skinflint seemed to like Mr Guy and Miss Stella well enough.

Suède shoes outside Mr Guy's door; smart, they were, but a nuisance to clean. She'd have to do them, she supposed, because the under-gardener would be sure to put polish on them by mistake.

And lastly Miss Stella's shoes, two pairs of them, the brogues she wore on the Heath, and the blue kid shoes she went to town in.

She put all the shoes in her apron, and carried them down the back-stairs to the scullery. Cook, Mrs Beecher, was in the kitchen, and called her in for a cup of tea. It made all the difference to you, thought Mary, being in a place where the cook was good-tempered. She went into the kitchen, and took her place at the table between Beecher and Rose. Rose was sitting with her elbows on the table, and her cup between her hands, eagerly recounting what had passed between the Master and Miss Stella in the library last night.

'. . . And then he told her straight he wouldn't have Dr Fielding making up to her under his roof. The names he called the doctor you wouldn't believe! And then he said that bit I told you, about the doctor being a fool with no prospects, and if you ask me it was that which set Mrs Matthews against the doctor, because against him she is, and no one'll make me believe different.'

'You didn't ought to listen to what wasn't meant for your ears,' said Mrs Beecher.

'It does seem a shame about the doctor and Miss Stella,' said Mary. 'I am sure no one could be more gentlemanlike.'

'Ah, there's more to it than that,' replied Beecher,

passing his cup across to his wife. 'They say he's a bit fond of the bottle. Not that I've ever seen him the worse for wear myself, but there's no smoke without a fire.'

'That I won't believe!' declared Mrs Beecher roundly. 'And what's more I'm surprised at you mentioning it, Beecher!'

Rose, avidly absorbing this fresh piece of scandal, said: 'There you are, then! and no wonder Mrs Matthews had one of her nerve-attacks! When I saw her I thought to myself at once – '

'Then you thought wrong,' interposed Mrs Beecher repressively. 'I haven't ever held with Mrs Matthews' nerves, and no more I ever shall, but if she had an attack, *which* I doubt, it wasn't along of Miss Stella whom she doesn't care two pins for, if you was to ask me, but because of Mr Guy being shipped off to Brazil.'

'Oh, the Master isn't ever going to do that, not really, is he?' exclaimed Mary, aghast.

'So I believe,' said Mrs Beecher, rising ponderously and moving towards the stove. 'Not that I'm one for nosing into other people's business, but I had it from Miss Harriet as long ago as last Thursday. It's time the Early Teas went up. Hand me over the caddy, Rose, there's a good girl.'

Rose complied with this request, and stood waiting while Mrs Beecher filled three little teapots, and one glass tumbler in a silver holder. 'You might carry Miss Stella's tray up for me, dear,' said Rose to Mary, receiving the tumbler of hot water from Mrs Beecher, and placing it upon a small tray.

Mary finished her own tea in two gulps, and got up. She had her own work to do, and plenty of it, but if you were only an under-housemaid it paid you to keep in with the upper servants. She picked up Miss Stella's tray, and followed Rose up the back-stairs, Beecher bringing

11

up the rear with the Master's and Mr Guy's trays poised on his capable hands.

Miss Stella was not awake, and, as usual, she had left her clothes scattered about the floor. Mary drew back the curtains, tidied the clothes, and slipped out of the room again. Miss Stella wouldn't thank you for waking her.

Mr Guy's tray was reposing on the table in the hall, and Rose was still in Mrs Matthews' room. Mary could hear Mrs Matthews' slightly plaintive voice raised behind the shut door. She was just about to go and fill the hot-water cans, when the door of the Master's room opened, and Beecher came out rather quickly.

Mary stared at him. There was a queer, scared look on his face. 'Anything wrong, Mr Beecher?' she asked.

He passed his tongue between his lips, and answered in a shaken voice: 'Yes. It's the Master. He's dead.'

Her lips parted, but she could find nothing to say. A kaleidoscope of impressions flashed through her brain. It was shocking, awful, and yet thrilling. There might be an Inquest. She didn't want to have anything to do with it; she wouldn't be out of it for worlds.

Rose came out of Mrs Matthews' room. 'Well!' she said. 'Anyone would think there was no work to be done in this house! Where are my cans?'

Mary found her voice. 'Oh, Rose!' she faltered. 'The Master's dead!'

'Somebody's got to tell Them,' said Beecher, glancing at the four shut doors. 'I don't know who.'

Rose solved this problem for him. She broke into noisy tears, not because she had been fond of the Master, or disliked the thought of a death in the house, but because she was startled. The sound of her hysterical sobs brought the ready tears to Mary's eyes too. It also brought Miss Matthews out into the hall, with her grey hair in curlers, and an aged flannel dressing-gown huddled round her.

She had forgotten her glasses, and she peered shortsightedly at the group before her.

'What is the matter? Rose – is that you, Rose? Disgraceful! If you've broken any of the china it will come out of your wages, and it's no use crying about it. The breakages in this house – '

'Oh, madam!' gulped Mary. 'Oh, madam, it's the Master!'

The door next to Miss Matthews' opened. Stella stood yawning on the threshold in peach silk pyjamas, and with her short hair ruffled up like a halo about her face. 'What on earth's all the row about?' she inquired fretfully.

'Stella! Your dressing-gown!' exclaimed her aunt.

'I'm all right. Oh, do shut up, Rose! What is it?'

Both maids were now sobbing gustily. Beecher said: 'It's the Master, miss. He's dead.'

Miss Matthews gave a shriek, but Stella, staring at Beecher for a moment, said: 'Rot! I don't believe it.'

'It's true, miss. He's – he's cold.'

Somehow that seemed funny. Stella gave an uncertain giggle.

Her aunt said: 'How can you stand there and laugh – ! I'm sure I don't understand you modern girls, and what is more I don't want to. Not that I believe a word of it. I shall go and see for myself. Where are my glasses? Mary! my glasses!'

'I'll go,' said Stella, walking across the hall.

'Stella, not in your pyjamas!' screamed Miss Matthews.

Stella began to laugh again, trying to stifle the unbecoming sound by biting her lips.

Her uncle's room was in the front of the house, separated from his sister-in-law's by a bathroom. Beecher had drawn back the curtains, and set the early morning tea-tray down on a table beside the bed. It was evident, even to Stella, looking on death for the first time, that Gregory Matthews would never drink tea again.

He was lying on his back in an uncomfortably rigid attitude, his arms tossed outside the bedclothes, the fingers gripping the sheet as though in a last convulsion. His eyes were open, the pupils contracted. Stella stood looking down at him, her face slowly whitening. She heard her aunt's querulous voice, her footstep in the hall, and moved towards the door. 'I say, Aunt Harriet!' she said jerkily. 'Don't come! It's beastly!'

Miss Matthews, however, fastening her pince-nez on her nose with trembling hands, pushed past her niece into the room, and walked up to the bed. 'Oh, he's dead!' she said superfluously, and recoiled. 'It's his blood-pressure. I knew it would happen! He ought never to have eaten that duck, and it's no use anyone blaming me, because I *ordered* cutlets for him, and if he wouldn't eat them nobody can say it was my fault. Oh dear, oh dear, he does look dreadful! I wish he hadn't gone like that. We may have had our differences, but blood's thicker than water, say what you will! And you'd never think it, but he was a *dear* little boy! Oh, whatever are we going to do?'

'I don't know,' said Stella, taking her arm, and pulling her towards the door. 'Let's get out of this room, anyway. Oh aunt, *don't*, for God's sake!'

Miss Matthews allowed herself to be led away, but continued to weep. Stella, unable to feel that Gregory Matthews' nature when a little boy could compensate her aunt for all the subsequent years of strife, was impatient of this facile grief, and thankfully gave her into Mary's charge.

Rose, still gulping, quavered a message from Mrs Matthews: Miss Stella was to go to her mother at once.

Mrs Matthews was reclining against her pillows in a most becoming bed-jacket, and had evidently had the presence of mind to wipe the expensive night-cream from her face, and apply a dusting of powder. She turned her

14

head as Stella came into the room, and held out a wavering hand. 'Oh, my dear child!' she said in an extinguished voice. 'Poor Gregory! It has given me a terrible shock. I had a *feeling* when Rose brought my hot-water.'

'Aunt Harriet says it must have been the duck he ate for dinner,' said Stella, still on the verge of a giggle.

Mrs Matthews gave a faint, pained sigh. 'No one knows dear Harriet's good points better than I do,' she remarked, 'but one can't help being a little sad that her first thoughts in face of a thing like this should be still of mundane things. Do you know, darling, that when Rose told me what had happened I could only think of those beautiful words: "God's ways are – "'

'Yes, I know,' interrupted Stella hastily. 'But the point is what ought we to do? Aunt Harriet's having a sort of hysterical fit. Shall I call Guy?'

'Poor Guy!' said his mother. 'One would give one's all to keep tragedy away from the young. Somehow – '

'Well, if it comes to that I'm three years younger than Guy,' Stella pointed out. 'Not that I think he'll be much use, but – '

Mrs Matthews laid a hand on hers and pressed it. 'Dearest, not that flippant tone, *please*! Try to remember that the Shadow of Death is over this house. And Guy is far, far more highly-strung than you are, dear.'

'Oh mother, do stop!' implored Stella. 'Honestly, I don't want to have hysterics, but I shall in a minute. What ought we to do first?'

Mrs Matthews removed her hand. 'My practical little daughter! Where should we poor Marys of this world be, I wonder, without our Marthas? And yet one does somehow yearn for just a little time to be quiet, to face our loss, before we plunge into the sordid side of what ought not to be sordid at all, but very, very beautiful.'

Stella gave a gasp, and went off into a fit of strangled

laughter. In the middle of this her brother walked into the room, looking tousled and a little dazed still with sleep. 'I s-say!' he stammered. 'Uncle's dead! Did you know? Beecher's locked the room, and gone to ring up Fielding. He says there's absolutely no doubt.'

'Hush, dear!' said Mrs Matthews. 'Stella, try to control yourself! A doctor should of course be sent for, but one shrinks, somehow, from the thought of Dr Fielding, whom your uncle disliked, coming at such a moment. Perhaps I am over-sensitive, and I suppose there is no help for it, but – '

'I can't see that it matters in the least,' said Guy. He grasped the rail at the foot of his mother's bed, and stood looking down at her with bright, uncomprehending eyes. 'I can't grasp it!' he announced. 'I mean, uncle's dying like that. Of course, everybody expected it in a way, I suppose. I mean, his blood-pressure. What do you think he died of? Do you suppose it was apoplexy? I always thought he'd have apoplexy sooner or later, didn't you, Stella? Will there have to be an inquest? I don't see why there should be, do you? I mean, everyone knows he had a weak heart. It's obvious he died of it.'

'Yes, dear, but we won't talk of it now,' Mrs Matthews said repressively. 'You are upset, and you let your tongue run away with you. You must try and realize what it all means to me. I sometimes think poor Gregory was fonder of me than of his own sisters. I do try always to see only the good in everybody, and Gregory responded to me in a way that makes me very happy to look back upon.'

'Oh Gawd!' said Guy rudely.

Mrs Matthews compressed her lips for a moment, but replied almost at once in an extremely gentle voice: 'Go and dress, Guy dear. A dark suit, of course, and *not* that orange pull-over. You too, Stella.'

'Actually, I hadn't thought of the orange pull-over,'

said Guy loftily. 'But I utterly agree with Nigel about mourning. It's a survival of barbarism, and, as he says – '

'Darling, I know you don't mean to hurt me,' said Mrs Matthews sadly, 'but when you treat sacred things in that spirit of – '

'You've simply got to realize that I'm a Pure Agnostic,' replied Guy. 'When you talk about things like death being sacred it means absolutely nothing to me.'

'Oh, shut up!' interrupted Stella, giving him a push towards the door. 'Nobody wants to listen to your views on religion.'

'They're not particularly my views,' said Guy, 'but the views of practically all thinking people today.'

'Oh yeah?' said Stella inelegantly, and walked off to her own room.

Mary's surmise that Dr Fielding had been called out before breakfast was proved to be correct. He had not returned to his house when Beecher rang up, and it was not until both Stella and Guy had bathed and dressed that he arrived at the Poplars. By that time Miss Matthews, recovering from her fit of crying, had also dressed, and had not only telephoned to her elder sister, Gertrude Lupton, but had found time to give a great many orders to Mrs Beecher for the subsequent using-up of the fish and the eggs already cooked for a breakfast she felt sure no one could think of eating. These orders were immediately cancelled by Stella and Guy, who were feeling hungry, and an altercation was in full force when Dr Fielding walked into the house.

He was a tall man in the middle-thirties, with very wide-set grey eyes, and a humorous mouth. As he stepped into the hall he exchanged a glance with Stella, who at once went forward to greet him. 'Oh Deryk, thank God you've come!' she said, taking his hand.

'Stella, not with your uncle lying dead upstairs!' begged Miss Matthews distractedly. 'Not that *I* disapprove, because I'm sure dear Dr Fielding – But after all Gregory said – though I daresay he feels quite differently now that he's passed on: I believe they do, though I've never been able to understand why. Oh dear, how very confusing it all is! If I'd ever dreamed it would all be so difficult and unpleasant I should have been the last person in the world to have wanted Gregory to die. It was the duck, doctor. I implored him not to eat it, but he would go his own way, and now he's dead, and there are two beautiful lamb cutlets gone to waste. Eaten in the kitchen! English lamb!'

Dr Fielding, returning the pressure of Stella's fingers, broke in on this monologue to request that he might be taken at once to Gregory Matthews' room.

'Oh yes!' said Miss Matthews, looking round in a flustered way. 'Of course! I should take you up myself, only that I feel I never want to enter the room again. Guy, *you* are the man of the house now!'

'No one need take me up,' replied Dr Fielding. 'I know my way.'

Beecher coughed, and stepped forward to the foot of the stairs. 'If you please, sir, I will escort you to the Master's room.'

The doctor looked at him. 'You were the one who found Mr Matthews, I think? By all means come up.'

At the head of the stairs he was met by Mrs Matthews. She was dressed in a becoming black frock, and greeted him in a voice rather more fading than usual. She was not a patient of his, because she mistrusted all General Practitioners, but as a man (as she frequently observed) she liked him very well. Now that Gregory Matthews' opposition had been cut short in this summary fashion she was even prepared to accept the doctor as a son-in-law. So there was just a suggestion of sympathetic understanding in the smile she bestowed on him, and she said: 'I expect Stella has told you. We can't realize it yet

18

– perhaps mercifully. And yet, when I woke this morning, I had a sort of presentiment. I can hardly describe it, but I think that people who are rather highly-strung, which I'm afraid I am, are more sensitive than others to – what shall I call it? – *atmosphere*.'

'Undoubtedly,' replied the doctor, who knew her of old.

'It was of course a heart-attack, following on acute indigestion,' stated Mrs Matthews. 'My poor brother-in-law was sometimes very headstrong, as I expect you know.'

'Yes,' agreed the doctor, edging his way past her. 'Very headstrong, I'm afraid.'

She let him go, and proceeded on her way downstairs while Beecher unlocked the door of Gregory Matthews' room, and ushered the doctor in.

He did not say anything when he saw the body lying on the bed, but bent over it with his brows drawn close. Beecher stood watching him while he made his examination, and presently said: 'I suppose it *was* a natural death, sir?'

Dr Fielding looked up quickly. 'Have you any reason to think that it was not?'

'Oh no, sir, only that he does look awful, and his eyes being open like that don't look right, somehow.'

'Is that all! If you take my advice you won't spread that kind of rumour about. It might get you into trouble.' Dr Fielding transferred his attention to the bed again, finished his examination, and straightened himself.

Beecher, opening the door for him, volunteered the information, in a rather offended tone, that the body had been cold when he had found it at eight o'clock. The doctor nodded, and passed out of the room to the head of the stairs.

Below, in the hall, the party had been augmented by the arrival of Mrs Lupton and her husband, who had motored over from their house on the other side of the Heath. The presence of Henry Lupton, a little, sandy-moustached man with weak, worried blue eyes, was generally felt to be insignificant, but Gertrude Lupton's personality made her a formidable and unwelcome visitor. She was a massively built woman of about fifty-five, extremely upright, and reinforced wherever possible with whalebone. She even wore it inserted into the net fronts which invariably encased her throat. Her hats always had wide brims and very high crowns, and her face-powder was faintly tinted with mauve. She had been the nearest to Gregory Matthews in age of all his family, and the most like him in temperament. Both resembled nothing so much as steam-rollers in their dealings with their fellow creatures, but the difference between them had lain in the fact that whereas Gregory Matthews had been subject to awe-inspiring rages no one had ever seen Gertrude lose one jot of her implacable calm.

She was perfectly calm now, though evidently in the grip of some powerful emotion. She stood resting one hand on the gateleg table in the middle of the hall while she delivered herself of various forceful statements. Dr Fielding, pausing on the top stair, heard her quell Harriet's volubility with a stern admonition to the unfortunate lady to control herself; and annihilate Mrs Matthews, who had unwisely repeated the history of her premonition, by saying: 'I have the greatest dislike for that kind of foolish talk, and I must say that I consider it quite uncalled-for in one who was no relation of my poor brother whatsoever. I sincerely trust, Zoë, that you will abandon any attempt to make yourself the central figure in this appalling affair, though I am bound to confess from my knowledge of you that it would be extremely like you to try to focus the limelight on yourself.'

The candour (and indeed the blunt truth) of this speech came as near to confounding Mrs Matthews as anything could. The doctor, descending the stairs, thought that it said much for her control that she was able to reply, with unimpaired charity: 'Ah, my dear Gertrude, I'm afraid that you strong-minded women don't always understand us highly-strung creatures.'

'I understand you perfectly, and I may say that I always have,' replied Mrs Lupton crushingly. She became aware of the doctor's approach, and wheeled round to confront him. 'Dr Fielding, I believe. I have heard of you from my brother.'

Her tone implied that she had heard no good of him. He answered somewhat stiffly: 'I have been attending Mr Matthews for some time, so I imagine you might.'

She looked him over. 'And what,' she demanded, 'was, in your opinion, the cause of my unfortunate brother's death?'

'In my opinion,' replied Fielding with a touch of sarcasm, 'your brother died from syncope.'

'What on earth's that?' inquired Stella, who had come out of the dining-room as soon as she had heard his voice.

'You will oblige me,' said Mrs Lupton, ignoring her niece, 'by being more precise.'

'Certainly,' said Fielding. 'Your brother, as no doubt you know, suffered from a high blood-pressure, coupled with a slight valvula affection of the – '

'I am quite aware of the fact that you have been treating my brother for heart-trouble,' interrupted Mrs Lupton, 'but I can only say that if he had a weak heart he was the only one of our family thus afflicted. I never believed in it. We come of extremely healthy stock. I am sure that such a thing as a weak heart was never dreamed of in our family.'

'Possibly not,' said Fielding. 'But the fact remains that your brother had – as you call it – a weak heart. I repeatedly warned him against over-excitement and injudicious diet, and as he invariably disregarded my advice I have very little doubt that his death was due to syncope, produced, in all probability, by an attack of acute indigestion.'

'The duck!' exclaimed Miss Matthews. 'I knew it!'

'Yes, dear,' said Mrs Matthews comfortingly. 'I thought at the time that it was a little unwise of you to have ordered duck, but I make it a rule never to interfere in your province. If only one could have foreseen the result!'

'What did your brother eat for dinner last night?' asked the doctor.

'Roast duck,' answered Miss Matthews, miserably. 'It never did agree with him, and there were two beautiful lamb cutlets which he wouldn't touch. I can't bear to think of them.'

'I am afraid,' said Mrs Matthews, recapturing the doctor's attention, 'that last night's dinner was not very suitable for anyone with a delicate digestion. There was a lobster cocktail for one thing – '

'Oh, but uncle didn't have that!' objected Stella. 'He took about one mouthful, and said it wasn't fit for human consumption.'

'Darling child, please don't interrupt!' said her mother. 'And soles with *rather* a rich sauce, doctor, and a cheese savoury, which I always consider most indigestible.'

'It sounds to me exactly the sort of ill-chosen meal I should expect you to order, Harriet,' said Mrs Lupton severely, 'but I have yet to learn that Gregory had anything wrong with his digestion. My own impression is that there is a great deal more in this than meets the eye, and I insist on seeing my brother's corpse immediately.'

Mrs Matthews winced, and closed her eyes. 'Please!' she said faintly. 'Not that terrible word, Gertrude!'

'I have no patience with that kind of sentimentality,' said Mrs Lupton. 'I believe in calling things by their proper names, and if you can tell me that my unfortunate brother is not a corpse I shall be very grateful to you. Henry, I am going up to Gregory's room. You had better come with me.'

Henry Lupton, who had up till now remained discreetly in the background said: 'Yes, my dear, of course!' and with a deprecating look in Dr Fielding's direction, started forward to follow his wife up the stairs.

No one said anything until the Luptons were out of earshot. Dr Fielding was looking at Stella with a rueful smile; Mrs Matthews had sunk into a chair, and was wearing a resigned expression. Harriet, whose lips had been moving in silent communion with herself, suddenly said with strong indignation: 'I shall never forgive her, never! I have been ordering meals for Gregory for years! None of the others killed him, so why should this one? Tell me that!'

'Ah, Harriet!' said Mrs Matthews, mournfully shaking her head.

'And don't say Ah, Harriet to me!' snapped Miss Matthews. 'If anyone killed him it was you, with all the worry and disturbance about Guy – and about Stella too, now I come to think of it!'

'Oh, Deryk!' murmured Stella, 'we're a dreadful family!'

Their fingers met and clasped for a brief moment.

'I wish you wouldn't all talk such rot!' suddenly ejaculated Guy from the dining-room doorway. 'It's obvious what uncle died of! Nobody killed him!'

'If anyone mentions the word duck again, I rather think I shall scream,' said Stella.

The sound of a door being shut upstairs warned them of Mrs Lupton's return. She came down the stairs with her lips tightly compressed, and she did not say anything at all until she reached the hall. Then she drew a hissing breath, and said with strong feeling: 'Terrible! I am inexpressibly shocked by what I have seen. My poor brother!'

'Yes, indeed,' said Henry Lupton, who was looking unhappier than ever. 'Terrible, terrible!'

'That will do, Henry. Talking will not mend matters,' said his wife. She bent her hard stare on the doctor. 'Do I understand that you are prepared to sign a death certificate?'

He looked frowningly back at her, a hint of uneasiness in his eyes. 'As a medical man – '

'Medical fiddlesticks!' said Mrs Lupton. 'I insist upon another's opinion being called in!'

A startled silence fell. It was broken by Mrs Matthews. Her voice jarred a little, though she still spoke in her dulcet way. 'Dear Gertrude, you are upset, and no wonder. I am sure you don't mean to hurt anyone's feelings.'

'I am unconcerned with anyone's sensibilities,' said Mrs Lupton. 'I repeat, I insist upon a second opinion.'

'Perhaps,' said Dr Fielding, looking her in the eye, 'you would like me to notify the Coroner of your brother's death?'

'Yes,' said Mrs Lupton. 'That is precisely what I should like, Dr Fielding!'

2

No one spoke for a minute. The implication of Mrs Lupton's words could not be misunderstood, but it took time for her meaning to be fully realized. Everyone stared at her a little blankly, except the doctor, who stood looking down, still frowning, at the table's polished surface.

Harriet was the first to break into agitated speech. 'You may just as well say at once that you think I poisoned him, and I'm astonished that you don't! And as for housekeeping, you may think you are much better at it than I am, but all I can say is I should be ashamed of the waste that goes on in your house! And if you think I gave Gregory duck on purpose to kill him there are the cutlets to prove I didn't!'

'No, there aren't,' said Stella unsteadily. 'Eaten in the kitchen.'

Mrs Matthews took a cigarette-case out of her handbag, and with trembling fingers selected a cigarette, and lit it. 'Stella! Please!'

Guy came forward a few paces. 'Do you mean you want a p-post-mortem?' he demanded. 'It's absolute rot! And I must say I should like to know what right you have to waltz in and interfere! Now uncle's dead I'm the head of this house, and – '

'No, my dear Guy, you are not,' said his aunt, quite unruffled. 'I have little doubt that you would like to think yourself the head of the family, and I am well aware of the machinations of you and your mother to induce your uncle to name you his heir. What I am not aware of is that he ever did so. That being so it is my duty to remind you that the head of this family is now your cousin Randall.'

Guy flushed angrily. 'Anyway, you're not the head, and you've no right – '

'If Randall is going to be dragged into this I shall remove myself at once,' said Stella disgustedly. 'I can put up with a good deal, but not with Randall. What's more, if anyone poisoned uncle I should think it was he.'

'That,' said Mrs Lupton, 'is a foolish remark which you will, I trust, regret having made once you have given yourself time to consider. I hold no brief for Randall. Far from it. But to accuse him of poisoning your uncle is absurd. Randall has not been down to Grinley Heath since last Sunday.'

'Are we not all of us a trifle overwrought?' interposed Mrs Matthews smoothly. 'Surely no one seriously thinks that poor Gregory died from anything but the results of acute indigestion? If there were the slightest reason for suspecting foul play I should be the first to demand a thorough investigation. But I am sure no one can have wanted his death, and really, Gertrude, when one considers the unpleasantness of – of inquests, and things – '

'I hope I am not one to shrink from unpleasantness,' said Mrs Lupton. 'And when you say that you are sure no one can have wanted Gregory's death I must beg to differ from you. Please understand that I make no accusations! But I am not ignorant of the dissensions in this household, and I cannot but see, painful though the thought may be, that his death benefits several people.'

Her husband entered unexpectedly into the discussion. He gave a little cough, and said nervously: 'Really, my dear, I think we should be guided by what the doctor says. You don't want to start any sort of scandal, do you? You would very much dislike to be dragged into – er – that kind of publicity, you know.'

'Kindly permit me to know my own mind, Henry,' said

Mrs Lupton freezingly. 'You and I at least can have no reason to fear an investigation.'

Henry looked rather frightened, and said: 'No, my dear, of course not, but hadn't we better think it over before we act?'

'Deryk, you don't think he was poisoned, do you?' asked Stella anxiously.

Fielding have her a brief smile. 'No, I don't. At the same time, if Mrs Lupton feels there is room for doubt I should naturally prefer that there should be a post-mortem examination.' He glanced at Mrs Lupton as he spoke, and added: 'As far as I am concerned there is no objection to the matter being put into the hands of the Coroner.'

'Well, I think there's every objection!' said Guy angrily. 'Everyone but Aunt Gertrude is perfectly satisfied with your diagnosis, and I utterly fail to see what point there is in having uncle cut up, and a lot of family linen washed in public! Of course he wasn't poisoned, but the instant we have an autopsy and an inquest people will start talking, and say there's no smoke without a fire, and life will be pure hell!'

'I must say, that is perfectly true,' agreed his mother. 'And one cannot help wondering whether it is quite what poor Gregory would have liked.'

'It isn't,' said Miss Matthews positively. 'He said he wasn't going to have anything more to do with doctors. And it isn't what I like either, though no one considers my feelings in this house, or ever has! I know what it will be. We shall all have to answer questions which have nothing to do with the case, and after all no one could possibly live with Gregory without quarrelling with him. And for my part I shall tell them quite frankly that it was Gertrude who always quarrelled most with him in the nursery, which is perfectly true, as poor Hubert and Arthur would bear me out if only they were alive to hear me!' This chance reference to her two deceased brothers caused her to burst into tears again. She brought out a large handkerchief from her pocket, and sniffed into it, saying: 'If only I had a Man to turn to! But my brothers are all dead, and even Mr Rumbold's away, and you can put upon me as much as you choose!'

'Don't be ridiculous, Harriet!' commanded her sister. 'No one suspects you of having anything to do with it.'

'That's what you say!' retorted Miss Matthews. 'But I haven't the least doubt they'll bring it home to the duck, and not believe a word about the cutlets! And if they don't say it's the duck you may depend upon it they'll fix upon poor Guy, because his uncle was going to send him to South America, which was just like Gregory, and if Guy *had* killed him there would have been some excuse. And so I shall tell them! Guy's the only one of you who has any affection for his poor old aunt, and it's my belief you're behaving like this out of pure spite, Gertrude!'

After delivering herself of this diatribe Miss Matthews was entirely overcome, and sobbed so gustily, and thrust her sister and sister-in-law away so violently that it fell to Guy and Stella to escort her up to her own room. Guy performed his share of this task without conveying any marked impression of fondness for his aunt, while Stella openly grimaced at Dr Fielding. She was obliged to remain with Miss Matthews until that afflicted lady had recovered some measure of composure, and by the time she was at liberty to go downstairs again Dr Fielding had left the house, and Mrs Matthews was bidding farewell to the Luptons in the porch.

Stella found her brother in the library, telephoning to Mr Nigel Brooke, with whom, a year ago, he had gone into a precarious partnership.

Mr Brooke's vocation was Interior Decoration, and since Guy coupled a leaning towards Art with a profound veneration for Mr Brooke, four years his senior, he had

had no difficulty in discovering the same vocation in himself. Both were alike in being the only sons of widowed mothers, but whereas Nigel had entire control over his inherited capital the little money which Arthur Matthews had been able to leave his son was left him in trust, the trustees being his wife, and his eldest brother, Gregory. Guy had owed his partnership to his mother's skilful handling of his uncle, Gregory Matthews, who liked a Pretty Woman, and who knew next to nothing of his nephew's abilities, and had allowed himself to be cajoled into putting up a thousand pounds for Guy's share in the virgin business. Since that day he had ample opportunity of appraising his nephew's capabilities, and the result of this study was that upon being asked for a further advance to support the struggling fortunes of the firm of Brooke and Matthews he had countered with an offer from a business acquaintance who had a vacancy for a young man in the office of his rubber plantations in Brazil. The coaxings and even the tears of a Pretty Woman had this time failed to melt Gregory. He apostrophized his nephew as a young waster, and stated, with unnecessary violence, his profound desire to be rid of him. For perhaps the first time in her life Zoë Matthews had found it impossible to get her own way. Her only means of gratifying her son's ambition, and of keeping him at her side, was to sell out some of her own capital for his use, and since her income was already quite insufficient for her needs this expedient was naturally out of the question. She did not even consider it. Nor did she permit her resentment to become apparent to Gregory Matthews, for that would have been very stupid, and might have led to the loss of an extremely comfortable home for which she was not expected to pay as much as one farthing. The home had its disadvantages, of course. It was not her own, and the presence of her sister-in-law was always an irritation, but since poor Harriet was the antithesis of everything Gregory Matthews thought a female should be it needed really very little trouble to enlist his support in any disagreement she happened to have with her sister-in-law. Patience and unfailing sweetness had achieved their object: at the end of a five-year sojourn at the Poplars Zoë Matthews had contrived to make herself, if not the mistress of the house, at least the cherished guest whose comfort must be everyone's first consideration. 'Such a ruthless woman – my dear Aunt Zoë,' Randall Matthews had once murmured, glancing maliciously up under his long lashes.

Randall was in Stella's thoughts as she waited for her brother to conclude his conversation with Nigel Brooke. When he put the receiver down at last she said abruptly: 'Do you suppose uncle left everything to Randall, Guy?'

'You bet he did – most of it, anyway,' replied Guy. 'Randall's been working for it for months, if you ask me – always turning up here for no known reason except to oil up to uncle by suddenly being attentive to him. It's so damned unfair! I come down from Oxford, and get a job absolutely bang-off, and stick to it, and all Randall does is to drift around looking willowy and run through a packet of money (because Uncle Hubert left a fair spot, so Aunt Harriet told me) and never do a stroke of work, or attempt to! It makes me sick! Besides, he's so utterly poisonous.'

Stella lit a cigarette. 'I suppose he'll turn up next. And say foul things to everybody in a loving voice. Do you think uncle's left mother any money?'

'Yes, I'm pretty sure he has,' said Guy confidently. 'Anyway, the main point is she's my sole trustee now, which means I shall be able to carry on with Nigel.' His brow clouded. 'Everything would be all right if it weren't for that blasted old harridan Aunt Gertrude! What the hell she wanted to stick her nose into it for I can't imagine.'

'Jealous of us,' said Stella negligently. 'She probably thinks mother's getting more out of uncle's death than she is. Of course it's fairly noxious, but I suppose it doesn't really matter – the post-mortem, I mean.'

'Oh, doesn't it matter?' said Guy with considerable bitterness. 'Well, for once in her life Aunt Harriet hit the nail on the head! We shall have the police barging in and asking damned awkward questions, and if that's your idea of a good time it isn't mine! Everyone knows I had a flaming row with uncle over his precious South American scheme, and when the police hear about that I shall be in a nice position.'

Stella, not much impressed, flicked the ash off her cigarette on to the carpet. 'But when they don't find poison in uncle they won't ask us any questions at all.'

'Yes, but what if they do find poison?' Guy demanded.

'They won't.' She looked up quickly. 'Good Lord, you don't – you don't really think he was done-in, do you?'

'No, of course not,' answered Guy. 'Still, we've got to face the fact that he may have been. Mind you, I don't believe he was, but that ass Fielding didn't seem any too sure.'

'Do you frightfully mind not calling Deryk "that ass"?' asked Stella frigidly. 'I happen to be going to marry him.'

'Well, you'll have a jolly job explaining that to the police,' retorted Guy. 'And you'll also be able to tell them what uncle said about it, *not* forgetting the bit about the Inebriates' Home.'

'Shut up!' Stella said fiercely. 'It isn't Deryk's fault that his father drank!'

'No, but it's definitely his misfortune,' mocked Guy. 'Particularly if it comes out that uncle, in his well-known playful way, threatened to blow the gaff if Fielding didn't lay-off you.'

Stella's hand as she raised her cigarette to her lips was

shaking, but she controlled her temper, and merely said: 'I suppose you have to be vulgar as well as spiteful?'

'I may be vulgar, but I'm not in the least spiteful,' replied Guy. 'I'm merely pointing out to you how and where you stand. *I* don't blame Fielding for having a Hopeless Inebriate for a father, but if you think Grinley Heath would be nice about it you've got another guess coming. A fat lot of practice he'd have had here by now if uncle *had* split! 'Tisn't as though he were even T.T. himself. Far from it, in fact.'

'You're a filthy, backbiting little cad!' Stella exploded, her cheeks flaming. 'If you're hinting that Deryk poisoned uncle, let me tell you that I'd a lot sooner believe you did!'

'Oh, you would, would you?' said Guy, suddenly furious. 'Thanks very much! Well, I didn't poison him, and I'll trouble you to refrain from suggesting that I did! Because if there's going to be any chat of that sort from you, there'll be quite a spot from me about your precious Deryk! Quite got that?'

'If you think that I'd – ' Stella broke off, staring across the room at him. She gave an uncertain laugh. 'What on earth did you start this futile argument for? You talk as though we knew uncle had been poisoned, and you know perfectly well it's all rot!'

'Yes, of course,' Guy said, his anger evaporating. 'Utter rot. Sorry; I didn't mean to be offensive. Only if there does happen to be trouble we've damned well got to stick together.'

'What's going to be done?' asked Stella, after a slight pause. 'Did Aunt Gertrude ring up the police?'

'No; Fielding's going to get on to the Coroner. They'll come and take uncle's body away, and I suppose we shan't know anything much for a day or two. I asked Fielding, and he said it would be a question of sending the organs up to the Home Office, or somewhere. I've

32

rung up uncle's lawyer, by the way, so no doubt he'll come down with the Will. Personally I can't see any reason why I shouldn't go up to town as usual.'

His mother, entering the room at that moment, overheard this last remark and read him a fond but reproving lecture on the respect due to the dead. When she perceived that this made very little impression on him she begged him to consider her feelings. Stella, realizing that her mother was going to expatiate sadly on the loneliness of widowhood, slipped out of the room, and went upstairs, only to run into her aunt, who had temporarily forgotten her woes in the discovery that owing to the window in Gregory Matthews' bathroom having been left open the new bottle of his medicine had been blown over into the washbasin, and smashed.

'I can't see that it matters,' said Stella crossly. 'You couldn't use up somebody else's tonic.'

'No, but the chemist always allows us something on the bottles,' said Miss Matthews severely.

Stella looked with faint repulsion at the assortment of objects in her aunt's clutch, and wondered how one could be expected to feel solemn about death when one's relatives behaved like Aunt Harriet. Miss Matthews had triumphantly collected from her brother's bathroom his sponges and face-flannel (which would all come in useful for cleaning-rags), a cake of soap, two toothbrushes (excellent for scrubbing silver filigree dishes), a half-used tube of toothpaste (which she proposed to use up herself as soon as her own was finished), a bottle of mouth-wash, and a loofah.

'I thought Guy might like the loofah,' said Miss Matthews. 'It's a very good one. There's the end of a stick of shaving-soap too.'

'If you take my advice you won't offer it to him,' said Stella. 'He's a bit squeamish.'

33

'If there's one thing I hate above all others,' declared Miss Matthews, 'it is waste!'

Her activities during the rest of the morning were surprising. Having ordered cold lamb and rice-pudding for lunch, spurning all Mrs Beecher's more appetizing suggestions on the score that no one would care what there was to eat on such an occasion as this, she announced her intention of having Gregory Matthews' room turned out. No sooner had his body been removed in an ambulance than she ordered both Rose and Mary upstairs to begin this work of purifaction. Rose at once started to cry, saying that she couldn't bear to enter the Master's room, but Miss Matthews, her own late qualms forgotten, told her not to be silly, but to gather up all the Master's discarded underclothing, and carry them to the dirty-linen basket. Rose immediately gave notice, and retired sobbing. Mrs Matthews came up to suggest that they should all of them devote the rest of this unhappy day to quiet and meditation, but was tartly informed that if a thing had to be done her sister-in-law did not believe in putting it off. She went away, routed, and since Guy was occupied in designing an overmantel for a house in Dorking, and flatly refused to meditate with his mother, and Stella could not be found, abandoned all ideas of a contemplative day, and ordered the chauffeur to motor her to town for the purpose of buying mourning clothes.

When Miss Matthews, busily engaged in inspecting the condition of Gregory's suits (with a view to selling them), heard of her sister-in-law's action she could scarcely contain herself. To go to London for no nobler purpose than to squander money on dress seemed to her the height of callousness. 'After all her talk about setting our minds on higher things! Meditation indeed! And I should very much like to know what right she has to take the car out without one word to me!' This aspect of the case soon outweighed every other. Miss Matthews went muttering about the house, and by lunch-time had muttered herself into a state of considerable agitation which found expression in a sudden announcement to her nephew and neice that she could not enjoy a moment's peace until she had seen Gregory's Will, and had the Whole Thing settled Once and for All.

One glance at the rice pudding which succeeded the lamb at luncheon drove Stella from the table. She said in a wan voice that she really didn't feel she could, and betook herself to the house next door.

Dr Fielding had come in from his rounds when Stella arrived, and had just gone in to luncheon. He was glancing through his notebook when Stella was ushered into the room, but at sight of her he threw the book aside, and jumped up. 'Stella, my dear!'

'I've come to lunch,' said Stella. 'There's nothing but mutton and rice *chez nous*, and I can't bear it.'

He smiled. 'Poor darling! Jenner, lay for Miss Matthews. Sit down, my dear, and tell me all about it. Have you had a difficult morning?'

'Ghastly,' said Stella, accepting a glass of sherry. 'Enough to make one wish uncle hadn't died.'

Fielding gave her a warning look, and said: 'I was afraid you'd have rather a bad time. All right, Jenner, we'll wait on ourselves.' He paused while the manservant withdrew, and then said: 'Stella, be careful what you say in front of people. You don't want anyone to get the impression that you wished your uncle to die.'

'I didn't wish him to,' replied Stella. 'I hadn't ever considered the possibility. He wasn't the sort of person you'd expect to die, was he?'

'Well, I'm a doctor,' said Fielding, smiling.

'You mean you did expect it? You never told me.'

'No, I didn't exactly *expect* it. Nor should I have told you if I had, my darling.'

Stella laid down her knife and fork. 'Deryk, please tell me one thing: Do you believe uncle was poisoned?'

'No, I don't,' he answered. 'But although there were no signs not compatible with death from syncope, I couldn't undertake to state definitely that he was not poisoned upon a purely superficial examination.'

She looked a little troubled, and presently said: 'I do wish there hadn't got to be a post-mortem. Whatever you may say, I believe you're secretly a bit afraid that they may find something.'

'I'm not in the least afraid of it,' said Fielding calmly. 'I hope they won't, for all your sakes, but if there's any doubt I want it cleared up.'

Stella was unappeased. 'Well, it's pretty beastly for the rest of us. I must say I hoped you weren't going to give in to Aunt Gertrude. Couldn't you have stopped it all?'

He raised his eyebrows rather quizzically. 'My dearest child! What about my professional reputation?'

'I don't know, but you said yourself you were prepared to sign a death certificate. I can't understand your wanting a post-mortem. Supposing they do find poison? Everyone knows uncle had a row with you about me, and it seems to me the police are quite likely to start suspecting you of having given him poison.'

'They can suspect what they like,' said Fielding coolly. 'But they'll be darned clever if they manage to prove that I ever administered poison to your uncle. Don't you worry your head about me, Stella: I haven't the slightest reason to fear a post-mortem.'

'Of course I didn't mean that I thought you really might have poisoned uncle,' said Stella. 'But it does seem to me that things are going to be fairly beastly one way and another. The only nice part of it is that we shall be able to get married now without an awful fight. I don't think mother really minds about it. She's much more wrapped up in Guy than she is in me.'

He stretched out his hand to her across the table. 'Well, that's a *very* nice part, anyway.'

She nodded. 'Yes, because I hate rows. I should have married you whatever uncle said, but it makes it easier now that he's dead.'

Fielding got up, and came round behind her chair. 'I'm going to ring for Jenner to bring in the next course,' he said, laying his hands on her shoulders. 'But first I must kiss you.'

She raised her face, and as he bent over her put her hand to caress his lean cheek. 'How many girls have you kissed, like that?' she asked, when she was able.

'Crowds,' he said, laughing.

She smiled, but said seriously: 'I expect that's true. You were keen on Betty Mason before you thought of me, weren't you?'

'Never!'

'Oh, I'm not throwing a jealous fit,' Stella assured him. 'You needn't mind admitting it. I think you're rather the type that can't help making love to girls who aren't actually cross-eyed or hare-lipped. I shall probably have an awful time with you when we're married.'

'It sounds as though it's I who will have the awful time,' he replied teasingly.

'Well, I must say I shouldn't like it if you got off with anyone else now that you're engaged to me,' admitted Stella.

'I'll watch my step,' he promised, walking over to the bell and setting his finger on it.

Jenner's entrance put an end to the conversation. He brought word of two patients awaiting the doctor in the surgery.

'Who are they?' asked Fielding.

'Young Jones, sir, and Mrs Thomas about her little girl's leg.'

'Oh, well, tell them I don't see patients until two o'clock. Put the clocks back, or something.'

'Very good, sir.'

'Don't think you've got to stay here because of me,' said Stella. 'I'm just going anyway.'

'It's nobody who matters,' he said lightly.

Stella looked at him with a hint of austerity in her candid eyes. 'You don't only care about the people who matter, do you, Deryk?'

'Of course not, but there's nothing urgent about these cases. Have some more cream?'

'No, thanks. If it's Mrs Thomas from North End Cottages I do wish you'd go. She told Aunt Harriet that Minnie dreads having her leg dressed, and I must say I'm not surprised. I hate kids to be scared, don't you? I used to be at the dentist's, and he always kept me waiting, which made it worse.'

He got up, pushing his chair back, and said ruefully: 'You're determined to keep my nose to the grindstone, young woman. Shall I ever be allowed to have a meal in peace when we're married?'

'Yes, lots,' said Stella, kissing her hand to him.

She finished her luncheon alone, and strolled back to the Poplars. She noticed as she walked up the drive that the blinds were all down in the front windows, and found, upon entering the house, that this had been brought about by the relentless hand of her Aunt Gertrude, who had returned to the Poplars, accompanied this time by her younger daughter, Janet.

In consequence of the gloom reigning over the library and the dining-room the family had been forced to sit in the drawing-room, a large and cheerless apartment at the back of the house, elegantly but uncomfortably furnished in the style of Louis XV. Mrs Lupton was discussing with her sister what had best be done with Gregory Matthews' clothing, and Janet, a pale, earnest-looking young woman

38

of five-and-twenty, was trying to be bright and intelligent over her cousin Guy's sketch of the overmantel for the house in Dorking. Stella paused on the threshold, meditating instant flight, but Guy cast her a supplicating look, and feeling that at least she had enjoyed a very good luncheon while he regaled himself on cold lamb and rice pudding she took pity on him, and advanced into the room. 'Hullo, Janet!' she said.

Mrs Lupton looked up, folding her lips. She was a just woman and she did not blame Stella for being much better-looking than either of her own daughters. She was merely sorry that Stella should ruin her complexion with make-up, and squander her mother's (or more probably Gregory's) money on ridiculously unsuitable clothes. 'Well, Stella?' she said. 'And where have you been, may one ask?'

'Out,' said Stella briefly.

Mrs Lupton was glad to think that her daughters would never dream of answering her in that rude way. 'I should have thought you could have stayed at home for one day,' she remarked. 'And have you nothing quieter to wear than that frock?'

'No, nothing.'

'You must have a black one.'

'All right,' said Stella equably. 'If she happens to think of it, I daresay mother will buy one for me.'

Mrs Lupton sat very straight in her chair. 'The least said about your mother's expedition to town the better,' she announced.

Guy looked up, a spark of anger in his eyes. 'Quite!' he said with a good deal of emphasis.

Janet, who hated people to quarrel, hurried into speech. 'Aunt Zoë has such wonderful taste!' she said. 'I'm afraid I never know what to buy, but of course I don't care for clothes, much. Or jewellery either. Isn't it funny? Because Agnes – '

39

'Not funny: tragic,' said Stella, with a smile that took the sting out of her words. 'You look heathenish in that hat too.'

'Oh, Stella, you are awful! Do I really?'

'Yes,' said Guy viciously.

'I know you're only teasing me, but I don't care. I think nearly everything is so much more important than mere clothes, don't you?'

'No,' said Stella. 'You can see I don't.'

Janet persevered. 'Oh, I know you only *say* that! Guy has been showing me a design for an overmantel. I think it's marvellous. I should never have thought of green marble. I'm not really a bit artistic. You'd shriek if you saw my attempts at drawing! It's funny, really, because Agnes used to sketch beautifully, and of course she has awfully good taste. By the way, mother rang her up as soon as she heard, and she sent her love, and said to tell you all how sorry she is. She'd have come down, only that Baby's cutting a tooth, and she doesn't like to leave him.'

'I shall give that baby an expensive christening present,' said Guy in a burst of gratitude.

Janet giggled. 'You are mad! You know he was christened ages ago, the dear mite! Why, he's actually six months old now! It doesn't seem possible, does it?'

As neither Stella nor Guy could think of anything to say in answer to this a silence fell. Janet broke it, saying in a lowered voice: 'It's funny, isn't it, the way one simply can't help talking of ordinary, everyday things even when something awful has happened? I suppose it is that one just doesn't realize it at first.'

'No, I think it is that uncle didn't really matter to any of us,' replied Stella thoughtfully.

'Oh, Stella, how can you?' cried Janet, shocked.

'But it's perfectly true,' Stella said, resting her chin in her cupped hands, and wrinkling her brow a little. 'When

40

he was here he made himself felt because for one thing he was a domestic tyrant, and for another he had a pretty strong personality. But he didn't matter to us because we didn't like him.'

'I'm sure I was always very fond of him,' said Janet primly.

Another silence fell. Miss Matthews' voice made itself heard from the other end of the room. 'All those lovely ivory brushes and things too! With G. M. on the backs, so they won't be any use to Randall, and it's obviously meant that Guy should have them. And I do think we ought to give something of Gregory's to Mr Rumbold.'

'I fail to see what claim Mr Rumbold has on any of Gregory's possessions,' said Mrs Lupton.

'Not a claim exactly, but he is such a close friend, and we had him to stay when Mrs Rumbold went to visit her sister. Really quite like one of the family, for I'm sure he treated this house like a second home, playing chess with Gregory, you know. Though I shall always feel it's a pity he ever married That Woman.'

'Harriet,' said Mrs Lupton, not mincing matters, 'you're a sentimental fool, and always have been.'

'I may be a fool,' said Miss Matthews with a rising colour, 'but I wish very much that Mr Rumbold weren't away, because at least he's a Man, in spite of being married to That Woman, and he could advise me.'

'I have very little opinion of men,' stated Mrs Lupton, 'and I fail to see that you stand in any need of advice. Nothing can be done until the Will has been read. I have no doubt that will make very unpleasant hearing, but at least it cannot come as a shock to those of us who have seen what has been going on under our noses for the past five years.'

Stella did not feel that she could let this pass. 'Yes,' she said across the room. 'Mother said today that she believed uncle was fonder of her than of either of his sisters.'

Mrs Lupton bent a cold stare upon her. 'I can well imagine that your mother may have said so, but if she supposes that your uncle had any real affection for anyone but himself she is a bigger fool than I take her for.' She turned back to her sister. 'Has anyone remembered to inform Randall of his uncle's death?' she demanded.

'I'm sure it's no use asking me,' replied Miss Matthews. 'I have had far too much to think of.'

'If there's one thing more certain than anything else it is that we don't want Randall coming here to make things ten times more unbearable than they are already,' said Guy.

'My opinion of Randall must be as well known to you as it is to him,' said Mrs Lupton, 'but personal feelings are beside the point. So far as we know Randall is his uncle's heir. He is certainly the head of the family, and he should be summoned.'

'I must say,' remarked Janet with an air of originality, 'that I don't like Randall. I know it's wrong of me, but I just can't help it. He's the sort of person I could never trust. I don't know why, I'm sure.'

'Oh, because he's like an amiable snake,' said Stella light-heartedly. 'Smooth, and fanged.'

The door opened. 'Mr Randall Matthews!' announced Beecher.

3

'Hell!' said Guy audibly.

There entered a sleek and beautiful young man who paused just inside the door, and glanced round at his assembled relatives with a bland and faintly mocking smile. He was dressed with the most finicking care, and nothing could have been more symphonic than the blend of his shirt with his silk socks and his expensive tie. His figure was extremely elegant; his hands were well-manicured; his jet-black hair was brushed into waves undisturbed by the slightest disorder; and his teeth were so gleamingly white and regular that they might have served for an advertisement for somebody's toothpaste. His mouth was a little too thin-lipped to be perfect, and curled too sarcastically to be pleasant, but his eyes, set under straight brows and fringed by long lashes, were remarkable for their colour and brilliance. They were of a startling and deep blue, very hard, generally half-hidden by drooping lids, and occasionally disconcerting in their sudden alertness. As he looked from one to the other of his relations they were smiling, and quite limpid.

'How lovely for me!' he said in a voice of honeyed sweetness. 'Not only my dear Aunt Gertrude, but my charming cousin Janet as well!' He walked forward, graceful and rather feline, and bent to kiss his aunt's cheek. 'My dear aunt! You look so nice in that hat.'

'Do you think so?' said Mrs Lupton unresponsively.

'I've thought so for years,' he said gently, and passed on to Miss Matthews. 'You must none of you bother to say how pleased you are to see me,' he said. 'I can read it in all your expressive faces.' He looked critically at Stella, and strolled across the room towards her. 'Yes, darling, that is quite a nice frock, but the handkerchief is not only the wrong shade of grey, but quite damnably tied. Let me show you, my sweet.'

Stella pushed his hand away. 'No, thanks!'

He was still smiling. 'How you hate me, don't you?' he murmured. 'And Guy? How are you, little cousin?'

Guy, who did not relish this form of address, glowered at him.

Mrs Lupton, still rigid with wrath at the edged compliment paid her, said sharply: 'I presume you have heard the news of your uncle's death?'

'Oh yes!' said Randall. 'You will notice that I am wearing an armband. I always like to observe the conventions. And which of you,' he inquired, looking amiably round, 'is responsible for dear Uncle's death? Or don't you know?'

This airy question produced a feeling of tension, which was possibly Randall's object. Mrs Lupton said: 'That is not amusing nor is this a time for jokes in bad taste.'

Randall opened his eyes at her. 'Dear aunt, did you think I was joking?'

'If uncle was poisoned, which I don't believe he was for an instant,' said Stella, 'you had a bigger motive for killing him than anyone else!'

Randall took a cigarette out of his thin gold case, and lit it in a leisurely way. 'True, my pet, very true, but you mustn't forget that I was several miles distant when he died. And while I am on the subject may I ask who was responsible for starting this *canard* that uncle was poisoned?'

'I was responsible for the post-mortem,' replied Mrs Lupton.

'Do you know, I thought perhaps you might be?' said Randall.

'I am by no means satisfied that your uncle died a

44

natural death. I accuse no one; I make no insinuations; but I shall be surprised if my suspicions are not found to be correct.'

'I know you like plain-speaking, my beloved aunt,' said Randall, 'so you will not mind my telling you that I find your behaviour extremely officious.'

'Indeed?'

'And ill-judged,' said Randall pensively.

'I am not concern – '

'Also more than a little stupid. But that was to be expected.'

'It may interest you to know – '

'Experience, my dear aunt, leads me to reply with confidence that whatever it is you have to say is not in the least likely to interest me.'

While Mrs Lupton fought for words Stella said curiously: 'Then you don't think uncle can really have been poisoned, Randall?'

'I haven't the slightest idea,' replied Randall. 'The question interests me almost as little as Aunt Gertrude's remarks.'

'Of course, I see what you *mean*,' said Janet. 'But if he was poisoned I'm sure we all want it cleared up.'

'Are you, darling?' said Randall solicitously.

'Well – well, you wouldn't want a thing like that to go unpunished, would you?' said Janet.

'If there's any doubt naturally we want it cleared up!' said Guy, looking defiantly at Mrs Lupton.

'That was not the tone you used this morning,' she commented dryly.

'You must not pay too much attention to Guy, Aunt Gertrude,' said Randall. 'He is only trying to impress you.'

'Damn you, are you hinting that I've any reason for wanting it hushed up?' demanded Guy angrily.

'Shut up! he's only trying to get a rise out of you,' said

45

Stella. She met Randall's ironic gaze, and said bluntly: 'Why are *you* so against a post-mortem?'

'Oh, I'm not!' Randall assured her. 'I was merely looking at it from your point of view.'

'Mine?'

'Yes, my sweet, yours, and Guy's, and Aunt Harriet's, and even my clever Aunt Zoë's. You ought all of you to be very thankful for uncle's timely decease. I do not like to see you looking a gift horse in the mouth. Could you not have induced your obliging medical friend to have signed the death certificate, Stella darling?'

She flushed. 'Dr Fielding was perfectly ready to sign the certificate without any persuasion from me. None of us wanted to start a scandal except Aunt Gertrude.'

'Of course we didn't,' corroborated Guy. 'In fact, I said everything I could to stop it.'

'Then do not assume a pious attitude now, little cousin,' said Randall. 'Believe me, it is nauseating.'

Miss Matthews, who had been opening and shutting her mouth in the manner of one awaiting an opportunity to enter into the conversation, suddenly exclaimed: 'How dare you say that I wanted Gregory to die? I never even thought of such a thing! I may not have been very fond of him, but – ' She broke off as Randall's smile grew, and said, trembling: 'You are insufferable! *Just* like your father!'

'My dear aunt,' said Randall, 'you were not in the least fond of uncle. Nor was Stella, nor was Guy, nor, even, was my clever Aunt Zoë.'

'And nor were you!' flashed Stella.

'And nor was I,' agreed Randall suavely. 'In fact, I can think of no one, with the possible exception of Aunt Gertrude, who was fond of him. Were you fond of him, aunt, or was it a mere question of affinity?'

'I'm sure I was very fond of poor Uncle Gregory,' said Janet unwisely.

'How very affecting!' said Randall. 'But perhaps you are also sure that you are very fond of me too?'

'I always try to see the best in people,' said Janet with a bright smile. 'And I'm sure you don't mean half the things you say.'

Randall looked at her with acute dislike. 'I congratulate you, Janet,' he said. 'Your cousins have been trying to silence me for years, but you have done it with one utterly fatuous remark.'

'May I ask, Randall, whether you came here with any other intention than of being offensive to my daughter?' asked Mrs Lupton.

'Why, certainly,' he answered. 'I came to satisfy my not unnatural curiosity.'

'You mean your uncle's death?'

'I mean nothing of the sort,' said Randall. 'I was already informed of that, and also of the impending post-mortem, by uncle's solicitor. I was curious to know how you were all behaving in this time of trial, and why it had not occurred to any of you to notify me of uncle's death.'

He looked round inquiringly as he spoke, and Guy immediately said: 'Because we didn't want you nosing about and creating unpleasantness!'

'Oh, I do hope I haven't done that?' said Randall in a voice of gentle concern.

'As a matter of fact,' stated Mrs Lupton fairly, 'I was telling your Aunt Harriet that you ought to be informed when you arrived. Not that I consider you have any cause for complaint. You are not more nearly concerned than Gregory's sisters. Please do not imagine that you need give yourself airs just because you happen now to be the head of the family! There will be time enough for that when we have heard your Uncle's Will read. Which reminds me, Harriet, that I must arrange with Mr Carrington when it will be convenient to him to come down here. In the ordinary course of events I suppose he would come immediately after the funeral, but in this case I am of the opinion that the sooner he comes the better.'

'I am glad of that,' said Randall. 'He is coming on the day after tomorrow.'

Mrs Lupton eyed him with something approaching loathing. 'Do I understand that you took it upon yourself to make this arrangement without a word to anyone?'

'Yes,' said Randall.

At this moment a not unwelcome interruption occurred. Mrs Matthews came into the room. She extended a gloved hand towards Randall, and said: 'I saw your car, and so guessed you were here. Janet, too! Quite a little family party, I see. I wonder if you thought to order any fresh cake, Harriet dear? I seem to remember that there was not a great deal yesterday. But I'm sure you did.' She dropped her hand on to her sister-in-law's shoulder for a moment, and pressed it. 'Poor Harriet! Such a sad, sad day. And for me too.'

'I understood that you had been shopping in town,' said Mrs Lupton.

Mrs Matthews gave her a look of pained reproach. 'I have been buying mourning, Gertrude, if you can call that shopping.'

'I do not know what else one can call it,' retorted Mrs Lupton.

Randall handed Mrs Matthews to a chair. 'How tired you must be!' he said. 'I find there is nothing so fatiguing as choosing clothes.'

'Oh,' said Mrs Matthews, sinking into the chair, and beginning to draw off her gloves, 'it was not so much choosing, as taking anything that was suitable. One doesn't care what one wears at such a time.'

'You have a beautiful nature, dear Aunt Zoë. But I feel sure that exquisite taste cannot have erred, shattered though we know you to be.'

Mrs Matthews fixed her soulful eyes on his face, and

replied gravely: 'Not shattered, Randall, but in a mood of – how shall I express it? – melancholy, perhaps, and yet not quite that. Gregory has been much in my thoughts.'

'Let me beg of you, Zoë, not to make yourself ridiculous by talking in that affected way!' said Mrs Lupton roundly. 'You will find it very hard to convince me for one that Gregory has been in your thoughts, as you call it, for as much as ten seconds.'

'And I'm sure I don't know why he should be!' added Miss Matthews, a good deal annoyed. 'I lived with Gregory all my life, and what is more he was my brother, and if he was in anyone's thoughts it was in mine, which indeed he was, for I have been sorting all his clothes, wondering whether we should not send most of them to a sale. Though there is an old coat which might very well be given to the gardener, and no doubt Guy would be glad of the new waterproof.'

'My thoughts were rather different, dear,' said Mrs Matthews. 'I was in Knightsbridge, and found time to slip into the Oratory for a few moments. The peace of it! There was something in the whole atmosphere of the place which I can hardly describe, but which seemed to me just right, somehow.'

'It must have been the incense,' said Miss Matthews doubtfully. 'Not that I care for it myself, or for joss-sticks either, though my mother used to be very fond of burning them in the drawing-room, I remember. Though why you should go into a Roman Catholic Church I can't imagine.'

'Nor anyone else,' said Mrs Lupton.

Janet said large-mindedly: 'I think I can understand what you mean, Aunt Zoë. There's something about those places, though one can't *approve* of Roman Catholics, of course, but I can quite imagine how you felt.'

'No, dear, you are too young to understand, mercifully

for yourself,' said Mrs Matthews, disdaining this well-meant support. 'You do not know anything of the dark side of life yet, and pray God you never may!'

'Oh, *mother*!' groaned Guy, writhing in acute discomfort.

'If all this grossly exaggerated talk refers to Gregory's death I can only say that I never listened to such nonsense in my life!' declared Mrs Lupton.

Randall lifted one long, slender finger. 'Hush, aunt! Aunt Zoë is remembering that she is a widow.'

'Damn you!' muttered Stella, just behind him.

'Yes, Randall, I am remembering it,' said Mrs Matthews. 'Now that Gregory has passed on I realize that I am indeed alone in the world.'

Randall made a gesture towards his scowling cousins. 'Ah, but, aunt, you forget your two inestimable Blessings!' He glanced down into Stella's wrathful eyes, and said softly: 'That will teach you to say damn you to me, my sweet, won't it?'

Under cover of Mrs Lupton's and Miss Matthews' voices, both uplifted in indignant speech, Stella said: 'You're a rotten cad!'

He laughed. 'Temper, Stella, temper!'

'I wish to God you'd get out, and stay out!'

'Think how dull you'd be without me,' he said, turning away. 'Dear, dear, surely my beloved aunts are not quarrelling?'

The dispute ended abruptly. 'Do you mean to stay to tea, Randall?' snapped Miss Matthews.

'No, Stella has expressed a wish that I should get out and stay out,' replied Randall, quite without rancour.

'Stella, dear! I'm sure you didn't mean that,' Mrs Matthews said.

'What a thing it is to be head of the family!' murmured Randall. 'I am becoming popular.' With which parting shot he blew a kiss to the assembled company, and walked out of the room.

He left behind him a feeling of tension which the succeeding days did nothing to allay. The family was uneasy, and the intelligence, conveyed to Stella by Dr Fielding, that the organs of Gregory Matthews' body had been sent to the Home Office for analysis was not reassuring. The suspense set everyone's nerves on edge, and the visit of Mr Giles Carrington, of the firm of Carrington, Radclyffe, and Carrington, to read the Will on Friday had the effect of causing a great deal of pent-up emotion to explode.

Everyone had nursed expectations; everyone, except Randall, was disappointed. Mrs Lupton was left a thousand pounds only, and an oil painting of her brother which she neither liked nor had room for on her already overcrowded walls, and was inclined to regard it as an added injury that she was referred to in the Will as Gregory's beloved sister Gertrude. Neither of her daughters was mentioned, and it was insufficient consolation to discover that Guy had been similarly ignored. Stella, in a codicil dated three weeks previously, was to receive two thousand pounds upon her twenty-fifth birthday on condition that she was not at that time either betrothed or married to Dr Fielding. The bulk of the estate was inherited by Randall, but a disastrous provision had been made for Mrs Matthews, and for Harriet. Gregory Matthews, with what both ladies could only feel to have been malicious spite, had bequeathed to them jointly his house and all that was in it with a sum sufficient for its upkeep to be administered by his two executors, Randall and Giles Carrington.

While Giles Carrington, who was a stranger to them, was present the various members of the family had for decency's sake to control their feelings, but no sooner had he departed than Mrs Lupton set the ball rolling by

51

saying: 'Well, no one need think that I am in any way surprised, for I am not. Gregory never showed the faintest consideration for anyone during his lifetime, and it would be idle to suppose that he would change in death.'

Randall raised his brows at this, and mildly remarked: 'This document is not a communication from the Other Side, I can assure you, aunt.'

'I am well aware of that, thank you, Randall. Nor would it astonish me to learn that you had a great deal to do with the drawing-up of the Will. To refer to me as his beloved sister, and then to leave me a portrait of himself which I never admired and do not want makes me suspect strongly that you had a finger in the pie.'

'Perhaps,' said Stella, looking him in the eye, 'it was you who had this bright notion of leaving me two thousand pounds with strings tied to it?'

'Darling, I wouldn't have left you a penny,' replied Randall lovingly.

'That would suit me just as well,' said Stella. 'I don't want his filthy two thousand, and I wouldn't touch it if I were starving!'

Agnes Crewe, who had come down with her husband to hear the Will read, said: 'I didn't expect uncle to remember *me* in his Will, but I must admit that it does upset me to think that Baby is not even mentioned. After all, the mite is the only representative of the third generation, and I do think uncle might have left him something, even if it were only quite a little thing.'

Owen Crewe, a quiet man in the late thirties, said pleasantly: 'No doubt he felt that my son was hardly a member of the Matthews family, my dear.'

Agnes, as fair-minded as her mother, and with her sister's invincible good-nature, replied: 'Well, there is that, of course, but after all, I'm a Matthews, and – '

'On the contrary, my dear,' said Owen, 'you were a Lupton before you married me.'

Agnes gave her jolly laugh. 'Oh, you men! You always have an answer to everything. Well, there's no use crying over spilt milk, and I shan't say another word about it.'

'That is an excellent resolve, my dear, and one that I hope you won't break more than three times a day,' replied Owen gravely.

Henry Lupton, who had made no contribution to the conversation till now, suddenly said with a deprecating little laugh: 'Blessed is he that expecteth nothing.'

'You may consider yourself blessed if you choose,' said his wife severely. 'I am far from looking at it in that light. Gregory was a thoroughly selfish man, though I am sorry to have to say such a thing of my own brother, and when I think that but for me he would be buried by now, and no one a penny the wiser as to the cause of his death I am extremely sorry that I did not wash my hands of the whole affair.'

'No, no!' remonstrated Randall. 'Think of the coals of fire you are heaping on his ghostly head!'

'Please do not be irreverent, Randall! I am not at all amused.'

'It seems to me that the whole Will is rottenly unfair!' exclaimed Guy bitterly. 'Why should Stella get two thousand pounds and me nothing? Why should Randall bone the lot? He wasn't uncle's son any more than I was!'

'It was because of my endearing personality, little cousin,' explained Randall.

'No one – *no* one has as much cause for complaint as I have!' said Miss Matthews in a low, trembling voice. 'For years I've slaved to make Gregory comfortable, and not squander the housekeeping money as others would have done, and what is my reward? It was downright wicked of him, and I only hope I never come across him when I die, because I shall certainly tell him what I think of him if I do!'

She rushed from the room as she spoke, and Randall

at once turned to Mrs Matthews, saying with an air of great affability: 'And what has my dear Aunt Zoë to say?'

Mrs Matthews rose nobly to the occasion. She said with a faint, world-weary smile: 'I have nothing to say, Randall. I have been trying to forget all these earthly, unimportant things and to fix my mind on the spiritual side of it all.'

Henry Lupton, who thought her a very sweet woman, looked round with a touch of nervous defiance, and said: 'Well, I think we may say that Zoë sets us all an example, don't you?'

'Henry,' said his wife awfully, 'I am ready to go home.'

Mrs Matthews maintained her air of resignation, but when alone with either or both of her children found a good deal to say about the Will. 'It is not that one *wants* anything,' she told them, 'but one misses the thought for others. Consideration for people's feelings means so much in this dark world, as I hope you will both of you remember always. I had no claim on Gregory, though since I was his brother's wife I daresay a lot of people would disagree with me on that point. As far as actual money goes I expected nothing, but it would have been such a comfort if there had been some little sign to show that I was not quite forgotten. I am afraid poor Gregory – '

'Well, there is a sign,' said Stella bluntly. 'You've got a half-share in the house, and it isn't to cost you anything to keep up.'

'That was not quite what I meant, dear,' said Mrs Matthews, vague but repressive. 'Poor Gregory! I have nothing but the kindest memories of him, but I am afraid his was what I call an *insensitive* nature. He never knew the joy of giving. In some ways he was curiously hard. Perhaps if he had had more imagination – and yet I don't know that it would have made any difference. Sometimes

54

I think that he was brought up to be selfish through and through. I was very, very fond of him, but I don't think he ever had a thought for anyone but himself in all his life.'

'He was rather a mean brute,' agreed Stella.

'No, darling, you must never think that,' said her mother gently. 'Try only to look on the best side of people. Your uncle had some very sterling qualities, and it wasn't his fault that he was hard, and selfish, and not always very kind to others. We cannot help our natures, though some of us do try.'

'Well,' said Stella, correctly divining the reason for these strictures on her uncle's character, 'one comfort is that Aunt Harriet can't live for ever.'

'That kind of person nearly always does,' said Mrs Matthews, forgetting for the moment to be Christian. 'She'll go on and on, getting more eccentric every day.'

Stella laughed. 'Cheer up, Mummy! She's years older than you are, anyway.'

'I only wish that I had her health,' said Mrs Matthews gloomily. 'Unfortunately I've never been strong, and I'm not likely to get better at my age. My nerves are not a thing I should ever expect your aunt to sympathize with – I've often noticed that people who are never ill themselves have not the faintest understanding of what it means to be more or less always seedy – but though I make a point of never letting anyone guess how very far from well I often feel, I do sometimes long for a little more consideration.'

'Aunt Harriet isn't such a bad old stick,' remarked Guy, glancing up from his book.

'You don't have to live with her all day,' replied his mother with a touch of asperity. She recollected herself, and added: 'Not that I don't fully realize all her good points, but I can't help wondering what induced your uncle to leave her a half-share in this great house. She would be far happier in a little place of her own. She's always complaining that this house is too big, and runs away with so much money, and we all know that she really is not capable of doing the housekeeping – which I've no doubt she'll insist on doing the same as ever.'

'But mother, you know your health would never stand the worry of housekeeping,' said Stella tactfully.

'No, darling, that is not to be thought of – not that I should consider my health for a moment if it weren't my duty to keep myself as well as possible for your sakes – but if I had my way I should install a competent housekeeper.'

'That's more or less what Aunt Harriet is,' said Guy.

'She is not in the least competent,' retorted Mrs Matthews. 'And really her mania for using things up, and saving money on sheer necessities, like coal, will drive me into my grave! It's all very well for you two: you have your own lives, and your own amusements, but at my age I don't think I'm unreasonable to want a house of my own, where I can entertain my friends without having Harriet grudging every mouthful they eat, and wanting to turn off all the lights at eleven o'clock!'

'If you mind frightfully,' said Stella, 'wouldn't your income run to a small flat, or something?'

'Not to be thought of!' said Mrs Matthews firmly. 'I have to be very careful as it is.'

It was evident that she was a good deal moved, and Stella, who had not before realized how confidently she had expected to be left in sole possession of the Poplars, did what she could to console her. This was not very much, since honesty compelled her to admit that Miss Harriet Matthews was an impossible companion for anyone of Mrs Matthews temperament. Honesty also compelled her to admit that Mrs Matthews herself was not the ideal housemate, but loyalty to her mother would not allow her to listen to her aunt's rambling complaints.

Guy, though quite fond of his aunt, always defended his mother from any criticism levelled at her by any other person than himself or Stella, so Miss Matthews was in the unfortunate position of having a grievance with no one to whom she could air it. She went muttering about the house, gave vent to dark sayings at odd moments, and was fast developing a tendency to behave as though mortally injured when Mr Edward Rumbold and his wife providentially returned from Eastbourne, where they had been staying during the whole of the past week.

Miss Matthews was delighted. She was genuinely attached to Edward Rumbold, who always treated her with courtesy, and never seemed to be bored by her discursive conversation. Moreover, she had a firm belief in the infallibility of the male sex, and had very often found Mr Rumbold's counsel to be good. Her brother had more than once warned her jeeringly not to make a fool of herself over a married man, but although this advice had the power to distress her she knew that there was Nothing Like That in her relationship with Edward Rumbold, and even had he not already possessed a wife she still would not have wished for a closer tie than that of friendship.

Randall had once remarked that Edward Rumbold seemed to have been created especially to be a Friend of the Family. It was certainly true that Miss Matthews' woes were not the only ones poured into his ears. Mrs Matthews, and Stella, and Guy all took him in varying degrees into their confidence, and if he found the recital of other people's troubles wearisome, at least he was far too well-mannered to show it.

He had of course seen the notice of Gregory Matthews' death in the papers, and came round to the Poplars after his return on Saturday to offer condolences, and any help that might be needed. Mrs Rumbold accompanied him, which was not felt by the two elder ladies of the house to be an advantage.

'One wonders what he saw in her,' and 'One wonders how she managed to catch him' were expressions frequently heard on Mrs and Miss Matthews' tongues, and they both persisted, in spite of his evident fondness for his wife, in pitying him from the bottom of their hearts. Miss Matthews usually referred to Mrs Rumbold as That Woman, while her more charitable sister-in-law spoke of her as Poor Mrs Rumbold, and said that That Type always pulled a man down. Occasionally she added that it was very sad that the Rumbolds were childless, and it was generally understood that this circumstance was in her opinion a further blot on Mrs Rumbold's character.

Actually it would have been hard to have found a couple more quietly devoted to each other than Edward and Dorothy Rumbold. They took little part in the social activities of Grinley Heath, but spent a considerable portion of the year in travelling, and always seemed to be content with one another's company. Edward Rumbold was a fine-looking man of about fifty, with iron-grey hair, very regular features, and a pair of steady, far-seeing eyes. His wife was less prepossessing, but persons not so biased as Mrs and Miss Matthews had no difficulty in perceiving wherein lay her attraction for Edward Rumbold. 'She must have been awfully pretty when she was young,' said Stella.

She was still pretty in a kind light, for she had large blue eyes, and a retroussé nose which gave a piquancy to her face. Unfortunately she was a blonde who had faded quickly, and she had sought to rejuvenate herself by the not entirely felicitous use of hair-dye, and rouge. Nature had intended her, at the age of forty-seven, to be grey-haired and plump, but Art and Slimming Exercises had given her bronze locks and a sylph-like silhouette. She was always rather lavishly made-up, and had lately taken to painting her eyelashes a startling blue, and her finger-nails a repulsive crimson. She was as kind as she was common, and Stella and Guy (though they vied with one another in inventing her past history) liked her, and said that she was a Good Sort.

She sat beside Miss Matthews on the sofa in the drawing-room when she came with her husband to condole, and said: 'You poor dear! It must have been a terrible shock. I was ever so upset when I read it in the paper. I couldn't believe it at first, not till I saw the address, and even then I couldn't seem to take it in, could I, Ned?'

'It was surely quite unexpected?' he said, his quiet voice in somewhat striking contrast to his wife's shrill tones.

This civil question had the effect of causing Miss Matthews to break into a torrent of words. Gregory Matthews' constitution, his disregard of his health, the duck he had eaten at his last meal, Mrs Lupton's spite, and the scandal of a post-mortem were all crammed higgledy-piggledy into one speech.

'I am exceedingly sorry! I had no idea!' Mr Rumbold said. 'Of course it must be most unpleasant for you all.'

'Why, whatever can have made Mrs Lupton go and say a thing like that?' wondered Mrs Rumbold. 'As though anyone would want to murder Mr Matthews! No, really, I do call it downright spiteful, don't you, Ned?'

'I expect she was upset,' he answered.

'So were we all, but we didn't say he'd been poisoned!' retorted Miss Matthews. 'I wished very much that you had been here to advise me. I shall always feel that something ought to have been done to stop it, no matter what anyone says!'

He smiled a little. 'I'm afraid you wouldn't have been able to stop it,' he replied. 'And after all, if there is any feeling of suspicion you'd rather have it put to rest, wouldn't you?'

'Yes, if it *is* put to rest,' agreed Miss Matthews. 'But it's my belief that as soon as you start stirring things up something shocking is bound to be discovered where you least expect it.'

'The idea that Gregory was poisoned is merely absurd,' said Mrs Matthews. 'Of that I am convinced.'

'Yes, I daresay you are, but you know very well Guy had been quarrelling with him, not to mention Stella.'

The effect of this speech was to turn Mrs Matthews from a Christian woman into something more nearly resembling a tigress at bay. There was even something faintly suggestive of a feline crouch in the way she leaned forward in her chair, with her hands gripping the arms of it. 'Perhaps you would like to explain what you mean by that, Harriet?' she said in a low, menacing voice. 'Please do so! And remember that you are speaking of My Children!'

Miss Matthews quailed, as well she might, and said tearfully that she meant nothing at all.

'Ah!' said Mrs Matthews, relaxing her taut muscles. 'I am glad of that, Harriet.'

Under her delicate make-up she was quite pale. Guy leaned over the back of her chair, and grinned down at her. 'Attaboy, ma!' he said approvingly.

She put up her hand to clasp his, but said only: 'Please don't use that vulgar expression, dear. You know I dislike it.'

'I'm sure,' said Miss Matthews, groping in her pocket for her handkerchief, 'you needn't turn on me, Zoë! Nobody could be fonder of Guy than I am – and of Stella too, of course. I was only thinking how it would look to an outsider.'

Mrs Matthews recovered her poise. 'Don't let us say any more about it. You naturally cannot be expected to understand a mother's feelings.' She turned to Mrs Rumbold, and said graciously: 'And has your stay at the seaside done you good, Mrs Rumbold?'

'Oh, I'm splendid, thanks!' replied Mrs Rumbold. 'It was only Ned who would have it I needed a change of air.' She threw him a warm look as she spoke, and added: 'You wouldn't believe the way he spoils me, that man!'

Mrs Matthews smiled politely, but made no remark. Miss Matthews, with a glance of hatred cast in her direction, asked Mr Rumbold to come and look at the plumbago, and bore him off in triumph to the conservatory. She was a keen horticulturist, and soon became torn between a desire to talk solely of her troubles and an even stronger desire to compare notes with him on the progress of their respective rarities. She contrived in the end to do both, but became somewhat muddled, and kept on handing him earthy pots of flowers (which he could have looked at just as easily without having to hold them) with a slightly inconsequent recommendation to him to Look at the way she's behaving now, just as though she owned the whole house! He escaped from her presently on the pretext of being obliged to go and wash his hands, and went upstairs to do so only to fall a victim, on his way down again, to Mrs Matthews, who was on the look-out for him.

Later, Stella accompanied both the visitors down the drive to the gate, and said with a twinkle: 'Did Mother tell you all her woes when Aunt Harriet had finished telling you hers, Mr Rumbold?'

He laughed. 'You're an irreverent minx, Stella. She did tell me a certain amount.'

'Well, I hope you smoothed them both down. They're rather on each other's nerves.'

'And I'm sure it's not to be wondered at,' said Mrs Rumbold kindly. 'A death in the house is enough to upset anybody, and when it comes to inquests and things,

I'm not surprised at your mother and your auntie being a bit on edge.'

'We all are,' Stella said, 'Uncle wasn't poisoned, of course, but somehow when a thing like that has been suggested you find yourself – sort of speculating on who might have done it. It's horrid.'

'I shouldn't think about it at all, if I were you,' said Edward Rumbold with calm good sense. 'Dr Fielding is much more fitted to judge than your Aunt Gertrude, you know.'

'Yes,' agreed Stella. 'Only if it did happen to be true, and the police come and ask us all questions won't it look rather black that Guy, and D – that Guy and I have been having rows with uncle?'

'Of course it won't,' said Edward Rumbold comfortingly. 'The police don't arrest people merely because they've been quarrelling, you know! You're too fond of meeting troubles halfway, young woman.'

'Well, all I can say is I hope they don't come,' said Stella unconvinced.

'I don't suppose they will,' said Mr Rumbold.

But at ten o'clock on Monday morning Beecher went to the store-room in search of Miss Matthews, and in ominous silence held out a silver tray with a visiting-card reposing on it.

The card bore the name of Detective-Superintendent Hannasyde, of the Criminal Investigation Department, New Scotland Yard. Miss Matthews gave a startled gasp, and dropped it as though it were red-hot.

'I've shown them into the library, miss,' said Beecher.

4

There were three people in the library. One was a middle-aged man, with grizzled hair, and eyes deep-set in a square, good-humoured countenance; the second was a thin man with a clipped moustache, and a very thin neck; the third was Dr Fielding. As Miss Matthews entered the room, clinging to her nephew's arm, the doctor stepped forward, and said in a grave voice: 'Miss Matthews, I am sorry to say that things are more serious than I had supposed. This is Superintendent Hannasyde, of Scotland Yard; and this,' he added, indicating the man with the moustache, 'is Inspector Davis, from the Police Station here.'

Miss Matthews looked at the Superintendent much as she might have looked at a boa-constrictor, and said Good-morning in a frightened whisper. The local Inspector she ignored.

'Good-morning,' Hannasyde said pleasantly. 'Inspector Davis and I have come to ask you one or two questions about your brother's death.'

'You surely aren't going to tell us that he really was poisoned?' exclaimed Guy. 'I don't believe it! Why on earth should anyone want to poison him?'

Hannasyde glanced towards him. 'I don't know, Mr – Matthews? That is one of the things I've come to find out.'

'But it's incredible!' Guy declared. 'I simply can't believe it!'

'I'm afraid there's no doubt, Guy,' interposed Fielding. 'The analysts discovered nicotine.'

Guy blinked. 'Nicotine? But he didn't smoke!'

'So Dr Fielding has been telling me,' replied Hannasyde.

Miss Matthews found her voice. 'Then it couldn't have been the duck!' she said.

'The duck?' repeated Hannasyde a little blankly.

'Yes, because if there had been any poison in that we should all be dead! And in any case I have the bill for two lamb cutlets, and anyone will tell you that they were ordered for my brother, even though he didn't eat them.'

'Miss Matthews was afraid that the roast duck which her brother ate that evening might have caused his death,' explained the doctor.

'I see,' said Hannasyde. 'No, it could hardly have been the duck, Miss Matthews. Can you remember what else your brother ate or drank on the night he died?'

She began to enumerate the dishes which had appeared for dinner, but he stopped her. 'No, later than that, Miss Matthews. Did he take anything on going to bed? A cup of Ovaltine, perhaps, or – '

'He couldn't bear anything with malt in it,' said Miss Matthews positively. 'Often and often I've begged him to try it, because he didn't sleep very well, but he never would listen to advice, not even when he was a little boy.'

'Did he take anything at all for his insomnia?' Hannasyde asked.

'Oh, it wasn't as bad as that!' said Miss Matthews. 'In fact, it's my belief he slept a lot better than he thought he did.'

Hannasyde turned his head towards the doctor, and raised his brows in a mute question.

Fielding said: 'I prescribed nothing. He may occasionally have taken aspirin. I don't know.'

'No, that I'm sure he did not,' said Miss Matthews. 'He didn't approve of drugs.'

'Then between dinner and bedtime he didn't, to your

knowledge, take anything at all? No drink of any sort? A whiskey-and-soda, for instance, or – '

'Oh, that sort of thing!' said Miss Matthews. 'He often had a whiskey-and-soda about half an hour before he went to bed. Not always, you know, but quite often. We have a tray brought into the drawing-room at ten o'clock. I myself think it's entirely unnecessary, and simply encourages young people to sit up late, drinking and smoking, and wasting the electricity.'

'Do you remember if your brother had a whiskey-and-soda, or any other kind of drink, on Tuesday evening? Perhaps you can help me, Mr Matthews?'

'I was just trying to remember,' said Guy. 'I don't think – '

'Yes, he did,' said Miss Matthews suddenly. 'Speaking to you reminded me of it, Guy. He had a small whiskey, and he said that when he asked for a small one he didn't mean he wanted it drowned in soda. And you said the syphon was rather "up". Don't you remember?'

'Was that the night he died?' asked Guy, frowning. 'Yes, I believe it was.'

'Did you pour out his drink for him, Mr Matthews?'

'Yes. I often did,' Guy answered.

'At about what time did he have the whiskey?'

'Oh, I don't know! The usual time, I think. Round about half-past ten.'

'Do you know when he went up to bed?'

'No, I was in the billiard-room with my sister.'

'My brother always went up to his room at eleven, unless we had visitors,' said Miss Matthews. 'We were all brought up to keep regular hours in my family, though I must say Gregory used to waste a lot of time pottering about his room before he got into bed.'

'You don't know what he did after he went upstairs, or when he actually got into bed?'

Miss Matthews was inclined to be affronted. 'Certainly not! I was not in the habit of spying on him!'

'I wasn't suggesting anything like that, Miss Matthews,' replied Hannasyde peaceably. 'You might have heard him moving about in his room.'

'Oh no, this house is very well built, and, besides, my room isn't next to his.'

'I see. Who did sleep next to Mr Matthews?'

'Well, my sister-in-law, in a way, but there's a bathroom in between,' explained Miss Matthews.

Hannasyde looked at Guy. 'At what hour did you go up to bed, Mr Matthews?'

'Haven't an idea,' said Guy carelessly. 'Sometime between half-past eleven and twelve, I should think.'

'Did you notice whether the light was still on in your uncle's room?'

'No, I'm afraid I didn't. My sister might know. She went up at the same time.'

'Yes, I should like to have a talk with Miss – Miss Stella Matthews,' nodded Hannasyde, consulting his notebook. 'And with Mrs Matthews too, if you please.'

'My mother doesn't get up till after breakfast, but I'll go and tell her,' volunteered Guy, and left the room.

Mrs Matthews was doing her hair at the dressing-table when her son knocked on the door. She smiled at him as he came in, and said: 'Well, darling, not gone off to work yet?'

'No, and a darned good job too!' said Guy. 'Haven't you heard? There's a chap from Scotland Yard down-stairs, cross-examining everybody!'

Mrs Matthews' comb was stayed in mid-air; in the mirror her eyes met Guy's for one startled moment. Then she put the comb down, and turned in her chair to face him. 'Scotland Yard,' she repeated. 'That means he was poisoned.'

'Yes, something to do with nicotine. I never heard of

66

poisoning anybody with nicotine myself, but that's what Fielding said. The Superintendent's interviewing Aunt Harriet now, and then he wants to see you and Stella. He's already asked Aunt Harriet and me a whole lot of questions. Aunt was scared out of her life at first, but personally I found it rather amusing.'

'What did your aunt say?' asked Mrs Matthews quickly.

'Oh, she drivelled on in her usual style! Mostly irrelevant. Except that she would insist on stressing the fact that it was I who poured out uncle's drink for him on the night he died.' He gave a little laugh. 'Actually it wouldn't be a bad plan if someone tipped her the wink not to talk so much. Given time she'll tell the police all the family details, down to what uncle was like in the cradle.'

Mrs Matthews began to put up her hair. 'I'll go down at once. Run along while I finish dressing, dear. Oh, and Guy! – Find Stella, and tell her I want her, will you? And just remember, darling, that the less you say the better. It isn't that there's anything to conceal, but you and Stella are inclined to let your tongues run away with you, and you very often give a totally wrong impression to people. I want you for all our sakes to be careful what you say.'

'Well, of course!' said Guy, rather impatiently. 'You don't suppose I'm going to give anything away, do you, mother?'

'There's nothing to give away, dear. All I mean is that I don't want you to talk in that silly, exaggerated way you and Stella so often fall into, particularly when speaking of your uncle.'

'All right, all right!' Guy said. 'I'm not quite a fool, mother!'

He went downstairs again, and found his sister in the hall, holding a low-voiced conversation with Dr Fielding. They both looked up as Guy rounded the bend in the stairs, and he saw that Stella was rather pale. 'Mother wants you,' he told her. 'Seen the giddy detective yet?'

'No. I'm scared stiff of him,' Stella confessed.

'You needn't be, Stella; he's not at all alarming,' said the doctor reassuringly.

'I shall go and blurt out something stupid. Policemen always terrify me,' said Stella with a nervous laugh. 'You know, in spite of talking about it, and wondering what would happen if uncle had been poisoned, I never really believed he had been, did you, Guy? Deryk says it was nicotine, which, as a matter of fact, I always thought was the stuff you get in tobacco.'

'Well, so it is,' said Guy. 'I didn't know you could poison people with it either. Is it often done, Fielding?'

'No, I don't think so,' replied the doctor shortly.

'I suppose he couldn't have taken it by accident, could he?' suggested Stella hopefully.

The doctor shrugged. 'I should say, very unlikely.'

'Well, but when could he have swallowed it if not at dinner?'

'My dear girl, what's the use of asking me? I don't know.'

'You needn't be stuffy about it,' said Stella mildly. 'It's my belief you know more than you pretend about this nicotine stuff.'

'Actually I know extremely little about nicotine,' answered Fielding. 'Sorry if that blights your faith in me, but it is not the sort of poison that comes in the way of general practice.'

'Jolly lucky for you,' remarked Guy. 'I mean, if it had been an ordinary sort of poison, like arsenic, they might have suspected you.'

'Why should they?' demanded Stella fiercely. 'There's no reason to suspect Deryk!'

Fielding smiled. 'Oh yes, there is, Stella! Guy is quite right, and I have no hesitation in freely acknowledging it:

68

It might easily have looked as though I could have done it, had the poison been one you'd find in a doctor's poison-cupboard. A great many people know that I was not on good terms with your uncle, and I imagine that all the members of your family know that he had threatened to – spread an unpleasant scandal which would in all probability have injured my practice considerably.'

'Yes, but we shan't say anything about it, you know,' said Guy, a little awkwardly.

'I don't wish you to conceal it, I assure you,' replied Fielding calmly. 'If I am asked I shall certainly tell the police the entire story.' He added with a slight smile: 'Nor do I imagine that Miss Matthews will be as discreet as you and Stella would be!'

In the library Miss Matthews was proving the justice of this mistrust of her. Having discovered that Superintendent Hannasyde was a sympathetic listener she had soon lost her first dread of him, and had told him any number of things which her family would no doubt have preferred her to have kept hidden. She told him the whole history of the duck; she told him how disagreeable Gregory used to be; and she complained bitterly to him of the wicked unfairness of the Will.

'I did think,' she said, 'that after the years I've lived with him my brother would have had the common decency to have left the house all to me. But that's just the kind of man he was. I'm sure it's no wonder he was poisoned. And if we could only see him I've no doubt he's laughing about it now in that sneering way of his. If you were to ask me, I should have to say that I believe he liked to make people uncomfortable, which he certainly has done, getting himself poisoned in this tiresome way, and leaving a most unfair Will.'

'You had lived with him a long time, Miss Matthews?'

'Oh yes, ever since my mother died, eighteen – or was it only seventeen? no, I'm sure it was eighteen – years ago. Not that I ever wanted to keep house for him; in fact, if it hadn't been for my sister I would much have preferred to work for my living, because I never did get on with Gregory, even when we were children. He always wanted to be top-dog, which I think very wrong myself, not that my opinion is likely to count with anyone in this family. But when you've looked forward for years to having the house to yourself one day, and then find you've got to share it with the last person in the world you'd choose – '

'The house is left to you and to someone else as well?'

'Yes, my sister-in-law,' nodded Miss Matthews. 'Oh, I've no doubt you'll think she's very sweet and charming when you see her! People do. But I know better. She's pleasant enough on the surface, but never in my life have I met anyone, I don't care who it is, who's more thoroughly selfish! That woman,' she said impressively, 'will go to any lengths to get her own way. My one comfort is that whatever she chooses to say I know she's just as disappointed in the Will as anyone else. I know very well that she counted on being left the house, and money too, if the truth be told. And if she tells you she's badly off, don't you believe it! She's got quite enough for one person; too much, if you ask me! In fact, I should have thought she could well have given some money to Guy, instead of expecting his uncle to do it!'

'Guy?' repeated Hannasyde. 'That is the nephew who came in with you a little while ago, isn't it?'

'Yes,' answered Miss Matthews. 'Such a nice boy! And I do hope you won't listen to any spiteful tales about him from my sister. Gregory was extremely unkind to him, and Guy had every reason to dislike him. The idea of sending a boy like that to South America! I shouldn't have been in the least surprised if he had poisoned his uncle. Not that he did, of course. I'm quite sure he didn't, and if you want to know I'd much rather think it

70

was Randall – my other nephew. Only he wasn't here at the time, so I'm afraid that's out of the question.'

Inspector Davis, who had been listening to this illuminating monologue with a slightly dazed but intent expression on his face made a stifled sound, and put up his hand to hide his mouth. But the Superintendent, though there was a twinkle at the back of his eyes, said with perfect gravity: 'Well, yes, at first glance that does seem to rule him out. And to what part of South America was Mr Matthews proposing to send his nephew?'

Miss Matthews who had seldom (except for Edward Rumbold) met with so encouraging an audience, answered with the utmost readiness: 'Some place in Brazil: I forget the name of it. So unsuitable! Guy doesn't like rubber at all, and besides, he's doing so well at his work, which is really most original – I mean the way he does it – and you can't expect a new business to make money right away, can you?'

'No,' agreed Hannasyde. 'What is his business, if I may ask?'

'Well, they call it Interior Decoration, and though I myself shouldn't want a gilded ceiling and black panels I can quite understand that tastes differ. But Gregory never did have any patience with Art, and besides, I don't think he liked Guy, and I must say that Guy was often needlessly rude to his uncle, though at the same time Gregory gave him plenty of excuse. And then about this South American business! Only there was a good deal of excuse for Guy over that too, because the poor boy felt quite desperate – he told me so himself – and no wonder! Altogether things have been very difficult, and though Gregory's death hasn't done as much good as one hoped it would, at least it has put a stop to all the incessant quarrelling and unpleasantness in the house.'

'That sounds as though others beside Mr Guy Matthews

71

have been at variance with your brother,' said Hannasyde, smiling.

'I should call it being at daggers drawn!' said Miss Matthews candidly. '*Most* unfortunately my niece, Stella, wants to marry Dr Fielding, and I need hardly say that Gregory had taken one of his unreasonable dislikes to the poor man. As though anyone could be blamed for what his father did! Not that I should mention any of that, and I'm not going to, for I was thoroughly ashamed of my brother's behaviour, and what is more I told him that to my mind it was nothing less than blackmail! But it's something I prefer not to talk about, so I beg you won't ask me any questions about it.'

'I quite understand,' said Hannasyde. 'It must have been very trying both for you and for Mrs Matthews. I hope for your niece's sake she does not also oppose the marriage?'

Miss Matthews gave a sniff. 'I'm sure I don't know what her views are, for I never believe a word she says. Besides, if she cares for anyone but herself it's for Guy, not for Stella. As a matter of fact, I was agreeably surprised in her over the South American business at first. I didn't know she had so much feeling and I certainly didn't expect her to quarrel with my brother about it. At one time I thought it was really going to come to a breach between her and Gregory, but the instant she realized she couldn't force Gregory an inch she turned completely round, and butter wouldn't have melted in her mouth. My sister Gertrude was right – not that I've any desire to quote Gertrude, because I consider she's behaved most unkindly to me, calling me a bad housekeeper, and I don't know what beside! It just serves her right that Gregory only left her a picture of himself and a small legacy, and for my part I call it a judgement, and I only hope that it will teach her a lesson, and that in future she won't go about demanding post-mortems right and left!'

The Inspector stiffened suddenly, and shot a look at Hannasyde. Hannasyde very slightly frowned, but he was watching Miss Matthews closely as he asked: 'Was it your sister who put the matter into the Coroner's hands, Miss Matthews?'

'Well, actually it was Dr Fielding who rang up the Coroner,' said Miss Matthews. 'But he never would have done so if it hadn't been for Gertrude. He didn't suspect poison at all; in fact, he was very much against a post-mortem, but that's Gertrude all over! She always wants to interfere. She made an absurd fuss, and of course the doctor had to give way about it, and I should like to know what good it's done? I mean, if Gregory's dead he's dead, and we can only be thank – well, perhaps not quite that, but you know what I mean.'

'Perfectly,' said the Superintendent. 'I wonder if you would be so kind as to find out if Dr Fielding is still in the house? If he is, I should like to have a word with him.'

Miss Matthews was a little disappointed at having her talk cut short, but she acquiesced with a fairly good grace, and went off to find the doctor. As he was still chatting to Stella in the hall this was not difficult, and the Inspector had had no time to say more than: 'That's something we didn't know, anyway,' when he entered the library.

'Come in, doctor,' said Hannasyde pleasantly. 'There are just one or two questions still that I should like to put to you.' He glanced down at his open notebook. 'I think you stated that when you saw the body of the deceased you noticed nothing that was not in your opinion compatible with death from syncope?'

'Quite right,' said the doctor. 'I doubt whether anyone could have detected poisoning from a superficial examination.'

Hannasyde nodded. 'You had been treating Mr Matthews for some little time, I believe?'

'About a year.'

'You were no doubt fairly intimate with the various members of the household – knew the ins and outs, in fact?'

The doctor hesitated. 'I hardly know how to reply. I have been very intimate with Miss Stella Matthews for some while – we are engaged to be married, in fact – and I have attended her aunt in a professional capacity. I know very little of the other members of the family.'

'You knew that there was a good deal of friction in this house, I take it?'

'Everyone knew that,' responded the doctor dryly.

'Had you that friction in mind when you decided to put the matter into the hands of the police, doctor?'

The doctor raised his eyes, and looked steadily across at Hannasyde. 'You are under a misapprehension, Superintendent,' he said. 'It was Mrs Lupton, not I, who insisted on an inquiry.'

'You did not tell me that,' said Hannasyde.

'I beg your pardon,' replied the doctor politely. 'I suppose it slipped my memory. In any case, it doesn't seem very material to me. Mrs Lupton herself will tell you that I was in no sense averse from having a post-mortem inquiry. Quite the reverse: if there was any suspicion of foul play I naturally was one of the first to want a full inquiry.'

The Inspector shot a question at him. 'Were you on good terms with the deceased?'

Fielding looked at him with a slightly amused expression on his face. 'No, Inspector,' he said. 'I was not.'

'Will you tell us why, doctor?' asked Hannasyde.

The doctor regarded his finger-nails. 'Since you ask me I am bound to tell you why,' he answered. 'It is not particularly pleasant for me to have to do so, but I have not the smallest desire to hinder you by keeping anything back which you may think of importance. Mr Matthews was bitterly opposed to my engagement to his niece.'

'Why?' asked the Inspector.

The doctor was silent for a moment. Then he said in a somewhat constricted tone: 'Mr Matthews had discovered – how, I don't know – that my father died in a Home for Hopeless Inebriates.'

The Inspector looked very much shocked, and coughed in an embarrassed way. Hannasyde said in his unemotional voice: 'It is naturally very distasteful for you to discuss such a matter, doctor, but did Mr Matthews impart this knowledge to Miss Stella Matthews?'

'It made no difference to her,' replied the doctor.

'I see. Had he any control over her actions?'

'We should have got married whatever he said, if that is what you mean.' Fielding paused, and looked from one to the other with a rueful smile. 'Come, Superintendent, why beat about the bush? You want to know whether he had been threatening me with exposure, don't you? Of course he had, and of course it would have been highly unpleasant for me if he had.'

'Thank you, doctor,' said Hannasyde, and turned his head as the door opened.

Mrs Matthews came into the room with Stella behind her. She looked charming in a black frock with touches of white at the throat and wrists, and if she had put her hair up in haste at least the ordered waves showed no signs of it. She checked on the threshold, and said: 'Oh, have we interrupted you? I'm so sorry, but my son told me that you wanted to see me, er – Superintendent.'

'No, please come in,' said Hannasyde, rising from his chair by the table. 'I needn't keep you any longer now, doctor.'

Mrs Matthews waited until Fielding had left the room, and then advanced towards Hannasyde, and sat down in a chair on the opposite side of the table, indicating to him with a graceful wave of her hand that he might resume his seat. Stella, admiring her exquisite poise, perched on the arm of her chair, and gravely regarded the Superintendent.

'You wanted to see my daughter too, didn't you?' said Mrs Matthews. She laid her hand on one of Stella's, and added with a laugh that seemed to take the Superintendent into her confidence: 'I know you won't mind my being here while you talk to her. I'm afraid she has a very guilty conscience, and is terrified lest you should ask her awkward questions about such things as driving without a rear light!'

Stella wriggled uncomfortably, and muttered: 'Mother, really!'

'That isn't my department, Miss Matthews,' said Hannasyde.

'I know,' replied Stella indignantly.

The pressure of her mother's fingers silenced her. 'Please ask me anything you like, Superintendent!' Mrs Matthews said kindly. 'One shrinks from discussing it, but I know that it is necessary, and one must try and overcome one's instinctive distaste. I was very much attached to my poor brother-in-law, and this has all been terribly upsetting to me. I ought to tell you that my nerves are not my strong point. But I'm quite ready to answer anything I can.'

'Thank you,' said Hannasyde. 'Naturally I understand how you must feel. You have lived under Mr Gregory Matthews' roof for some years, I believe?'

She bowed her head. 'I have lived here for five years. My brother-in-law was very good to me at a time of deep sorrow, and I shall always think kindly of him for that reason alone.'

'My father died five years ago,' interrupted Stella. 'My uncle was joint guardian and trustee with my mother for my brother and me.'

'I see,' said Hannasyde. 'It was in the capacity of guardian that Mr Matthews proposed to send your son to South America, Mrs Matthews?'

Mrs Matthews raised her brows. 'That absurd scheme! I'm afraid I didn't take that very seriously, Superintendent. You have been listening to my sister-in-law, haven't you? She is a very dear soul, but, as I daresay you've realized, she is rather apt to exaggerate. Naturally I should not say so in her hearing, but she didn't understand her brother. I think that is so often the way when two people don't get on together. There is just that lack of sympathy which gives one insight into another person's character. I sometimes think that no one understood my brother-in-law as well as I did.'

Inspector Davis caught the Superintendent's eye for an instant. His own glance spoke volumes. It seemed to him that the Matthews household consisted entirely of voluble females.

'But was there not a serious plan to send your son to Brazil, Mrs Matthews?' asked Hannasyde.

'My brother-in-law certainly thought it might be a good opening for him, but – '

'And you? Did you agree?' interrupted Hannasyde ruthlessly.

Mrs Matthews threw him an indulgent little smile. 'You would not ask me that question if you were a woman, Superintendent,' she said. 'I am Guy's mother. I could never agree to be parted from my boy unless it were for some very, very good reason.'

'In fact, you opposed it, Mrs Matthews?'

She gave a wise laugh. 'Well, yes, I suppose you may say that I *opposed* it. But I have told you that I understood my brother-in-law, and I knew that his plan wouldn't come to anything.'

Hannasyde glanced at Stella. She was sitting perfectly still with her eyes cast down and her mouth set rather

77

sternly. His gaze returned to Mrs Matthews' face. 'Was there any bad feeling between you over the affair?'

'Thank God, no!' she replied. 'When he died we were on the same affectionate terms as ever.'

'There had been no quarrel between you?'

She sank her voice a tone. 'There *had* been – not a quarrel, but a feeling of – of – how shall I put it? – of *hurt* on my side, and I'm sorry to say a little bitterness. I did allow myself to be cross with him when he first broached the question of Brazil. It was mother-instinct, but very foolish of me, and I am thankful to say that I got it under. I knew all the time that my brother-in-law would never insist on doing anything against my wishes. One just had to be tactful. You do not know what a comfort it is to me to be able to say that at the time of Gregory's death there was no shadow of coolness between us.'

'I can well imagine that it must be,' replied Hannasyde.

It was over an hour later when he and Inspector Davis left the Poplars, and the Inspector was frankly exasperated. As he walked beside Hannasyde down the drive he said: 'Well, I always heard that the old lady was a caution, but if you ask me Mrs Matthews is the worst of the two! I'm darned if I know what to make of her, and that's a fact!'

'Yes, she's difficult,' agreed Hannasyde. 'It's always hard when dealing with that type of woman to know when they're speaking the truth as it was, and when they're speaking of it as they think it was . . . Hullo, Hemingway!'

Sergeant Hemingway, a brisk person with a pair of bright eyes and an engaging smile, who had been waiting for his chief outside the gate, fell into step beside him, and said cheerfully: 'I'll tell you something, Super. We aren't going to like this case, not by a long chalk. You know what it smelt like in the servants' quarters? Pea-soup!'

The Inspector, who was not acquainted with Hemingway, looked a little puzzled, and said: 'Eh?'

'Figure of speech,' explained the Sergeant. 'Get anything your end, Super?'

'Not much,' replied Hannasyde. 'It's early yet.'

'Early or late I don't like poisoning cases,' said the Sergeant. 'Give me a nice clean bullet-wound where I've got something to go on, and not too many doctors to mess the case up disagreeing with one another! Ever handled a case of nicotine-poisoning before, Inspector?'

'No, I can't say I have,' admitted the Inspector.

'If I know anything about it you won't want to handle another by the time we're through with this,' prophesied the Sergeant. 'Nor me either. The Superintendent here doesn't believe in premonitions, but I've got one right now.'

'You've had them before,' remarked Hannasyde unkindly.

'I won't say I haven't,' replied the Sergeant, quite unabashed. 'This case remind you of anything, Super?'

'No,' said Hannasyde. 'But you'd better tell me, and get it off your chest. What does it remind you of?'

The Sergeant cocked an eye at him. 'The Vereker Case,' he said.

'The Vereker Case! That was a stabbing affair!'

'I'm not saying it wasn't, but when I got the hang of the *décor* here, and a squint at some of the *dramatis personæ* that's what flashed across my mind.'

'What I don't like about it,' said the Inspector slowly, 'is this nicotine. It seems to me the doctors don't properly understand it, judging from that report you showed me, Superintendent. I mean, if there wasn't no more than a slight trace of it in the stomach, so as to make them think he can't have swallowed much, and yet they find by the state of the blood – and the mouth, wasn't it? – that – '

'Mucous membrane and tongue,' interjected the

79

Sergeant knowledgeably. 'They tell me you always look for nicotine in the mouth. Liver and kidneys too. It's a mystery to me why anyone wants to be a doctor.'

'Well, what I'm getting at is how did he have all that poison in his innards?' said the Inspector.

'It is quite possible,' said Hannasyde, 'that he didn't swallow any poison at all.'

'What?' demanded the Inspector.

'Cases have been known,' continued Hannasyde, 'where nicotine has either been injected subcutaneously, or even absorbed through the skin, with fatal results. There was apparently an instance once, years ago, of a whole squadron of Hussars being made ill by trying to smuggle tobacco next to their skins.'

'There you are! What did I tell you?' said the Sergeant. 'Nice, simple case we've got when we don't even know whether the poor fellow drank the dope or had it poured over him! One thing, it looks as though whoever did the murder knew a bit about poisons.'

'Y-es. Or had read it up,' said Hannasyde. 'As far as I can see it ought not to be a very difficult matter – given a little chemical knowledge – to prepare nicotine. What did you get out of the servants, Hemingway?'

'Plenty,' answered the Sergeant promptly. 'A sight too much for my taste. According to them any one of the family would have been glad of the chance to do old Matthews in. Proper sort of tyrant he seems to have been. The cook thinks it was Mrs Matthews, on account of the old man wanting to ship his nephew off to Brazil, but what's the use of that? I don't say it isn't good psychology. It is. But so far I don't get any sort of line on the Matthews dame. No evidence. Then there's a classy bit of goods, calling herself Rose Daventry. If you was to ask me what I think about her, Super, I'd tell you only that I wouldn't like to use a word that might shock the Inspector.'

Inspector Davis grinned. 'I know her,' he said.

'Well, she thinks the niece did it, because her uncle didn't cotton to her marrying the doctor. At least, that's the reason she gave me, but what she meant was that Miss Stella Matthews makes a lot more work in the house than little Rosebud likes. After that I had a go at the under-housemaid. Country girl, name of Stevens. She doesn't think anything, never having been brought up to it. Ruling out a couple of gardeners and the kitchen-maid, there's the butler. I've got his evidence taped for you, Chief, and it's the best of a bad lot, which is all I'll say for it. Main points being that when he went up to bed a few minutes after eleven he saw Miss Harriet Matthews come out of her brother's room.'

'Did he indeed?' said Hannasyde. 'That's interesting. She gave me to understand that she didn't see Matthews, after he went up to bed.'

'Well, if you're pleased, Super, it's OK by me,' said the Sergeant. 'But if you know what motive she had for doing the old boy in, you know a sight more than I could find out.'

'She's a very eccentric kind of woman,' said the Inspector thoughtfully. 'Regular cough-drop.'

'Well, I'm bound to say I haven't so far come across a case of anyone doing a murder just because they were eccentric,' said the Sergeant, 'but that isn't to say I won't. Maybe you'll like my next bit of evidence. According to Beecher, there was a brand-new bottle of some tonic or other blown over into the washbasin in Matthews' bathroom, and consequently smashed. Miss Harriet found it, and disposed of the bits of glass by dropping them into the kitchen-stove. Seems a funny thing to do, to my way of thinking, but the servants made nothing of it. Said it was the sort of silly trick she would get up to. My last titbit is highly scandalous. They say the doctor drinks. Beecher-the-Butler has it firmly wedged in his head that

Matthews had got something on the doctor, but unless it was him being over-fond of the bottle he doesn't know what it may have been.'

'The doctor gave me a perfectly straightforward account of that,' replied Hannasyde. 'Matthews appears to have threatened to broadcast the fact that Fielding's father died in an Inebriates' Home if Fielding didn't leave his niece alone.'

The Sergeant opened his eyes at that. 'What things they do get up to in the suburbs!' he remarked admiringly. 'Now, some people might call that blackmail, Super.'

Hannasyde nodded. 'I do myself.'

'Blackmail's one of the most powerful motives for murder I know, Super.'

'Admittedly. But I didn't get the impression that Fielding was so desperately in love with Miss Stella that he'd commit murder on her account.'

The Inspector, who had been listening with knit brows, said: 'It wouldn't surprise me if the doctor thought Miss Stella was going to inherit a tidy little fortune. I'd have gone bail myself Matthews would have left the lot to her, or most of it anyway. Very fond of her he was, judging from all I hear. Gave her a Riley Sports car only six months ago, and he wasn't the sort to give anything to someone he didn't like a good bit.'

Hannasyde was silent for a moment. Then he said: 'Why nicotine? He's been attending Matthews, and we know that Matthews' wasn't a good life. If he'd wanted to murder him wouldn't he have done it gradually, so that no one would ever have suspected?'

'There's that, of course,' agreed Hemingway. 'On the other hand, nicotine looks to me like the very poison you wouldn't expect a doctor to use. How's that, Chief?'

'Yes, I had thought of that,' said Hannasyde.

'That's where psychology comes in,' said the Sergeant briskly. 'What's our next move?'

'I've got to see Mrs Lupton, Matthews' elder sister. It transpired that it was she who demanded the PM.'

'Well, well, well!' said the Sergeant. 'So it wasn't Plausible Percy after all? Now we are getting somewhere!'

'If you mean that it wasn't Fielding,' said Hannasyde patiently, 'no, it wasn't. But as he seems, according to all the evidence I've heard yet, to have been perfectly willing, and even anxious to have the PM, I don't think we're getting as far as you imagine. We'll see what Mrs Lupton has to tell us, and then I must pay a call on the heir.'

'Who's he?' inquired the Sergeant.

'He,' said Hannasyde slowly, 'is Gregory Matthews' eldest nephew. He lives in town, and I shall be interested to make his acquaintance. From all I can gather he seems to be an extremely unpopular and unpleasant gentleman.'

'This is a new one on me,' remarked the Sergeant. 'Where does he come into the case?'

Hannasyde gave a laugh. 'That's the snag, Skipper. He doesn't. And I can't help feeling that he's the very person who ought to!'

5

'Women!' said the Inspector, half-an-hour later. 'Women!'

They had just come away from an interview with Gertrude Lupton, and there was some excuse for the Inspector's voice of loathing. Hannasyde laughed, but Sergeant Hemingway, always interested in new types, said: 'Now this is what I call a nice morning. You wouldn't believe anyone would start a scandal in the family just for the fun of it, would you?'

'Not fun, jealousy,' Hannasyde corrected. 'And she happened to be right.'

'Right or wrong, it's my belief she hadn't a bit of reason for wanting that post-mortem,' said the indignant Inspector. 'I'm not surprised her husband looked so uncomfortable. More shame to him, letting her run riot the way she does!'

'Poor devil!' said Hannasyde. 'All the same, but for her there wouldn't have been a case at all, so really we've nothing to grumble about, whatever her motive may have been.'

The Sergeant scratched the tip of his nose in a reflective manner. 'No motive. Bit of womanly intuition, if you ask me. Funny things, women.'

'You don't believe in that, do you?' asked the Inspector scornfully.

The Sergeant looked at him with a penetrating eye. 'You a married man, Inspector?'

'I'm not.'

'That was what you call a rhetorical question,' said the Sergeant. 'I know you aren't. You'd believe in woman's instinct fast enough if you were. Why, they're always having fits of it, even the best of them, and about once in a dozen times it turns out to be right. Granite-faced Gertrude had a Feeling someone did her brother in, and if you knew as much about woman's Feelings as I do, you wouldn't go around saying she did it out of spite. Not she! What she thought was: "I don't like any of the people in this house." And believe me, Inspector, once a woman gets a thought like that into her head she'll develop a Feeling against the whole lot in double-quick time.'

'It wouldn't surprise me,' said the Inspector, who had taken an unreasoning dislike to Mrs Lupton, 'if we found she did it, and was acting like this to put us off the scent.'

The Sergeant exchanged an indulgent glance with Hannasyde. 'Bad psychology,' he said. 'She's all right.'

'Wasting our time!' snorted the Inspector. 'There wasn't a thing she could tell us we didn't know already. Don't you agree, Superintendent?'

Hannasyde, who had not been paying much attention, said: 'Agree? Oh! No, I don't agree with either of you. I think she had more than a Feeling, and I think she did tell us several things.'

The Sergeant nodded. 'I thought you were on to something,' he remarked.

'You were wrong,' said Hannasyde calmly. 'But this Lupton woman, though unpleasant, is scrupulously honest. In the Matthews household we interviewed a number of people who were all frightened, and who therefore said whatever they thought would be safest. Mrs Lupton isn't afraid of me or of any other policeman, and she was rigidly determined not to make the smallest accusation against anyone. She isn't being spiteful; she's out for justice. Which makes what she did say quite valuable. When a woman like Miss Matthews says that her sister-in-law is equal to anything, I disbelieve her, just as I discount Mrs Matthews' delicate implication that Harriet would have liked to have seen her brother put quietly out of the way. But when an uncompromisingly honest woman like Mrs Lupton tells me that her sister-in-law will go to any lengths to get her own way, I begin to sit up and take notice. The people she suspects are Mrs Matthews, the boy Guy, and the doctor.'

'Sweeping sort of suspicion,' commmented the Inspector.

'No, I don't think so,' said Hannasyde. 'She ruled out the girl, Stella, and I got the impression that she dislikes that girl cordially. But she said positively that Stella would not have done such a thing, which to my mind gave a good deal of weight to her pronouncement that any one of the other three have it in them to commit murder. I know nothing about female intuition, Hemingway, but if Mrs Lupton suspected foul play it wasn't because she detected anything odd about her brother's body, but because she knew that the situation at the Poplars had been tense enough to end in murder. Which is what I wanted to find out.'

The Sergeant nodded. 'Right, Chief.'

Inspector Davis was not so easily satisfied. 'Yes, but what I'd like to know is, how did Matthews take that poison? It's worrying me a lot, that is, because so far we haven't discovered a blessed thing he swallowed that the others didn't, barring the tonic he may have had after dinner.'

'Guy Matthews might conceivably have dropped the poison into that whiskey-and-soda from a phial concealed in his hand,' suggested Hannasyde.

The Inspector gave a disparaging sniff.

'Don't you fret, Inspector,' said Hemingway. 'The Chief's after something a bit more recondite. Am I right, Super?'

'More or less. Anyway, we'll go back to town now, and look up Randall Matthews.'

Parting from Inspector Davis at the Police Station, Hannasyde and his subordinate travelled back to London on the Underground Railway. Randall Matthews rented a flat in a road off St James's Street, but was not in at one o'clock, when the Superintendent called. His manservant, eyeing the police with disfavour, declined to hazard any opinion of the probable time of his master's return, but Hannasyde and his Sergeant, coming back at three o'clock, found a Mercédès car parked outside the house, and rightly conjectured that its owner was Mr Randall Matthews.

This time the manservant, instead of addressing them through the smallest possible opening of the front door, reluctantly held it wide for the Superintendent to pass through.

The two men were ushered into a small hall which was decorated in shades of grey, and left there while Benson went to inform his master of their arrival.

The Sergeant looked round rather dubiously, and scratched his chin with the brim of his bowler hat. 'What you might call Arty,' he remarked. 'Ever thought that *décor* is highly significant, Super? Take that divan.'

'What about it?' asked Hannasyde, glancing a little scornfully at the piece in question, which was wide, and low, and covered with pearl-grey velvet.

'Not sure,' replied the Sergeant. 'If it had upwards of a dozen cushions with gold tassels chucked on it careless-like I should have known what to think. But it hasn't. All the same, Super, we can write this bird down as having expensive tastes. Would you call the pictures oriental?'

'Chinese prints,' replied Hannasyde briefly.

'I wouldn't wonder,' agreed the Sergeant. 'It all fits in with what I was thinking.'

The looking-glass door at one side of the hall opened

at this moment, and Randall Matthews strolled towards them, holding Hannasyde's card between his finger and thumb.

'More *décor*,' muttered the Sergeant.

It could hardly have been by design, but Randall was dressed in a suit of pearl-grey flannel that harmonized beautifully with the background. He raised his eyes from the card, and said: 'Ah, good afternoon, Superintendent! I might almost say, Welcome to my humble abode. Won't you come in?' He made a gesture towards the room he had come from. 'Both of you, of course. You must introduce me to your friend.'

'Sergeant Hemingway,' said Hannasyde, his calm eyes slightly frowning.

'How do you do, Sergeant?' said Randall affably. 'Ah, Benson, take the Sergeant's hat.'

The Sergeant, equal to this as to any other occasion and growing more bird-like with interest every moment, handed his hat to the servant, and followed Hannasyde into a room that looked out on to the street, and seemed, with the exception of its book-shelves, to be entirely composed of Spanish leather.

Randall picked up a box containing Russian cigarettes, and offered it to his visitors. It was declined, so he selected one for himself, and lit it, and waved his hand in the direction of two chairs. 'But won't you sit down? And before we go any further, do tell me how my poor uncle was poisoned!'

Hannasyde raised his brows. 'Did you then think that he had been poisoned, Mr Matthews? I understand that you described Mrs Lupton's suspicion as a *canard*.'

'I'm sure that must be correct,' agreed Randall. 'It is very much the sort of thing I should unhesitatingly say of my dear Aunt Gertrude's pronouncements. But I have so much intuition, my dear Superintendent. Your genial presence convicts me of error. I am not at all ashamed to acknowledge my mistakes. I make very few.'

'You are to be congratulated,' commented Hannasyde dryly. 'Your uncle *was* poisoned.'

'Yes, Superintendent, yes. You would not otherwise be here. Is it permitted that I should know how?'

'He died from nicotine poisoning,' replied Hannasyde.

'What a shame!' said Randall. 'It sounds very common – almost vulgar. I think I will throw away the rest of my cigarette.'

'I don't propose to take up your time – '

'My valuable time,' interpolated Randall gently.

' – any longer than I need, Mr Matthews, but as I find that you are not only the heir to your uncle's property but also the head of the family, I thought it only right to call on you. It will be necessary for the police to go through the deceased's papers.'

'Ah, you want my uncle's solicitor,' said Randall. 'I am sure you will like him.'

'I don't think I have his name,' Hannasyde said.

'Perhaps you would be good enough – '

'Certainly,' said Randall. 'His name is Carrington.'

Hannasyde looked up quickly from his notebook. 'Carrington?'

'Giles Carrington. I think there are more of them, and I am sure I went to Adam Street to visit them.'

'Thank you,' said Hannasyde. 'I know Mr Giles Carrington very well. Now, if you would answer one or two questions, Mr Matthews, I need not detain you. When did you last see your uncle?'

Randall wrinkled his brow. 'Do you know, I seem to have heard those words before? Ought it not to be *father*?'

Hannasyde was aware of rising annoyance. He curbed it, and replied evenly: 'When was it, please?'

'Surely the Civil Wars?' said Randall. 'Oh, I'm so

sorry, I thought we were talking about pictures! I last saw my uncle on the Sunday before he died. That would be – '

'May 12th,' said Hannasyde. 'You were at Grinley Heath on that day?'

'I was indeed,' said Randall with a faint shudder.

'You will forgive my curiosity, Mr Matthews, but have you any particular reason for remembering the occasion?' asked Hannasyde, observing the shudder.

'It is quite indelibly printed on my mind,' said Randall. 'My visit coincided with that of my cousin, Mrs – I think it's Crewe, but I'm not altogether sure.'

'Is that all!'

'No,' said Randall. 'It was by no means all. She brought her regrettable offspring with her, and appeared to think it a fortunate circumstance that I should be present to admire it.'

Hannasyde ignored this, and said in his curtest tone: 'And that was the last time you saw the deceased?'

'Yes,' said Randall.

'Were you on good terms with him?'

'Quite,' said Randall indifferently.

'Intimate terms, Mr Matthews?'

Randall looked at him through his lashes. 'I shall have to ask you to construe, my dear Superintendent.'

'Let me put it this way: were you in his confidence?'

'I shouldn't think so,' replied Randall. 'There is just that indefinable something about me which does not lead my family to confide in me.'

'You cannot tell me, then, whether he had any enemies?'

'No,' said Randall softly. 'And I cannot tell you whether he had any friends either.'

'Oh!' Hannasyde cast him a shrewd glance under his brows. 'Do you know of anyone who had any reason to wish him dead?'

'Other than myself?' asked Randall.

The Sergeant jumped. Hannasyde answered: 'Had you reason, Mr Matthews?'

Randall smiled at him. 'My very dear sir, I'm the heir. Now do let us understand each other! There's not the least need for you to ask me careful questions. I shall be delighted to answer anything you choose to ask me. In fact, I'm positively burning to assist you to track down the murderer.'

'Thank you,' said Hannasyde.

'Not at all,' replied Randall. 'Only you mustn't be shy. You would like to know the state of my Bank balance, for one thing. That's not the sort of question I can answer offhand, but I will give you a letter of introduction to my Bank manager.'

'I should prefer it if you would give me an account of your movements on May 14th,' said Hannasyde.

'What could be easier? I was naturally at Newmarket,' answered Randall at once.

'You are fond of racing, Mr Matthews?'

'Very,' said Randall, moving over to his desk, and beginning to jot down something on a half-sheet of notepaper. 'Returning to town after the 3.30 race, in the company of one Frank Clutterbuck, whose address I am going to give you, I came back to this flat, changed my clothes – *vide* my man Benson – and repaired to Duval's – a restaurant no doubt known to you. Mention my name to the *maître d'hôtel*. I was joined there by two friends, whose names and addresses I am at the moment writing down for you. From Duval's we went to the Palladium – Row B, in the stalls – 8, 9, and 10. Leaving the Palladium shortly before the end of the performance, I became a slave to duty, and drove – but I stupidly omitted to take the taxi-driver's number – to South Street, where I made a belated but graceful appearance at Mrs Massingham's dance. I will give you her address too. Somewhere in the region of three o'clock I left South Street, came back to this flat, and went to bed.' He rose, and handed the sheet of paper to Hannasyde. 'Where I remained, Superintendent, until Mr Giles Carrington rang me up, somewhere between eleven and twelve in the morning, to inform me that my uncle was dead, a medical inquiry in progress, and a police inquiry imminent.'

Hannasyde folded the paper, and put it away in his notebook. 'Were you surprised, Mr Matthews?'

'Would not you be?' said Randall.

'I think I should – if I knew of no one who could have had any motive for the murder.'

Randall smiled, and answered rather mockingly: 'Ah, I think you must be referring to – er – family dissensions. Which of my relatives would you like me to incriminate by some damaging statement? I have hardly any preference.'

'I don't want you to incriminate anyone, thank you, Mr Matthews, but if you know anything relevant to the case I should like to hear it.'

Randall stretched out his hand and took a cigarette from the box beside him, and began to tap it on his thumbnail. 'But I don't think I do know anything relevant,' he said sadly.

'In that case we won't take up any more of your time,' said Hannasyde, and got up.

Randall touched a bell on his desk, and upon Benson's appearance instructed him, in his languid way, to show the visitors out.

As he walked down the stairs beside the Superintendent, Sergeant Hemingway said: 'A little too smooth-spoken, Chief. Just a little too smooth.'

Hannasyde grunted.

'Alibi and all,' pursued the Sergeant. 'Very pat. Gave it out as though he was darned pleased about it. Pick-a-hole-in-that-if-you-can. Question is, can we?'

'I shouldn't think so. You can check up on it – as a matter of form. I'm going to see Mr Carrington.'

'What you might call the bright spot in a bad day,' remarked the Sergeant. 'Funny thing, running slap into him right on top of my mentioning the Vereker Case. I wonder if Miss Vereker – oh, she's Mrs Carrington now, isn't she? I wonder if she still breeds bull-terriers?'

'I'll ask him,' said Hannasyde.

'You might ask him at the same time whether young Vereker has got himself hanged yet,' recommended the Sergeant.

Mr Giles Carrington did not keep Superintendent Hannasyde waiting for long. He got up from his big, untidy desk as Hannasyde was ushered into his room, and came forward with his hand held out. 'Well, this is indeed a pleasant surprise!' he said. 'How are you, Hannasyde? Sit down!'

Hannasyde shook hands warmly, and accepted a chair and a cigarette. 'How are *you*, Mr Carrington? And Mrs Carrington?'

'Oh, we're both very fit, thanks!'

'And Mr Vereker? Hemingway – you remember him? – wants to know if he's got himself hanged yet. Those pen-and-ink sketches he did of the police still rankle!'

Giles laughed. 'He went abroad immediately the case was over, and I'm happy to be able to tell you that a marriage has now been arranged, and will shortly take place.'

'Miss Rivers? That's splendid. I hope you'll give him my best wishes.'

'I will, with pleasure. If you like to drop in and see us one evening you can give them to him yourself. He's staying with us at the moment.'

'Nothing I'd like better,' said Hannasyde. 'But the sight of me might bring up what must be pretty painful recollections, mightn't it?'

'You never know with Kenneth,' replied Giles. 'Quite probably not.' He cast the Superintendent an appraising look. 'By the way, what does the sight of you portend, Hannasyde? Business or pleasure?'

'Both,' returned Hannasyde. 'It was a great pleasure to me to work with you, you know.'

'Very nicely put, but it won't wash. I know nothing about the late Gregory Matthews.'

The Superintendent's eyes twinkled. 'Now, now, Mr Carrington! None of that Holmes-stuff! Of course it's the Matthews case.'

'Was he poisoned?' asked Giles.

'Yes, he was. Nicotine. I shall want to go through his papers.'

'All right. Tomorrow suit you?'

Hannasyde nodded. 'We shan't find anything. We're five days behind this murder. And they have to put me on it! Tell me what you know about Matthews, Mr Carrington.'

'Nothing much. He's been a client of ours for about five years. Digby Bryant used to handle his affairs, and Matthews came to us when he died. I gather he didn't hit it off with young Bryant. He hasn't troubled us much. A few routine jobs. I wasn't in his confidence.'

'Know how he made his money?'

'Oh, sort of financial punter, wasn't he? He had an office in the City, and I think played about with stocks and shares. Started life in a broker's office, I believe, and I suppose struck lucky.'

'We'll take a look at that office of his. Do you know anything about the rest of the family?'

'Nothing except what I saw when I went down to read the Will.'

'You're not being at all helpful,' complained Hannasyde. 'What did you make of Randall Matthews?'

Giles tipped the ash off the end of his cigarette. 'Well,

since you ask me, I can't say I took to him much,' he replied.

'Nor did I. Know anything about him?'

Giles shook his head. 'Young man-about-town: not in my line of country. Are you interested in him?'

'I'm interested in anybody connected with this case. Hemingway says it's like pea-soup. It's this damned nicotine, Mr Carrington. It may have been swallowed, and the probability is that it wasn't. There was a bad scratch on the back of the deceased's left hand.'

'Borgia-stuff!' said Giles incredulously.

'Sounds like it, doesn't it? But one of our experts is of the opinion that the poison could have been absorbed that way. Well, the sister, Harriet Matthews, was the last person to be with Matthews on the night he died – though she didn't admit that to me. We can say, if you like, that she inflicted the scratch, but – '

'With a pair of poisoned nail-scissors,' interrupted Giles derisively. 'Go on, I like to see you becoming romantic.'

Hannasyde smiled. 'I know. But it's no joke, Mr Carrington. Suppose she inflicted the scratch, seemingly by accident, and then bathed it with lotion into which she'd dropped her poison?'

'Just a moment,' said Giles. 'Is Harriet Matthews the eccentric lady with the economy-mania?'

'That's the one.'

'Out of all your suspects what a choice to make! She wouldn't have the sense, let alone the knowledge.'

'Voluble and eccentric ladies aren't always so guileless as they seem, Mr Carrington. Not that I think it was she. I don't. But the trouble is there's no one I think it was. On the face of it the heir's the likeliest suspect. He lives high, probably beyond his income, and, if I'm not much mistaken, bets a lot. Clever fellow, and looks pretty cold-blooded. What's more, he presented me with a detailed alibi which I don't expect to pick the smallest hole in.

And I haven't, so far, a thing on him. He says he heard of his uncle's death through you. How did he take it?'

Giles reflected. 'It was over the telephone, you know. Quite calmly, I think. I merely said that Matthews was dead, and added that there was to be an autopsy.' He paused. 'He sounded distinctly annoyed about that, but I think one would be. No one likes a scandal in the home circle, after all.'

'What did he say?'

'I don't remember. Something about the incompetence of doctors, and that he'd better come round and see me.'

'Oh, he came to see you that day, did he? When?'

'Shortly before one. He was perfectly self-possessed. He came to arrange with me about reading the Will, and various other business matters.'

'He knew he was the heir, I suppose?'

'Oh yes! He's my fellow-executor.'

'Did he seem at all anxious to find out what had been happening down at Grinley Heath?'

'Not more than was natural. He wanted to know who was the fool who had started the murder-scare, but as I didn't know – '

'Who told him there was any question of murder? Did you?'

Giles looked at him. 'No, I don't think I did. But it rather leaps to the mind when you hear there's to be a post-mortem, doesn't it? I suppose he assumed there was a suspicion of poisoning, same as I did. He didn't seem to me to set much store by it, though. He said he had no doubt that the various members of his family were running entirely true to type, and added that the temptation to go down and watch them making fools of themselves was too strong to be withstood. I believe he did go down to Grinley that afternoon.'

'I've no doubt,' said Hannasyde. 'Very understandable that he should – and if there was any evidence at the

96

Poplars waiting to be destroyed, even more under-standable.'

'You sound a trifle peevish, my dear chap. Not like yourself.'

'Well, it's enough to make a saint swear, Mr Carrington: it really is! A man is poisoned on the evening of the 14th May. His own doctor finds natural causes, and is ready to sign the certificate, but one member of the family objects, so they think they'll have a post-mortem. The Divisional Surgeon makes no more of it than the family doctor, but the organs are sent up to the Home Office, as per regulations. No one at Grinley taking it seriously; no official action being taken. Result, it's five days before we get the case, during which time everyone connected with it has not only known that an inquiry was being conducted, but has also had plenty of time to dispose of whatever evidence there may have been. Dead man's room all nice and tidy, bottle of tonic providentially broken, everything cleared away.'

'Ah, I see!' smiled Giles. 'You want the corpse dis-covered *in situ*, with the incriminating letter in the waste-paper basket, the glass (with traces of poison) on the table, and everything under lock and key until you arrive.'

Hannasyde gave a reluctant laugh. 'Well, you'll admit it would be a lot easier to handle. By the way, you've got the dead man's keys, haven't you?'

'Yes, but I only took charge of them on Friday. Randall gave them to me, pending the result of the investigation.'

Hannasyde stared at him. 'Thinks of everything, doesn't he? Very proper behaviour on the part of Mr Randall Matthews. And the rest of the family hates him.' He tapped his fingers on Giles' desk for a moment. 'Get the Department to look into Mr Randall Matthews. Are you busy, Mr Carrington?'

'What do you want me to do?'

'Go with me to Gregory's office.'

Giles glanced at his watch. 'All right, but I must be back at five. I've got an appointment.'

A taxi bore both men to a big block of flats in the City. During his lifetime Gregory Matthews had rented a single room on the fourth floor where he had apparently transacted his business. It was a small apartment, containing a desk, and a couple of leather chairs, a table with a typewriter on it, a large waste-paper basket, a filing-cabinet, and a safe. It was very tidy, and smelled stuffy from having been shut up.

'No torn-up letters here, Hannasyde,' Giles remarked. 'One of those nice modern buildings where the char-woman lets herself in with a pass-key, and cleans the place each morning before you arrive.' He sat down at the desk, and began to inspect the keys on the ring he was holding. 'What would you like first? Desk, safe, or cabinet?'

Hannasyde had picked up a diary from the table, and was looking through it. 'I don't mind. Desk,' he said absently. 'Parker and Snell – they sound as though they might be his brokers. Apparently he had an appointment with them on the 14th May. Doesn't tell us much.'

'Yes, they're his brokers,' said Giles, fitting a key into the top drawer of the desk. 'Here you are.'

'Just a moment.' Hannasyde was turning the leaves of the diary backwards. 'Practically no engagements recorded. Share prices jotted down each day. Seems to have had a catholic taste in investments . . . Monday 13th May: Lupton, 12.0 P.M.' He lowered the book. 'Lupton? That's the brother-in-law. I wonder what he wanted to see him about?'

'Was Lupton the desiccated little man with the over-powering wife?' asked Giles.

'That's the fellow. Now why did Matthews make an appointment with him here when they lived in the same place? Might be useful to know that.'

Giles regarded him in some amusement. 'You have a fearful and wonderful mind, Hannasyde. I can think of a dozen reasons.'

'Oh, so can I, but you never know. Do you happen to know anything about a lady called Gladys Smith, living at 531 Fairleigh Court, Golders Green?'

'Never heard of her,' answered Giles, picking up some papers from the drawer he had opened. 'Has she got anything to do with the case, or are you going to tell me an anecdote?'

'Her name and address are written here on the 9th May, that's all. No time mentioned, so it may not necessarily have been an appointment.'

'You seem to be catching at straws,' remarked Giles, glancing cursorily through the papers in his hand.

Hannasyde made a note of Mrs Smith's address. 'Not much else to catch at. Sometimes important, too – straws. What have you got there? Anything?'

'Nothing of interest,' Giles said.

They went through the rest of the desk together, and turned next to the safe. Very little of importance was discovered there, but Hannasyde commandeered a Bank book, and a big ledger, and retired with them to the desk, and studied both for some time in silence.

Giles began to fill a pipe, and presently remarked: 'I call this boring.' Hannasyde grunted. 'Anything in the Bank book?' inquired Giles.

'Not at first glance. Seems to have kept his records a bit casually. Doesn't always show what he sold in order to buy some of these blocks of shares.' He sighed, and closed the book. 'I shall have to go into it more thoroughly. Let's take a look at this filing cabinet.'

This revealed nothing of any interest. They went quickly through the little that was contained in it, and Giles, yawning, remarked that he was glad he was not a member of the CID.

'A lot of people would be surprised if they knew how dull most of our work is,' replied Hannasyde. 'I want to take charge of the Bank book, and the ledger, and that diary, Mr Carrington. I don't think there's anything else here. We'll hope for better luck at his house. Could you meet me at the Poplars at ten o'clock tomorrow morning?'

'I'll motor you down there,' said Giles. 'I suppose you're now going to call on Gladys Smith?'

'Gladys Smith wants explaining,' answered Hannasyde imperturbably. 'Who is she, and why does she figure all amongst Stock Exchange quotations, and appointments?'

'I don't know, but I'm sure you'll find out,' said Giles cordially. 'You'll probably find she's a typist who applied for a job with Matthews, but I admire your zeal.'

'No sign that he ever employed a typist.'

'That doesn't prove that he wasn't going to,' retorted Giles.

'You're probably right,' said Hannasyde placidly.

But on the following morning, when he got into Giles' car, he said: 'My straws are beginning to make a rope, Mr Carrington. She wasn't a typist in search of a job.'

'What?' said Giles. 'Oh, Gladys Smith! So you did go and see her! What was she like?'

Hannasyde struck a match, and began to light his pipe. 'She's a pretty little woman. Not very young, and distinctly common. What you might describe as a comfortable creature. Nice eyes, and a motherly smile.' He paused, and added between puffs. 'She'd never heard of Gregory Matthews.'

Giles burst out laughing. 'Oh, that's even better than I expected! My poor Hannasyde, what a blow for you!'

'I didn't take it like that,' said Hannasyde, pressing the tobacco down into the bowl of his pipe with one square thumb. 'I thought it the most interesting circumstance that has yet come to light. You're not doing yourself justice, Mr Carrington. Don't you think it's a trifle odd that she should never have heard of a man who has her name and address written down in his diary?'

'Perhaps she knows him under an assumed name,' suggested Giles lightly. 'Strong aroma of intrigue about this. Was there a *liaison*?'

'Oh, no, she didn't even recognize his photograph,' said Hannasyde. 'No doubt about that.'

'I admit it does seem a trifle queer,' said Giles. 'Not altogether helpful, though. Where does the rope you mentioned come in?'

'She took me into her drawing-room,' said Hannasyde. 'Cosy little room. Lots of cushions and knick-knacks. You know the style, I expect. There was a large portrait of a man bang in the middle of the mantelpiece. She told me it was her husband.'

'Perhaps it was,' said Giles charitably.

'I don't think so,' replied Hannasyde in his unemotional way. 'It was a photograph of Mr Henry Lupton.'

6

'Henry Lupton?' repeated Giles, a little blankly. 'You don't mean the hen-pecked brother-in-law? Is he keeping a mistress? How extremely funny!'

'May not be so funny,' said Hannasyde. 'That's about the size of it, though. I didn't get much out of Gladys Smith. She said her husband was a commercial traveller, and often away from home. Great air of respectability about the whole thing. Poor devil!'

'Who? Henry? Seems to have found consolation.'

'Not much consolation if it comes to his wife's ears.'

'Well, what's it all about? What have Lupton's peccadilloes to do with Matthews' death?'

'Perhaps nothing. But if you remember, Mr Carrington, Gladys Smith figured in Matthews' diary on May 9th. On the 13th he had an appointment to see Lupton. Doesn't that seem to you to hang together?'

Giles frowned. 'Yes, it might, I suppose. Matthews found out about Gladys Smith and threatened Lupton with exposure if he didn't jettison her. Is that what you mean? Was he very fond of his sister?'

'He seems to have been fonder of her than of the rest of his family. And from what I've heard of him a ruthless piece of blackmail like that would have been just about his mark.'

'He looked a bit of a brute,' commented Giles. 'I take it Lupton now steps into the rôle of Chief Suspect, as Kenneth would say. I'm sorry about that: I had some news I hoped would please you.'

'What's that?' Hannasyde asked.

Giles smiled. 'Oh, only your friend Randall. He rang

102

me up last night to find out what you were up to – or so I gathered. Anyway, he's meeting us at the Poplars today.'

'What for?' demanded Hannasyde.

Giles shrugged. 'Well, he has every right to be present when you go through Matthews' papers. He's one of the executors, you know.'

'Oh, I've no objection,' Hannasyde said. 'But I'd like to know why he wants to be there.'

'You'd better ask him,' replied Giles. 'I didn't.'

'Quite right,' approved Hannasyde, and relapsed into meditative silence.

Randall's car was not to be seen when they arrived at the Poplars, but the first sound that met their ears when they were admitted into the house was that of Mrs Lupton's voice. A man's hat lying on the table beside a pair of brown leather gloves seemed to indicate that her husband might also be present. Hannasyde looked at the hat without appearing to do so, and turned to greet Miss Harriet Matthews, who came out of the library towards him. She was looking flustered, and annoyed, and spoke in an even more disjointed fashion than usual. 'Oh, you've come!' she said. 'Well, I'm sure it's nothing to do with me – oh, how do you do, Mr Carrington? I didn't see you! – but I must say I can't see what poor Gregory's private papers have to do with the police, and I consider it *most* officious – not that anyone pays the least heed to what I say. You needn't think you're going to find anything, because I know perfectly well there's nothing to find, and if there did happen to be any letters about the Brazilian business it proves nothing at all, whatever my sister may have told you to the contrary, as I've no doubt she did!'

Mrs Lupton came out of the library in the middle of this speech, followed by her husband, and said with her customary air of majesty: 'Do not make yourself ridiculous, Harriet. Good-morning, gentlemen. I understand you wish to inspect my brother's papers?'

'It has nothing whatever to do with you, Gertrude!' said Miss Matthews excitedly. 'I won't be treated like a cypher in my own house! You've no business here at all, behaving as though you were the one who had to be consulted! No one asked you to come, and no one wanted you!'

'Ah, good-morning, Mr Carrington!' cooed a voice from the stairs. Mrs Matthews had made her appearance, and bestowed a gracious smile on Giles, and a more formal one on the Superintendent. 'Such a lovely morning, isn't it? Dear Gertrude! What a surprise! And Henry, too!'

Miss Matthews eyed her with smouldering resentment. 'Well, you're down very early, Zoë!' she said. 'Quite remarkable! Of course, none of us can guess why. Oh, no!'

'Perhaps it was not quite wise of me,' agreed Mrs Matthews. 'But on a day like this one feels glad to be alive.' Her smile was once more directed towards Giles. 'I'm afraid they will tell you that I am rather a hopeless old crock, Mr Carrington.'

'If you mean me, Zoë,' said Mrs Lupton witheringly, 'I should not tell Mr Carrington anything of the sort. I do not propose to discuss you with him at all, but were I to do so I should not describe you as a hopeless crock, but as a *malade imaginaire*. Mr Carrington, I believe you are in charge of my brother's keys. Kindly come this way.'

Mrs Matthews gave a shudder. 'All these sordid details! I suppose it has to be.'

'Yes, I'm afraid it has,' said Giles in his pleasant way.

'If anyone has a right to object it is I, and certainly not my sister-in-law!' snapped Miss Matthews. 'Not that I do object. Why should I?'

At this moment Randall Matthews walked into the

104

house. Apparently he was in time to overhear his aunt's remarks, for he said as though he had been taking part in the conversation: 'No one has any right to object. Dear me, what can have brought my dear Aunt Gertrude here, I wonder?'

'You don't know what we were talking about!' said Miss Matthews angrily.

'No, but I feel sure my answer was the right one,' replied Randall. His gaze returned to Mrs Lupton. 'You are not unexpected, my dear aunt, but, believe me, superfluous.'

'I shall not pretend to be ignorant of your meaning, Randall,' announced Mrs Lupton. 'In your eyes I've no doubt I am superfluous, but I suppose I am concerned at least as much as you are with my brother's death. If light is shed by his private papers I expect to be told of it.'

'If so singular a phenomenon occurs the whole world shall be told of it,' promised Randall. 'Carrington, you have the key to Bluebeard's chamber. Do come and open it!'

A storm of protest broke out at this piece of flippancy. Without paying the least heed to it Randall conducted Giles and Hannasyde to his uncle's study, and waited unconcernedly while the key was fitted into the lock.

As one making civil conversation Hannasyde said: 'I'm sorry the ladies should be distressed about this, Mr Matthews. These things are always rather painful for the rest of the family.'

Randall's eyes flickered to his face. 'Well, you never know, do you?' he said. 'Lots of little things in our lives we should prefer to bury in decent oblivion.'

'Such as, Mr Matthews?'

'I haven't seen my uncle's correspondence yet,' replied Randall sweetly.

Giles turned the key in the wards, and pushed open the door. They went into the study, a square room with a

Turkey carpet, and solid furniture. Randall strolled to the window, and opened it, and remained there, his hands in his pockets, and his shoulders propped against the wall. He evinced no interest in the discoveries made by Hannasyde, which were not, indeed, of an interesting nature. There were some bills, many receipts, several typewritten letters referring to Guy Matthews' future in Brazil, and one brief note from Henry Lupton, dated 13th May. Giles, finding it, handed it to Hannasyde without comment.

It seemed to have been written in haste, and began abruptly: '*Further to our conversation of even date, I must see you again before doing anything. I trust you have by this time thought better of it, and warn you you will have cause to regret it if you drive me to take desperate action.*'

Hannasyde read this through, and was about to fold it up when Randall moved away from the window, and came forward. 'Ah, do you mind?' he murmured, and took the letter out of his hand.

'It is of no particular moment,' Hannasyde said, a little shortly.

'I expect that was why you were interested,' said Randall in his most dulcet voice. He read the letter, and gave it back. 'Dramatic little man,' he said.

'Do you know to what this letter refers, Mr Matthews?'

'Do you?' smiled Randall.

'Yes, Mr Matthews, I think I do.'

'Then why ask me?' inquired Randall. He glanced down at the drawer Giles had pulled out. 'How very disappointing! I'm afraid my uncle must have destroyed his more lurid correspondence.'

The drawer held an untidy collection of oddments. Hannasyde turned over a packet of labels, disclosing a pair of horn-rimmed sun-glasses underneath, a scattering of paper-clips, and a tube of seccotine. For the rest there was a quantity of stamp-paper, some sealing-wax, a pen-knife, a bottle of red ink, and a roll of adhesive tape. These articles the Superintendent turned out on to the desk, but there was nothing hidden under them.

Randall was looking at the heterogeneous collection, a slight frown between his eyes.

'The usual odds-and-ends drawer,' said Giles, beginning to put the things back.

Randall's eyes lifted. 'As you say,' he agreed politely. 'It is all very disheartening.'

The remaining drawers were equally barren of interest. Giles had just closed the last of them when a gentle knock fell on the door, and Henry Lupton looked deprecatingly into the room. 'I hope I don't intrude?' he said. 'The fact is, my wife would like to know – We only looked in, you see, just to inquire how things were going, and time presses, you know. So if we are not needed – ?' He left the end of the sentence unfinished, and looked from Hannasyde to Giles, and back again.

Hannasyde replied: 'Will you come in, Mr Lupton? As a matter of fact, there are one or two questions I want to ask you.'

Henry Lupton, though he closed the door, did not advance farther into the room. He said hurriedly: 'Oh, of course! I should be only too glad if there were anything I *can* answer, but really, you know, I'm as much in the dark as anyone. A most incomprehensible affair! I was only saying so to my wife last night. I was never so shocked in my life as when I heard of it.'

Randall took out his cigarette-case. 'Don't overdo it,' he said, his smile remarkably like a sneer.

Hannasyde turned his head. 'I don't think I need keep you any longer, Mr Matthews.'

'I rather fancy that you may discover a need for me,' returned Randall, flicking open his cigarette-lighter. 'I may, of course, be wrong, but – no, I'm not wrong.'

The door had opened again, this time without any preliminary warning, and Mrs Lupton sailed into the room. 'May I ask what is going on in here?' she said in tones of considerable displeasure. 'You are perfectly well aware that I have a busy morning before me, Henry. I must say I should have thought you had time to have delivered my message twice over by now.' She bent her magisterial frown on Hannasyde. 'Unless my presence is required I am now leaving,' she announced.

'Certainly,' said Hannasyde. 'I want, however to have a few words with your husband, if you will excuse us for a minute or two.'

'With my husband?' repeated Mrs Lupton. 'And pray what have you to say to my husband, Superintendent?'

Henry Lupton, who was looking rather sickly, said: 'Well, you see, my dear, the – the Superintendent wants to have a word in private with me, if – if you don't mind.'

'Indeed!' said Mrs Lupton. 'I have always understood a husband and wife to be one person.' She again addressed Hannasyde. 'You may speak quite freely in front of me, Superintendent. My husband and I have no secrets from each other.'

'It is not a question of secrets, Mrs Lupton,' replied Hannasyde. 'It is merely that I prefer – '

'If you have anything to ask my husband, you may ask it in my presence,' interrupted Mrs Lupton. 'No doubt I shall be a good deal more competent to answer anything relevant to the affairs of this house than he.'

'I'm afraid you don't understand, Mrs Lupton,' intervened Giles. 'Superintendent Hannasyde has to proceed in the – er – customary way. There is no – '

'Henry!' said Mrs Lupton, unheeding. 'Will you kindly inform the Superintendent that you have no objection to my presence?'

'Well, my dear, naturally I – naturally I – '

'It is now obvious to us all that he has every objection,'

108

said Randall. 'You know, you had very much better withdraw, my dear aunt. I feel sure that Uncle Henry's double life is going to be exposed. My own conviction is that he has been keeping a mistress for years.'

Giles could not forbear casting a quick look from Randall's handsome, mocking face to Henry Lupton's grey one. The little man tried to laugh, but there was no mirth in his eyes. Superintendent Hannasyde remained immovable.

Mrs Lupton flushed. 'You forget yourself, Randall. I am not going to stand here and see my husband insulted by your ill-bred notions of what is funny.'

'Oh, I wasn't insulting him,' said Randall. 'Why shouldn't he have a mistress? I am inclined to think that in his place – as your spouse, my dear Aunt Gertrude – I should have several.'

Across the room Giles' eyes encountered Hannasyde's for one pregnant moment. It was evident that Randall had at last succeeded in startling the Superintendent.

Mrs Lupton seemed to swell. 'You will either apologize for your impertinence, Randall, or I leave this room. Never have I been spoken to in such a manner!'

'Dear aunt!' said Randall, and kissed his fingers to her.

Mrs Lupton swept round, and stalked from the room.

Randall inhaled a deep breath of tobacco smoke. 'I said you might need me,' he remarked, and lounged towards the door.

Henry Lupton said in a strangled voice: 'Wait, Randall! What – what do you mean by this – this very questionable joke?'

Randall glanced contemptuously down at him. 'My good uncle, I have got you out of one mess: get yourself out of this!' he said, and walked negligently out of the room.

Giles would have followed him, but Lupton, a tinge of

colour now in his cheeks, stopped him, saying: 'Please don't go, Mr Carrington! I – really, I should prefer you to remain! You are a legal man, and I – '

'I cannot undertake to advise you, Mr Lupton,' Giles said, 'I am here merely as the late Mr Matthews' solicitor.'

'Quite, quite! But my position – '

'By all means stay,' interposed Hannasyde. He laid his own letter before Henry Lupton. 'Did you write this, Mr Lupton?'

Lupton glanced unhappily at it. 'Yes. That is – yes, I wrote it. We – my brother-in-law and I – had a slight disagreement over a – a personal matter. Such things will happen in the best regulated families, you know. I thought it would be best if we met and talked it over. Without prejudice, you know.'

'Did you meet him?' Hannasyde asked.

'No. Oh, no! You see, he died before there was really time.'

'Did he answer your letter, Mr Lupton?'

'Only by telephone. Just to let me know that he couldn't manage an appointment.' He gave a nervous laugh. 'I was very much annoyed at the time – well, my brother-in-law had a sort of *manner* that rather put one's back up, if you know what I mean.'

Hannasyde said in his measured way: 'Mr Lupton, I want you to realize one thing. Except in so far as they may have a bearing on this case I am not concerned with your private affairs. Nor, I can assure you, have I any desire to make wanton trouble in your family circle. But when I went through the late Mr Matthews' papers at his office, with Mr Carrington here, I found the name and address of a lady calling herself Gladys Smith. You will understand that I had of course to follow this up. I called on Mrs Smith at her flat yesterday, and what I saw and heard there were sufficient to convince me that you are – intimately acquainted with her.'

Henry Lupton looked towards Giles for support, and getting none said in a blustering voice: 'Well, and what if I am? I should like to know what bearing it can have on this case?'

'That is what I also want to know, Mr Lupton.' Hannasyde left a pause, but Henry Lupton said nothing, and after a minute he continued: 'You had an appointment to see your brother-in-law on Monday, 13th May.'

Lupton moved uneasily in his chair. 'Yes, certainly I had. But this is – is quite ridiculous! There is no reason why you should drag in Mrs Smith's name.'

'Are you going to tell me, Mr Lupton, that your appointment with the late Mr Matthews had no bearing on Mrs Smith – whose name and address I found in his diary?'

It was evident that Henry Lupton hardly knew what to reply. He mumbled something about consulting his solicitor, seemed to think better of it, and chancing to catch sight of his own letter to Gregory Matthews, said with a good deal of agitation: 'I didn't poison him, if that's what you suspect! Yes, yes, I know very well what's in your mind, and I admit I was a fool to write that letter. That ought to convince you – for I never dreamed that anything like this would happen.'

'I don't suspect anything,' said Hannasyde calmly. 'But it is obvious to me that at the time of his death you were on bad terms with Gregory Matthews; equally obvious that the existence of Mrs Smith had something to do with that. I think Mr Carrington, in the absence of your own solicitor, would advise you to be frank with me.'

Giles said nothing, but Henry Lupton, dropping his head into this hands, groaned, and answered: 'Of course I've no desire to obstruct the police. Naturally I – I appreciate your position, Superintendent, but my own is – is extremely equivocal. My wife has no suspicion – I

111

have my daughters to consider, and my whole object is to – is to – '

'Please understand, Mr Lupton, that I am not here to investigate public morals,' said Hannasyde coldly. 'I can only tell you in all honesty that your relations with Mrs Smith are more likely to become known through a refusal on your part to be frank with me than through a voluntary statement made to me now.'

'Yes,' agreed Lupton unhappily. 'I see that, of course. I suppose you'll make inquiries, and it'll get round.' He gave a shudder, and lifted his head. 'I have – known Mrs Smith for a number of years,' he said, not meeting Hannasyde's gaze. 'I needn't go into all that, need I? My work takes me about the country a good deal. I – there has always been plenty of opportunity without creating suspicion. I've been very careful. I don't know how my brother-in-law found out. It's a mystery to me. But he did find out. He asked me to call at his office. I'd no idea – I thought it odd, but he was a strange man, and it didn't cross my mind . . . anyway, I went, and he taxed me with – with my connection with Mrs Smith.' His face twitched. He clasped his hands tightly on his knee, and said in a constricted voice: 'He knew all about it. He even knew when I'd last been with her, and how they thought – the other people in the block, I mean – that I was a commercial traveller. He must have made the most minute inquiries. It was no use denying it. He knew everything – oh, things one wouldn't have thought he could know! He – was very unpleasant about it.' He broke off, and turned with a kind of appeal towards Giles. 'You knew him, Carrington. It's no good trying to explain to the Superintendent. No one who was unacquainted with Gregory would understand.'

'I didn't know him well,' Giles answered.

'You must have seen the type of man he was. Power! That's what he liked! He didn't care about my wife,

112

you know. Not enough to make him threaten me with exposure. That wasn't it. It was – a cruel streak in his nature. They're all of them like that, the Matthews, in a way. He wanted to pull the strings and see the puppets dance. Well, I told him he couldn't do that with me. I – I have danced, often, in – in minor things, but this was different. I don't want you to think of it as a mere sordid intrigue, because I swear it's not like that. Mrs Smith – well, she's just the same as a wife to me. I'd marry her if I could, but, you see, it's all so impossible. There are my daughters, for one thing, and my position, and – and my wife, of course. I've even got a grandson. One can't, you know. But that's what I meant when I wrote that.' He pointed to the letter, lying on the desk before Hannasyde.

Hannasyde picked it up. 'The phrase, *you will have cause to regret it if you drive me to take desperate action* – that meant that you were seriously contemplating divorce, Mr Lupton?'

'Yes, I think I meant that. I don't know. I was terribly worried. I couldn't see my way out of the trouble. I wrote that to try and frighten him. I thought he might hesitate to push me too far if he knew I was prepared to stand by Gladys, and let everything else go to the devil. After all he wouldn't want an open scandal in the family, and it wasn't as though my wife suffered in any way through Mrs Smith.'

'I quite understand that,' said Hannasyde. 'You asked him for a second interview, but he refused it, didn't he?'

Henry Lupton nodded, and gulped. 'Yes, he refused it. That was the last time I spoke to him. On the morning of the day he died, just over the telephone. He rang me up from his office. I never saw him again.'

'At what time did he ring you up, Mr Lupton?'

'Oh, quite early! Not later than eleven.'

'I see. And what did you do then?'

Lupton stared at him. 'Nothing. That is, I was at my office, you see. I had my work. I couldn't do anything.'

'You didn't make any attempt to see Mr Matthews – during lunch-time, for instance?'

'No. It wouldn't have been any use. I knew Gregory. I had lunch by myself. I wanted time to think.'

'Where did you lunch, Mr Lupton?'

'At my usual place. It's a quiet little restaurant called the Vine. They know me there. I'm sure they'll be able to bear me out.'

'And after lunch?'

'I went back to the office, of course. As a matter of fact, I left earlier than I generally do. Well, before tea.'

'Where did you go?'

'To Golders Green. I wanted to see Mrs Smith.'

'Ah, yes,' Hannasyde said suavely. 'You naturally wished to discuss the matter with her.'

'Well, no. No, actually I didn't speak of it. I meant to, but – but I still hoped there might be some way of getting round it, and – you see, we never spoke of my – my home-life. And I didn't want to upset Gladys. I haven't told her anything about what's happened. Just that we have had a death in the family.'

'Oh!' said Hannasyde. 'At what hour did you leave Mrs Smith?'

'I don't really know. I was home in time for dinner. I mean, I went straight home from Golders Green.'

'And after dinner?'

'We had some people in for Bridge. I didn't leave the house again until next day, when we came here.'

'Thank you.' Hannasyde was jotting something down in his notebook. His tone conveyed nothing.

Lupton looked anxiously at him. 'I don't know if there's anything more you want to know, or if I can go? My wife will be – '

'No, there is nothing more at present,' said Hannasyde.

114

Henry Lupton got up. 'Then – ?'

'By all means,' said Hannasyde.

The little man withdrew, and Giles came away from the window, where he had been standing, and said: 'Poor devil! What a mess to have got himself into! You don't like his story?'

'I don't like his alibi.'

'Which one? Oh, Gladys Smith! I should think he probably did go there. Vague idea of seeking comfort. Rather pathetic.'

'Anyway, she'll swear he was with her,' Hannasyde said.

'Probably, but I don't quite see how he could have come here at that hour without being seen by some of the household, if that's what you're driving at.'

'Easily,' said Hannasyde, with a touch of scorn. 'There are more ways of getting into this house than by the front-door, Mr Carrington. There's a garden-door, for instance, which opens out of a cloakroom on to a path at the side of the house. Anyone would use that door if he wanted to be unobserved. The backstairs come down just by the cloakroom. He would only have to choose his moment. The family and the servants would all be having tea. He might reasonably bank on the coast's being clear.'

'Yes, but what would have been the use?' asked Giles. 'Matthews wasn't at home then. Into what would he have dropped his poison?'

'I'm thinking of that bottle of tonic – so providentially smashed,' said Hannasyde.

Giles wrinkled his brow. 'Would he have known where it was kept? And how could he have arranged to smash it?'

'He might have known. Simple enough to smash it when he came round next morning with his wife.'

'Oh!' said Giles doubtfully. 'Think it's quite in keeping with his character? Such a weak little man!'

115

'He was feeling desperate, Mr Carrington. He admitted that himself. I should say this Gladys Smith is about the biggest thing in his life.'

'Divorce seems to me to be a solution more likely to appeal to him than murder,' said Giles.

Hannasyde shook his head decidedly. 'I don't agree with you. He wouldn't face up to that sort of a scandal. Probably fond of his daughters too. If he did the murder it was because he thought he could get clean away with it. He couldn't have got clean away with a divorce – not with that wife. There'd have been the hell of a row.'

'All very well,' objected Giles, 'but he couldn't have been sure that by killing Matthews he was protecting himself. Matthews might have told someone else. In fact, he did. That young sweep, Randall, wasn't drawing a bow at a venture. He knew.'

'He knew, yes, but, if you noticed, Lupton was amazed that he knew. He probably believed Matthews had so far kept the secret to himself.' He picked up Lupton's letter, and placed it in his pocket-book. Then he looked thoughtfully at the desk, and pulled open one of the drawers, and frowned. It was the odds-and-ends drawer. 'I wish – I wish very much that I knew what Mr Randall Matthews found to interest him amongst this collection,' he said.

'Was he interested? I didn't notice.'

'I'm nearly sure he was. But whether it was in something which he saw, or in something which he expected to see, and didn't, I don't know. Setting aside his duties as executor – which I don't fancy would worry him much – why did he want to be here when we went through his uncle's papers? What did he think we should find?'

'Perhaps the very thing we did find. That letter of Lupton's.'

Hannasyde considered this for a moment. 'It might have been that. It's quite probable, if old Matthews had

116

taken him into his confidence. But what is there in this drawer?'

'You may be right in thinking it is something which is *not* in the drawer.'

'I may. There is just one thing that strikes me as unusual: there's practically no old correspondence, either here or at Matthews' office.'

'Some men habitually tear up letters as soon as they've answered them,' said Giles. 'Are you suggesting that someone's been at work amongst Matthews' papers?'

'I'm suggesting nothing,' replied Hannasyde. 'But it does seem to me that if Matthews destroyed all his letters himself, it must have amounted to a mania with him.'

'The fell hand of Randall,' said Giles, with an amused look.

Hannasyde smiled reluctantly. 'I know you think I've got him on the brain. I ought to tell you that I can't find that he came anywhere near this place between May 12th and May 15th.' He added ruefully: 'You're quite right: I am suspicious of him, and I'm suspicious of his alibis. They're so good that they might have been created on purpose. But I tell you frankly, Mr Carrington, I don't see how he can possibly have committed this murder.'

'You sound regretful,' said Giles, laughing.

'No, not that. Just plain worried. Groping about in a fog, and all the time I've got an uneasy feeling I'm on the wrong track. If I could only discover the medium through which the poison was administered! It may have been the whiskey-and-soda Guy Matthews poured out for his uncle; Matthews may have bathed his scratched hand with poisoned lotion – but all the lotion I found in this house was a brand-new bottle of Pond's Extract with the paper sealing the cork down still intact. It may have been the tonic – and the bottle was smashed. I've racked my brains to think of something else – something that might have been doctored at any time, perhaps days before

117

Matthews' death. Well, I thought of aspirin tablets, but he didn't use drugs. Hemingway put all the servants through a hair-sieve, so to speak, but he couldn't discover that Matthews had eaten or drunk anything the rest of the family hadn't, barring that whiskey, and the tonic.' He broke off, and rose. 'Well, it's no use sitting and talking to you about it, Mr Carrington. I've got to get on with the job, and I've no doubt you're itching to get back to town.'

'I don't know about itching, exactly, but I certainly ought to go,' said Giles, glancing at his watch. 'I'm glad I don't leave Lupton in the rôle of Chief Suspect,' he added with a twinkle. 'I'm sorry for the poor wretch.'

'Oh, he's a suspect all right,' Hannasyde answered. 'I shall have to check up closely on him. But it's too clever, Mr Carrington. If Lupton did it, it must have been on the spur of the moment, and because he was desperate. Well, I may be wrong, but it doesn't look like that to me. It's been carefully planned, this murder, down to the very poison that was used. The ordinary man doesn't hit on a thing like nicotine on the spur of the moment.'

'I see. You think research is indicated.'

'I do. Research, and a cool, clever brain,' said Hannasyde, putting his pocket-book away, and moving across the thick carpet to the door. He opened it, and nearly collided with Miss Matthews. 'I beg your pardon!'

She was holding a bowl of flowers between her hands, and said in her hurried way: 'Oh, what a start you gave me, Superintendent! Just going to replenish my flowers. I always do it in the cloakroom, because it makes such a mess.'

She ended on one of her breathless, inane laughs, and sped on through the baize door at the end of the passage. The two men's eyes met. 'She was listening,' said Giles softly.

'Yes,' replied Hannasyde non-committally. 'She has a reputation for being extremely inquisitive.'

118

7

Randall, leaving the study in the wake of his aunt, did
not follow her to the library, where he could hear her
voice raised in denunciation of himself, but strolled
instead to the foot of the stairs, and after a brief glance
round the empty hall went up, not hurriedly, but soft-
footed. There was no one on the upper landing. The first
door led into Gregory Matthews' bedroom, and was not
locked. Randall turned the handle, and went in, and
quietly closed the door behind him.

The room, which was large, and gloomy with mahog-
any, had the unfriendly look that uninhabited apartments
wear. The bed was draped by a dust-sheet; the windows
were shut; and the dressing-table, the chest of drawers,
and even the mantelpiece were swept bare of all personal
belongings.

Randall glanced about him, and presently moved
towards the wardrobe, a huge, triple-doored piece that
took up nearly the whole of one wall. Gregory Matthews'
clothes were neatly arranged in it, but they did not seem
to concern Randall, for after a brief survey he closed the
doors again, and went across to the dressing-table. There
was nothing in either of its drawers, except a watch and
chain, and a box containing cuff-links and studs, and the
chest at the opposite side of the room contained only
piles of underclothing.

Randall shrugged, and walked over to the door which
communicated with his uncle's bathroom. Here the same
barrenness met his gaze; not so much as a razor-strop
had been left to remind him of his uncle's erstwhile

presence. He went at once to where a small medicine-chest hung, but it was quite empty. He slowly shut it, and turned away towards the door leading out on to the landing. He opened it, and stepped out of the room just as Stella came running lightly up the stairs.

She checked at sight of him, and stared, a frown slowly gathering on her brow. Randall met the stare with his faint, bland smile, and closed the bathroom door behind him. 'Good-morning, my precious,' he said.

She remained with her hand still resting on the big wooden knob at the head of the banisters. 'What were you doing in there?' she asked, her voice sharp with suspicion.

'Just looking over the scene of the crime,' he answered. He held out his open cigarette-case. 'Will you smoke, my love?'

'No, thanks. What were you looking for?'

He raised his brows. 'Did I say I was looking for something?'

'I know you were.'

'Well, whatever it was I was disappointed,' said Randall. 'Someone has been busy.'

'Aunt Harriet turned everything out the day uncle died,' Stella said shortly.

Randall lit a cigarette, and said in a meditative tone: 'I often wonder whether Aunt Harriet is the fool she appears to be, or not.'

'Good heavens, you don't think she did it to destroy evidence, do you?' exclaimed Stella, unable to believe in such forethought.

'I am quite unable to make up my mind on that point,' Randall replied. 'Cast your little feather-weight of a brain backward, my sweet. What did our dear Aunt Harriet take out of uncle's medicine-chest?'

'Oh, I don't know! All sorts of things. Corn-plaster, and iodine, and Eno's Fruit Salts.'

120

'And uncle's tonic, of course,' said Randall, watching the blue smoke rise up from the end of his cigarette.

'No, that was broken. New bottle, too.'

He raised his eyes rather quickly. 'Broken,' he repeated. 'Was it indeed? Well, well! and who broke it, my little one?'

'No one. Uncle must have left it on the shelf over the wash-basin, and the wind blew it over.'

'Any questions asked about it?' inquired Randall.

'Do you mean by the police? Yes, I think so. Not to me.'

Randall sighed. 'I wonder who regrets Aunt Gertrude's officiousness most,' he said. 'The Matthews family, or Superintendent Hannasyde?'

'I don't know, but talking of Aunt Gertrude, what on earth have you been saying to her? She says she's never been so insulted in her life.'

'I shouldn't think she has,' said Randall.

'What *did* you say?' persisted Stella.

'Merely that if I were married to her I should keep several mistresses,' Randall replied.

She could not help giving a gurgle of laughter, but she said: 'Well, really, I do think that's about the limit! It's about the rudest thing you could say.'

'I couldn't think of anything ruder at the time,' acknowledged Randall. 'It got rid of her most successfully.'

'You can't go about being filthily rude to people just to get rid of them!'

'I can and do,' he replied imperturbably.

'You do, yes,' Stella said hotly. 'You're the most poisonous-tongued person I know!'

'So you have often informed me,' bowed Randall. He regarded her with a curious smile. 'You can't bear me, can you, little Stella? What have I done?'

'Nothing. You don't,' Stella said contemptuously. 'You

121

just say spiteful things, and drift about like a lounge-lizard. I used to hate you when we first came to live with uncle.'

'My darling, you still do.'

'I don't think twice about you,' said Stella. 'You were horrid to me when I was a kid – '

'A gawky, clumsy flapper,' murmured Randall, closing his eyes. 'I remember.'

'I wasn't!'

'Also callow, ignorant, and without grace.'

She reddened. 'All girls are at that age!'

'Possibly, but I see no reason why I should be kind to them.'

'You're not kind to anyone. You were beastly to Guy, and you still are.'

'I am but human, my love. If he will rise to my bait, bait he shall have.'

'I wouldn't mind betting you used to pull flies' wings off when you were a boy,' said Stella with deep loathing.

'One of my favourite pastimes.'

'And – if it interests you – I very much object to your habit of sneering at my mother!'

His eyelids drooped. 'At my clever Aunt Zoë? How you misjudge me! I am quite her most appreciative admirer.'

'That'll do, thanks!'

He raised his brows. 'There's no pleasing you, sweetheart. What can I find to say about the boy-friend?'

'You can leave Deryk alone! He and I are engaged to be married.'

A malicious glint came into his eyes. 'Oh, is that still on?'

She reddened, hesitated for a moment, and then said bluntly: 'Now look here, Randall! If you think you're getting a rise out of me you're mistaken. I suppose you've got hold of some silly, exaggerated story about Deryk and the Fosters. You would! It's perfectly true that he partnered Maisie Foster to the Hopes' dance, but considering I couldn't go, and he's known Maisie quite as long as he's known me, I'm not – strangely enough – jealous about it.'

Randall's smile broadened. 'I seem to have got a better rise out of you than I had hoped for, darling. This is all news to me.'

She bit her lip. 'Then what were you hinting at?'

'Oh, nothing, nothing!' said Randall airily. 'Tell me more of this rival. Where does she live?'

'She lives on Park Terrace, and she is not a rival.'

He opened his eyes. 'It sounds very promising. An extremely well-to-do locality. I hope she's an only child?'

She was spared the necessity of answering by the arrival of her brother, who at this moment came along the landing from his own room. Randall promptly transferred his attention to him, and said with an assumption of artless surprise: 'Well, well! Can it really be my little cousin? Are you now a gentleman of leisure, Guy, or has the firm of Brooke and Matthews gone into liquidation?'

Guy, who was looking worn, and rather pale, scowled at him. 'No, it hasn't. You're not the only one who has a right to be here!'

'A little out of spirits?' murmured Randall. 'Not quite our bright self today?'

'I don't see how anyone can be bright with a thing like this hanging over us all,' said Guy jerkily.

'I contrive to maintain my usual equanimity,' said Randall. 'Have a cigarette: very soothing to the nerves.'

Guy took one mechanically, but stood with it between his fingers until Randall, his brows lifting, produced his lighter, and snapped it open. Guy gave a start. 'Oh, thanks!' he said awkwardly, and bent to light the cigarette. As he straightened his back again, he said: 'Have they finished downstairs?'

'Do you mean the police?' inquired Randall. 'Should I otherwise be here?'

Guy glanced at him and away again. 'They didn't find anything, did they? There wasn't anything to find.' He paused interrogatively, but as Randall made no remark said angrily: 'You can answer, can't you?'

'I thought you had spared me the trouble,' said Randall blandly. 'You said there was nothing to find. I expect you know.'

'Damn you, I haven't been tampering with uncle's papers!'

'Guy!' said his sister sharply. 'Don't be such a fool! Can't you see he's only trying to get a rise out of you?'

Guy gave a short laugh, and said: 'It's what he thinks, all the same.' He hesitated, and looked at Randall again. 'What line are they taking? What does that Superintendent-fellow make of it?'

'My poor child, do you imagine that I am in his confidence?' said Randall.

'I thought you might have gathered something. They're baffled, aren't they? I don't see how they can be anything else. There's nothing to show who did it. Anybody might have, but how are they going to prove which it was?'

'I haven't the slightest idea,' replied Randall. 'I imagine it might be helpful if they discover how the nicotine was administered, but I gather they haven't yet arrived at that. There may, of course, be some startling disclosures at the inquest tomorrow. I hope you've learned your piece, by the way?'

'Oh, you're thinking of that blasted whiskey-and-soda, are you?' said Guy. 'So easy for me to doctor it with the whole family sitting round!'

'Well, I don't know,' said Randall pensively. 'I think I could have done it.'

'You! I daresay you could. Probably would have if you'd had half a chance.'

124

Randall gave his soft laugh. 'But I hadn't half a chance, little cousin. I wasn't here. I'm afraid you'll have to rule me out. A pity, of course, but there it is.'

'Oh, do shut up!' begged Stella. 'What's the use of going on like this? It makes everything ten times worse than it is already. I can't see what you're worrying about, Guy. *We* know you didn't do it, and if the police think you did at least they can't do anything about it, because they've nothing to go on. I mean, they can't even test the glass uncle drank out of, because it was washed up days before they came here.'

'Guy isn't worrying about that,' Randall said, watching Guy's face from under his lashes. 'Perhaps it wasn't in the whiskey-and-soda.'

Guy's mouth twitched. 'Of course it wasn't. I'm not exactly worrying about anything, but this – this atmosphere of suspicion gets on my nerves. My own belief is that the whole thing will fizzle out for lack of evidence. After all, the police don't solve every crime by any means.'

'I wish to heaven Aunt Gertrude hadn't started the rotten business,' remarked Stella.

'God, I could *strangle* her!' Guy said, his voice shaking with suppressed emotion. He saw them both looking at him, and forced a laugh. 'Well, I'd better go down, and see what they're up to,' he said, and brushed past his sister at the head of the stairs, and ran down.

Randall watched him go, carefully put out the stub of his cigarette in a bowl of ferns at his elbow, and said: 'Dear me!'

'It's enough to get on anyone's nerves,' said Stella defiantly. 'You don't live here, so you don't know what it's like.'

'I hesitate to proffer advice unasked,' drawled Randall, 'but if I were Guy's fond sister I would tell him to go to work as usual. For one thing, it would look better.'

'He won't. I did say I thought he ought to carry on; in fact, I even got Mr Rumbold to advise him to go back to work, but he's frightfully highly-strung, and things do get on his nerves very easily. I think it's through having too much imagination. Because he has, you know.'

'Judging by the only example of his work which I have been privileged to behold I should describe his imagination as being not only excessive, but morbid,' said Randall.

Stella, who was not an admirer of her brother's decorative schemes, made no reply to this, but merely said: 'Well, I'm going down again. And I may as well warn you, Randall, if the police ask me I shall tell them how I saw you coming out of uncle's bathroom.'

'A very good idea,' said Randall cordially. 'Let us start a General Information Bureau. You can inform about me in uncle's bathroom, and I can counter with some of Guy's remarks.'

'You rotten cad!' Stella flashed.

He smiled. 'Do you want a truce, my sweet?'

She stood quite still, gripping the banisters, for a moment, and then, without a word, flung round on her heel, and ran downstairs. Still smiling, Randall followed her at his leisure.

Mrs Lupton had not waited for her husband to join her, but after having delivered herself of some sweeping strictures on her elder nephew's manners and morals, had left the house to attend a meeting of the local Nursing Association. Henry Lupton had just come away from the study when Randall reached the hall, and was hovering about in an uncertain fashion near the front-door. He looked a little surprised when Stella, with the briefest of greetings, went past him into the library, but a moment later he saw Randall on the bend of the staircase, and started forward. 'I want to speak to you!' he said in an urgent undertone.

'Do you?' said Randall, continuing his languid progress down the stairs.

'Yes, I do! I – ' He cast a quick look behind him to be sure that Stella had shut the library door – 'I want to know what you meant by the – the disgracefully rude things you said to your aunt!'

'The desire evinced by so many people of apparently normal intelligence of being informed of what they know very well already is a source of constant wonder to me,' remarked Randall. 'However, I'm quite willing to oblige you if you're sure you want me to.'

Henry Lupton looked up at him, his own eyes strained and questioning. 'What did your uncle tell you about me?' he demanded. 'That's what I want to know! That Sunday before he died, when he asked you into his study. I might have known! I might have guessed he'd tell you!'

'You might, of course,' agreed Randall. 'Did you suppose he wouldn't? He thought it would appeal to my sense of humour.'

'I've no doubt it did,' said Lupton bitterly.

'Up to a point,' said Randall. 'Have we now finished this discussion?'

'No. I want to know – I insist on knowing what you mean to do!'

'What I mean to do?' repeated Randall, dropping the words out disdainfully one by one. 'Is it possible – is it really possible that you imagine I am going to concern myself with your utterly uninteresting love-affairs?'

Lupton flushed, but his muscles seemed to relax. 'I don't know. I'd believe anything of your family, anything! As for you, if you saw a chance to make mischief you'd take it!'

'In this case,' said Randall unpleasantly, 'it affords me purer gratification to dwell upon the thought of my dear Aunt Gertrude duped and betrayed.'

'Your aunt doesn't suffer through it!'

'What a pity!' said Randall.

The baize-door at the back of the hall opened at this moment, and Miss Matthews came through carrying her replenished bowl of flowers. 'Oh, Henry! Gertrude's gone,' she said. 'And I must say, Randall, I think it was most uncalled-for, whatever it was you said to her. Not that I know what it was, for I don't, and I'm sure I don't want to. And if you mean to stay to lunch I do think you might have let me know, because whatever your Aunt Zoë's ideas of housekeeping may be mine are different, and there won't be enough.'

'Fortunately,' said Randall, 'I have no such intention.'

'Well, I hope I am not inhospitable,' said Miss Matthews, slightly mollified, 'but I must say I'm glad to hear it. There are quite enough people to feed in this house without adding to them. I've already had to make it plain to Zoë that I'm not going to have her friends coming here to meals all day and every day, and behaving as though the drawing-room existed just for them to play Bridge in. I know very well what her idea is, and I'm not going to put up with it! The house is just as much mine as it is hers. More so, if everyone had their rights, and so is the car, and I won't have it used without her even asking me if I want it! . . . Yes, Zoë, I am talking about you, and I don't care who hears me!'

Mrs Matthews who, possibly attracted by her sister-in-law's voice, had come out of the library, said sweetly: 'Were you, dear? Well, you can talk about me as much as you like, if you want to.'

'I shall,' said Miss Matthews. 'And I hope you heard what I said!'

Mrs Matthews gave her an indulgent smile. 'No, dear, I'm afraid I didn't. I came to remind you that I shall want the car this afternoon, if you are sure it is *quite* convenient to you.'

'Well, it isn't,' said Miss Matthews, with ill-concealed triumph. 'Pullen has taken it to be decarbonized.'

Mrs Matthews' smile faded, and a certain rigidity stole over her face. After a slight pause she said, carefully polite: 'My dear Harriet, surely you knew that I have an appointment to have my hair done this afternoon? I distinctly remember telling you about it, and asking whether you wanted the car yourself. Surely the car might have been decarbonized another day?'

'Pullen said it ought to be done,' replied Miss Matthews obstinately.

Mrs Matthews compressed her lips. There was a distinctly un-Christian light in her eyes, but she said smoothly: 'I am sure you did it for the best, Harriet, but in future perhaps it would be wiser if we consulted one another before giving *quite* such arbitrary orders. Don't you agree?'

'No, I don't!' snapped Miss Matthews, and walked off to put her flowers down in the drawing-room.

Randall watched her go, and glanced down at Mrs Matthews. 'My poor Aunt Zoë, do you find life very trying?' he said softly.

She was looking after her sister-in-law, but at Randall's words she turned. She met his cynical eyes, and said without a trace of annoyance in her voice: 'No, Randall, not at all. When you reach my age you will have learned not to judge people harshly, my dear boy. I am very, very fond of your Aunt Harriet, and all those little idiosyncrasies which you young people are so impatient of mean just nothing to me. You should always try to look beneath the surface, and remember that when people do things that are not very kind there may be a very good reason for it.'

'I am silenced,' bowed Randall.

She came to the foot of the stairs, and laid her hand on his arm for a moment as she passed him. 'Try to be more

129

tolerant, Randall dear,' she said thrillingly. 'It is always such a mistake to condemn people's little foibles. One should try to understand, and to help them.'

She gave his arm a faint squeeze, and went on up the stairs. Randall looked anxiously at his sleeve, smoothed it, and said: 'After that I feel that anything else would be in the nature of an anti-climax. I shall go home.'

'Your aunt is a very sweet woman,' Henry Lupton said warmly. 'I admire her more than I can say.'

'So do I,' said Randall. 'I always have.'

'And I think you might at least refrain from sneering at her!'

'That,' said Randall, 'is the second time today I have been accused of sneering at my clever Aunt Zoë. I am quite guiltless, believe me. In fact, my admiration for her is growing by leaps and bounds.'

Henry Lupton stared at him suspiciously, but Randall only gave a tantalizing smile, and walked across the hall to pick up his hat and gloves. 'I suppose you'll come down for the Inquest?' Lupton said.

Randall yawned. 'If nothing more amusing offers, I might,' he answered. 'Not if it is going to be held at some unearthly hour of the morning, of course. Convey my respectful farewells to my aunts if you see them again.' With which casual recommendation he strolled out of the house, leaving his uncle half-indignant and half-relieved.

Contrary to the expectations of his relatives he did not put in an appearance at the Inquest next morning, a circumstance which caused his three aunts to form a whole-hearted if brief alliance. Mrs Lupton supposed him to be ashamed to look her in the face, but considered that decency should have compelled him to be present; Miss Matthews read in his absence a deliberate slight to his uncle's memory; and Mrs Matthews, more charitable, feared that there was a callous streak in his nature, due, no doubt, to his youth.

130

The other members of the family all attended the Inquest. Even Owen Crewe came, though reluctantly. Agnes, looking brightly cheerful, but speaking in the hushed tones she considered suitable to the occasion, explained audibly to her mother that she had had quite a fight with Owen to get him to come, but had felt that he really ought to, if only to support her.

'I cannot see what the affair has to do with either of us,' said Owen in the disagreeable voice of one dragged unwillingly from his work.

'I suppose you will permit Agnes to feel some concern in her uncle's death?' said Mrs Lupton austerely.

Owen, who never embarked on an argument with his mother-in-law, merely replied: 'I can see no reason why I should be called upon to waste an entire morning over it,' and moved away to a seat as far removed from her as possible. When he discovered that Randall was not present he gave a short laugh, and said: 'Wise man!' the only effect of which was to make his wife say with unimpaired jollity that Owen was always cross in the mornings.

Mrs Rumbold, beside whom Owen had seated himself, said in a confidential voice: 'It is kind of horrid, isn't it? I mean, knowing poor Mr Matthews, and all.'

Owen looked round at her with the instinctive distrust of a shy man accosted by a stranger, and said: 'Quite,' in a stiff voice.

Mrs Rumbold smiled dazzlingly. 'You don't remember me, do you? Well, I'm sure I don't know why you should! My name's Rumbold. We knew poor Mr Matthews very well. We live next door, you know.'

Owen blushed, and half rose from his seat to shake hands. 'Oh, of course! I'm sorry, I'm afraid I'm very bad at remembering faces. How do you do? Er – very nice of you to come.'

'Well, we sort of felt we had to,' whispered Mrs Rumbold. 'I must say I'm not one for this sort of thing

131

myself, but those two poor old dears wanted Ned – that's my husband – to come, so here we are. Ned doesn't think anything much will happen, though.'

'Nothing at all, I should imagine,' replied Owen, dwelling fondly on the thought of Mrs Matthews' emotions could she but have heard herself described as a poor old dear.

'We're not the only people outside the family here, that's one thing,' remarked Mrs Rumbold. 'Half Grinley seems to have turned up. Just curiosity, if you ask me. Oh, there's Dr Fielding come in! Well, he doesn't look as if he was worrying much, I must say.'

'No reason why he should,' said Owen.

'Well, I don't know,' said Mrs Rumbold doubtfully. 'I mean, he didn't seem to know Mr Matthews had been poisoned, and him a doctor! Ned keeps on telling me no one can blame him, but what I say is, if he's a doctor he ought to have known. Don't you agree?'

'Really, I don't understand these matters,' replied Owen, who, though not particularly observant, had by this time taken in not only Mrs Rumbold's blue eyelashes, but also her arresting picture-hat, with its trail of huge pink roses, and was in consequence feeling acutely self-conscious at being seen with anyone so spectacular. He said something about wanting to have a word with his father-in-law, and retreated to a place beside Henry Lupton just as the Coroner came into court.

The Inquest, in the opinions of those people who had come to it in the hopes of witnessing a thrilling drama, was most disappointing. Beecher was called first, and described how he had found his master's body on the morning of the 15th May. Very few questions were asked him, and he soon stood down to give place to Dr Fielding.

It was generally felt that the proceedings were now going to become more interesting, and a little stir ran through the courtroom as the doctor got up. Several ladies thought that he looked very handsome, and one or two people confided to their neighbours, very much as Mrs Rumbold had done, that he looked as cool as a cucumber.

He was indeed perfectly self-possessed, and gave his evidence with easy assurance, and no waste of words. Questioned, he admitted that he had not discovered, upon a cursory examination, anything about the body incompatible with his first verdict of death from syncope. He became rather technical, and one half of his audience thought: Well, even doctors can't know everything; while the other half adhered to its belief that doctors ought to know everything. Questioned further, Fielding gave a still more technical description of the cardiac trouble for which he had been treating the deceased. When asked what circumstances had led him to communicate his patient's death to the Coroner he said at once: 'The dissatisfaction expressed by a member of the family with my diagnosis.'

This reply, delivered though it was in a calm voice, caused another stir to run through the court-room. It was felt that the details of some shocking family scandal were at any moment going to come to light, and when Mrs Lupton got up to give her evidence everyone stared at her hopefully, and waited in pent silence to hear what she was going to divulge.

But Mrs Lupton, who made nearly as good a witness as the doctor, divulged nothing. She knew of no reason why her brother should have been poisoned; simply she had felt that his death had not been due to natural causes. No, she did not think she could explain why she had had this feeling. It had attacked her forcibly on her first sight of the corpse. Her instinct was seldom at fault.

'What did I tell you?' whispered Sergeant Hemingway to the Superintendent.

Mrs Lupton sat down amid a general feeling of disappointment. People eyed the rest of the Matthews family, wondering which of them would next be called. The Coroner said something to the Clerk, and Superintendent Hannasyde finally annihilated all hope in the breasts of the curious by getting up and asking for an adjournment pending police inquiries. This was granted, and there was nothing left for the disgusted spectators to do except go home, and indulge their imaginations in a good deal of fruitless surmise.

Owen Crewe, threading his way out of the court-room in the wake of his wife, said into her ear: 'I told you you were wasting your time,' and began to feel much more amiable, and forbore to snub Janet when she squeezed her way up to him and announced that she was so thankful nothing more had happened. Once outside the building he firmly declined an invitation to lunch with his mother-in-law, told his wife that while she might do as she pleased he had every intention of returning to town, and walked off purposefully to where he had parked his car. Agnes would have liked to have talked it all over with her mother, but as her ideal of matrimony was founded largely on the theory that wives should whenever possible accompany their husbands, she bade her family a regretful farewell and went dutifully away with Owen.

Miss Matthews, who had attended the Inquest armed with a shopping-basket, and a list of groceries, darted off in the direction of the High Street; and Mrs Matthews, leaning slightly on her son's arm, smiled wanly on those of her acquaintance whom she happened to notice, and proclaimed her utter spiritual exhaustion. 'I feel,' she said in a solemn voice, 'that I must have just a little interval of quiet. Stella dear, I wonder if you can see Pullen anywhere?'

'Yes, he's waiting on the other side of the square,' said Stella.

'Tell him to bring the car here, dearest. Oh, he has seen us!' She turned to bestow one expensively gloved hand on Edward Rumbold. 'I haven't thanked you for coming,' she said deeply. 'I think you know what we feel. To know that one had a friend at one's side during that terrible ordeal – ! Is it foolish of me to be so sensitive? To me it was an agony of the spirit. All those hundreds of eyes, fixed on one!' She shuddered, held Mr Rumbold's hand an instant longer, and then released it. 'If only one could feel that one had left all the unpleasantness behind in that stuffy court!'

'You must try not to let it upset you,' said Edward Rumbold kindly. 'Of course it's all very distressing for you, and we're very sorry about it.'

She gave a faint, brave smile. 'I can't talk of it now,' she said. 'When I have had time to collect my thoughts . . . Will you come in and see us a little later on? At tea-time, perhaps?'

'Yes, I'll come if you want me, of course,' he replied. 'But – '

'Oh, do!' said Stella suddenly. 'It's too ghastly when there's no one but Family in the house.'

He could not help laughing. 'After that highly flattering invitation, how could I refuse?' he said teasingly.

'Well, *I* didn't mean it quite like that,' she admitted. 'And of course you'll bring Mrs Rumbold too.'

'Darling,' said Mrs Matthews reproachfully. 'that goes without saying, as Mr Rumbold knows.'

Whether Mr Rumbold knew it or not, he did not bring his wife to tea at the Poplars, but explained to Stella, who met him half-way down the drive, that she had another engagement.

'I don't blame her,' said Stella candidly. 'Ours is a Godforsaken household. And to make things worse we've been fending off reporters all day. They've been simply clustering about the place, and of course Mother let

135

herself be interviewed, so God knows what we shall see in the papers tomorrow.'

'Nonsense, you're letting yourself feel all this too much, Stella.'

'I can't help it,' she replied, falling into step beside him. 'It has absolutely got me down. Oh well, you pretty well know, don't you? It isn't only uncle's death: it's Aunt Harriet as well. I don't hold any brief for Mummy – '

'Then you should,' interposed Rumbold.

'Well, I know perfectly well she can be most frightfully annoying,' said Stella defensively. 'But actually what I was going to say when you *most* rudely interrupted me was that *though* I don't hold any brief for Mummy I do think Aunt Harriet is treating her awfully badly. She does every blessed thing she can think of to put a spoke in Mummy's wheel, and if Mummy so much as moves a table half an inch out of its usual place she kicks up a row, and says she ought to have been consulted.'

Edward Rumbold was silent for a moment, but he said presently: 'I shouldn't let that worry me too much, if I were you. Both your mother and your aunt are very much on edge, and – well, they are both of them disappointed at not being left in sole possession of the house, aren't they?'

The twinkle in his eyes was reflected in Stella's. 'I should think they jolly well are!' she said.

'Yes, well, you must give them time to get over that,' he advised. 'You'll probably find that they'll settle down quite comfortably in the end.'

'I hope they may,' said Stella. 'I only know that I'm definitely not going to go on living here as things are at present. Aunt Harriet's all right with Guy, but she doesn't like me, and doesn't leave me alone for a minute. Everything I do is bound to be wrong. I told Mummy last night I couldn't stick it much longer.'

He looked concerned, but said cheerfully: 'Well, you

won't have to, will you? When are you going to get married?'

She did not answer at once, and when she did it was in a studiedly offhand tone. 'Oh, not for a year, anyway! We never meant to get married this year, you know, and now that all this has happened we both think we ought to put it off at least till everything's been cleared up and I'm out of mourning.'

He took hold of her wrist, and made her stand still. 'My dear child, there's nothing wrong, is there?'

'Oh, good lord, no!' said Stella. 'As a matter of fact, it was my idea that we'd better wait a bit. I practically insisted on it, because there's Deryk's practice to be considered, and – and if we've got a murderer in the family he might like to think twice about marrying into it.'

'Not if he's a decent chap,' Rumbold said.

'Well, naturally, he didn't say that. But he does quite agree with me about not plunging into marriage until things have blown over. What I want to do is to share a tiny flat with a girl I knew at school. She's taken up dress-designing, and I thought I might get some sort of a job too. Do you think I'd be any good as a mannequin?'

'No, I don't,' he replied. 'What does your mother say about it?'

'Oh, she's against it, of course, but I expect she'll come round to it in time. She had to admit that it's pretty frightful at home now, but I got fed-up, because she would keep on moaning about it's being far worse for her than for Guy and me.'

They had reached the house by this time, and were met in the hall by Miss Matthews, who greeted Mr Rumbold effusively, and bore him off to the drawing-room, so that she could have a little talk with him alone, before her sister-in-law came downstairs from her room.

This scheme, however, was doomed to failure, because

137

Mrs Matthews had elected to curtail her afternoon rest, and was already seated on the sofa in the drawing-room, with a small piece of fancy-work in her hands, and a cigarette burning in an ash-tray beside her.

Miss Matthews, thoroughly put out, at once exclaimed that the room reeked of smoke, and rushed to open all the windows. Mrs Matthews paid not the slightest heed to this act of hostility, but rose and shook hands with Edward Rumbold, and invited him to sit beside her on the sofa.

The door then opened to admit Beecher, carrying the tea-tray, and as there was a sharp wind blowing, the window-curtains all flapped inwards, a vase of flowers was knocked over, and the butler was only just in time to save the door from slamming-to behind him. This misadventure forced Miss Matthews to shut the windows again, which annoyed her, and by the time the water from the flower vase had been mopped up, the vase restored to its place, and Guy had walked in and demanded to know what all the commotion was about, her temper had reached a dangerous pitch, and even vented itself on Guy, who was usually immune from attack.

It was at this quite inauspicious moment that the door opened again, and Randall, looking like a symphony in brown, came languidly into the room.

8

To the outside observer the effect caused by Randall's entrance could not be anything but comic. Mr Edward Rumbold, after one swift glance round the assembled company, became afflicted suddenly by a cough which made it necessary to shade his mouth with his hand for several moments. Mrs Matthews' sweet smile vanished abruptly; Miss Matthews broke off short in the middle of what she was saying and glared at Randall; and Guy said: 'Oh, *God*!' as though his endurance was at an end.

Randall looked round with a glint in his eyes, and said affably: 'How nice it is to see you all looking so happy and comfortable!'

'What the devil do you want?' said Guy disagreeably.

'Guy dearest!' said his mother, mildly reproving.

'Ah, how do you do?' said Randall, shaking hands with Edward Rumbold. 'I'm quite delighted to see you. I was afraid I should find unadulterated family. Do not trouble to ring the bell, dear Aunt Harriet: Beecher knows I am here.'

'I wasn't going to!' said Miss Matthews, quivering with annoyance. 'I'm sure I don't know why you've elected to come here. I noticed that you didn't trouble yourself to come to the Inquest.'

'No, I thought it would be much kinder to let you tell me all about it,' said Randall, drawing up a chair, and carefully hitching up his trousers before sitting down in it.

'I don't want to discuss it in any way, least of all with you!' snapped Miss Matthews.

139

'Really?' said Randall incredulously. 'And to think I nearly refrained from visiting you today for fear I should find you all talking about the Inquest in that peculiarly reiterative way you have!'

'If you had one spark of decent feeling, Randall, you would have been present at the Inquest!' said Miss Matthews, moving the cups about with a good deal of clatter. 'Not that I expected it. I've given up expecting you to behave in anything but a thoroughly selfish manner. Just like your uncle! Though you're not the only person I could mention who thinks of no one but themselves. I name no names, but those whom the cap fits can wear it,' she added darkly.

Mrs Matthews intervened at this point, and said in a grave voice: 'Isn't this a little undignified? When one thinks that only a week ago Death visited this house, doesn't it seem to you that we should all of us try to turn our minds away from petty squabbles to something higher and better?'

Guy made an impatient movement, and strode away to the window, and stood with his back to the room, fidgeting with the blind-cord.

'Certainly, my dear aunt!' said Randall, who had listened to her with an air of courteous interest. 'Let us by all means try! But you must suggest the subject. No one else is nearly so fit.'

'I think each one of us could think of something if we tried,' said Mrs Matthews gently. 'Even you, Randall.'

'I can tell you a story about a golfer who went to heaven,' said Randall, 'but I'm afraid that exhausts my repertoire of higher and better things.'

'If you are trying to shock me, Randall, I can only assure you that I am not shocked, but only very sad to think that you can joke about things which to me are sacred.'

'Aunt Zoë,' said Randall, 'you never disappoint me.'

Edward Rumbold felt that it was time to intervene. He said: 'The younger generation are most of them distressingly irreverent, Mrs Matthews. I met a "sweet young thing" the other day who propounded the most startling views on the Christian religion!' He drifted easily into anecdote, and succeeded in diverting not only Mrs Matthews, but Harriet Matthews as well.

Guy came away from the window as Mr Rumbold's story ended, and began to hand round the tea-cups. Stella entered the room almost immediately, nodded to Randall, and sat down on a floor-cushion by her mother.

Randall regarded her with a pained expression. 'My little love, do you not see that I am present? Have you no exclamation of mingled dismay and loathing to greet me with?'

'I saw your car in the drive, so I knew what to expect,' retorted Stella. 'I suppose you've come to hear about the Inquest. The police asked for an adjournment, so we're just where we were before.'

'If they're wise they'll give it up,' said Guy. 'No one'll ever know the truth. Don't you think they'll chuck it fairly soon, Mr Rumbold?'

'I don't know, Guy. It depends how much they've got to go on.'

'They haven't got anything. Aunt Harriet saw to that,' said Guy, with a little laugh.

'I'm sure if I'd ever dreamed there was going to be such a fuss made over my clearing up poor Gregory's things I wouldn't have touched one of them!' said Miss Matthews agitatedly. 'Anyone would think I did it on purpose! No one told me I ought not to, and my motto is, If a job has to be done sometime, do it at once! Besides, there wasn't anything that could possibly have had poison in it, as I told the Superintendent. "If you think there's poison in a bottle of iodine and a packet of corn-plaster," I said, "you can take them and see for yourself."'

'And did he take them?' inquired Mr Rumbold.

Miss Matthews sniffed. 'Yes. Such nonsense! I could understand him wanting to take the salts and the liver-pills, but I've yet to hear of anyone's drinking iodine. Anyway, I gave him everything I took out of poor Gregory's medicine-chest, and I only hope he's satisfied.'

'But my dear Miss Matthews, what did you *do* with your brother's personal effects?' asked Rumbold.

'I didn't do anything with them!' she replied hotly. 'I left all his clothes, and his ivory brushes, and his watch and chain, and things tidily put away in his wardrobe! The only things I threw away were things like his sponges, which were no good to anybody. And if the police want to see them I'm extremely sorry, but they went into the boiler with all the rest of the rubbish!'

'I see,' said Rumbold. 'A sort of clean sweep.'

'Well, what was the use of keeping a lot of things no one could ever use?' demanded Miss Matthews. 'Next I suppose I shall be blamed for having the room swept!'

'My dear, I don't think anyone blames you,' said Mrs Matthews. 'You couldn't know. After all, we none of us dreamed there was any truth in Gertrude's suspicions. And if perhaps you quite unwittingly burned something which contained the poison, do you know I am almost glad? Nothing can bring Gregory back to us, and isn't it better that we should remain in ignorance?'

'We seem to be likely to,' muttered Guy.

Stella was frowning. 'No!' she said. 'If he was poisoned we've got to know who did it. Good God, how could we go on when we know that one of us is a murderer?'

'How dare you, Stella!' gasped her aunt.

'But it's true!' persisted Stella. 'That's what's so ghastly.

142

You don't seem to see it, but can't you realize that if the police don't discover who did it we shall wonder which of us it was all our lives?'

'Morbid rot!' said Guy. 'I'd a lot sooner wonder than have a foul scandal, anyway.'

'Would you?' said Stella, looking up at him with a vague horror in her eyes. 'When it might have been me, or even Mummy?'

'Oh, don't talk such drivel!' said Guy roughly.

Mrs Matthews gave a little laugh, and dropped her hand on to Stella's shoulder. 'My darling, you mustn't let your imagination run away with you quite so fast!'

'But the fact remains that she has spoken nothing but the truth,' said Randall. 'I congratulate you, Stella.'

Mrs Matthews met his look with one very nearly as limpid. 'I'm afraid I can't agree with you, my dear Randall. Stella was speaking in that exaggerated way which I've so often deplored. I hope that she wouldn't suspect her mother or her brother of having committed such a terrible crime any more than I could ever suspect either of my children.'

'I think you are all of you making a mistake,' said Edward Rumbold. 'There's no reason to suppose that Matthews was murdered by any one of you. Are you so sure that there was no one outside his family who could have done it?'

Guy stared at him. 'Who on earth?' he asked bluntly.

'I don't know, but I think that if I were you I would rather believe that it must have been an outsider than make myself ill with quite groundless suspicions of my own people,' said Rumbold gently, but with a look that sent the blood rushing to Guy's cheeks.

'I'd rather have it cleared up,' said Stella decidedly.

Rumbold said, smiling down at her: 'Well, that's a sure

143

sign you don't really wonder whether your mother or your brother committed the crime,' he said.

'I never heard of such a thing!' said Miss Matthews. 'Oh, you're not going, Mr Rumbold? Why, you've barely finished your tea!'

'He is probably going to supplement it elsewhere,' remarked Randall. 'And I'm sure I don't blame him,' he added, casting a glance at the somewhat meagrely furnished cake-stand. 'There is a certain Lenten spirit clinging to my dear Aunt Harriet's tea-parties which only the few know how to appreciate.'

Stella gave a giggle, and even Mrs Matthews bit her lip. Harriet Matthews sat bolt upright in her chair, and said: 'I did not ask you to tea here, Randall, and I did not ask Mr Rumbold either, though I am always glad to see *him*, as I hope he knows. And if he finds my tea insufficient – '

'Thank you, thank you, but I have had an excellent tea!' Rumbold said hastily. 'You know how much I like those little scones of yours, Miss Matthews. I tell my wife she never gives me anything half as good. Now, please don't any of you disturb yourselves! I can find my way out.'

In obedience to a glance from his mother Guy put down his plate and got up. But Randall also had risen, and waved Guy back to his chair. 'Don't lose your chance of the last slice of cake,' he said. 'You, after all, are going to dine here. I will show Mr Rumbold out.' He moved to the door as he spoke, and opened it, and held it for the elder man to pass through.

'There's really no need for you to bother,' said Rumbold, picking up his hat from the hall-table.

'It is a pleasure,' replied Randall. 'The society of my relatives can only be enjoyed with frequent intervals.'

Rumbold looked at him, half in amusement, half in

144

reproof. 'Why do you come if you feel like that?' he asked. 'If you'll forgive my saying so, your presence isn't exactly conducive to peace.'

'No, but don't you think it's nice for them to have someone to vent their feelings on?' said Randall in his most urbane voice. 'They are all of them just a trifle on edge, as you may have noticed.'

'It's an extraordinarily unpleasant situation for them,' replied Rumbold seriously.

Randall strolled with him out of the house. 'Oh, extraordinarily,' he agreed. 'Did anything of interest transpire at the Inquest?'

'Nothing at all. The police asked for an adjournment as soon as Mrs Lupton had given her evidence.'

'Considering all things, that was to be expected,' said Randall. 'I take it that our engaging young doctor figured largely?'

'He was one of the witnesses, yes. I thought he made a very good one.'

'He probably would,' said Randall. 'And did everyone seem quite satisfied with his evidence?'

'Quite. There was no reason why they shouldn't be, you know. He's behaved perfectly properly throughout.'

'Yes, I noticed that,' said Randall. 'Not one to lose his head, our ambitious doctor.'

The sneer was thinly veiled. Rumbold hesitated, and then said: 'I won't pretend not to know what you're hinting at, but why do you do it? Have you anything against Fielding?'

'I find him entirely insupportable,' replied Randall calmly.

'That may make you wish to suspect him, but it is hardly a reason for doing so,' said Rumbold.

'I stand rebuked,' bowed Randall.

They had reached the gate by this time. Rumbold

turned, and held out his hand. 'Well, I don't know that I actually meant to rebuke you,' he said, 'but I am a much older man than you are, Matthews, and perhaps you will allow me to advise you not to drop that sort of remark in your cousin's hearing. For one thing, it isn't particularly kind, and for another I have an idea that she's got quite enough to worry her in that quarter without having anything added.'

Randall's eyes opened wide. Edward Rumbold was momentarily startled by their curious brilliance, and could not be sure that the expression they held was a pleasant one. The next instant the insolent lids had drooped over them again. 'Is that so?' Randall said. 'I am quite in your debt.'

He wended his way back to the house, and entered the drawing-room to find his two aunts, their own differences forgotten for the moment, engaged in extolling the virtues of their late guest, and deploring the vulgarity of his wife.

'Such a cultured man!' sighed Mrs Matthews. 'One cannot help wondering – '

' – what he saw in her,' cut in Stella. 'He saw a pretty face, and a kind heart.'

'That hat!' shuddered Mrs Matthews. 'The commonest shade of pink! And at her age, too!'

'Most unsuitable,' agreed Miss Matthews. 'Not at all the sort of hat to wear at an Inquest. I was quite shocked.'

Stella got up from her floor-cushion, and moved away to the other end of the room. The two elder ladies continued their stimulating conversation, and by the time they had agreed that the sole reason why Mr Rumbold, who must really be extremely wealthy (because all wool-exporters were), should live in quite a moderate-sized house, like Holly Lodge, was that his wife was probably only accustomed to a Council house, perfect harmony reigned between them, to vanish abruptly, however, upon

146

Mrs Matthews' ringing the bell to have the tea-things cleared away. This made it necessary for Miss Matthews immediately to pour herself out another cup, and as it was not only overpoweringly strong but also tepid, her temper became once more impaired, and the respective perfections and imperfections of Edward and Dolly Rumbold were forgotten in her own rankling grievances.

Guy, who seemed unable to occupy himself in any rational way, made another attempt to find out from Randall what line the police were following. Randall professed complete ignorance, and when Guy showed a disposition to pursue the subject, got up with a world-weary air, and quite firmly took his leave.

No one evinced any desire to accompany him to the front door, so he strolled out by himself, and had got into his car, and switched on the engine when he suddenly perceived Dr Fielding striding up the drive towards the house. Randall watched him, a singularly unpleasant expression in his eyes, and after a moment switched his engine off again. By the time the doctor came abreast the saturnine look had vanished, and the thin lips curled into the semblance of a smile. 'Ah, how do you do, doctor?' Randall drawled, and drew off one washleather glove, and extended his hand.

Fielding did not look particularly pleased to see him, but he shook hands, and said that it was some time since they had met. 'I missed you at the Inquest,' he remarked.

'That was hardly surprising,' said Randall. 'I wasn't there.'

'Oh, weren't you?' said Fielding.

'No,' said Randall. 'I thought it would be dull, and probably vulgar. But I'm sorry I didn't hear your evidence,' he added politely. 'I understand you provided the star-turn of an otherwise mediocre performance.'

'Indeed!' The doctor looked at him somewhat warily. 'In what way, I wonder?'

'In your demeanour, my dear doctor, which I understand to have been little short of noble. And in your testimony, of course, which I'm sure was masterly.'

Fielding drew in his breath. 'You're too kind. I am not unaccustomed to giving evidence in my professional capacity.'

'But in such difficult circumstances!' said Randall. 'And so many witnesses show a lamentable tendency to lose their heads. Not that I expected you to do that, I need scarcely say.'

'Thank you,' said Fielding, with heavy irony. 'There was no reason why I should lose my head.'

'No,' agreed Randall, 'everything seems to have been conducted in the politest way. No awkward questions asked, no nerve-racking cross-examination. I have always felt that to be cross-examined would be enough to shake the stoutest nerve.'

'Let us hope then that you will never be called upon to face such an ordeal,' said Fielding.

'That is very nice of you, and seems to call for a like response,' said Randall. 'I can do no less than hope that you will not be called upon to face it either.'

'I am not much alarmed by the prospect,' replied Fielding with a slight smile. 'If this business comes to a trial, I shall naturally have to appear.'

Randall shook his head. 'It has all been most unlucky,' he remarked. 'For the murderer, I mean. Who could have supposed that my dear Aunt Gertrude would have been the instrument chosen to upset one of the neatest murders of the century?'

'I could wish for the family's sake that the truth had never come to light, certainly,' said Fielding. 'It is most unpleasant for them.' He met Randall's satirical look fair

148

and square. 'It is even rather unpleasant for me,' he continued deliberately. 'Quite a number of people, I imagine, think that because I am a doctor I ought instantly to have realized that Matthews died from a somewhat obscure poison.'

'Oh, there is bound to be talk,' Randall answered cheerfully. 'People have such suspicious minds. I daresay they attach a ridiculous amount of importance to that bottle of tonic which was so fortunately smashed.'

'Fortunately?' repeated Fielding. 'Hardly fortunate from my point of view!'

'Did I say fortunately?' inquired Randall. 'I meant unfortunately, of course.'

'Happily the tonic was not made up at the dispensary,' said Fielding.

'No, I didn't expect that it would be,' said Randall.

Fielding's jaw became a shade more prominent. 'More-over,' he said, 'nicotine is hardly a poison which a doctor would use, as you, with your medical training, of course, know, Matthews.'

Randall had been gazing meditatively through his windscreen, but he turned his head at that, and said with a crooked smile: 'So you know that, do you?'

'Oh yes!' said Fielding. 'Your uncle mentioned it once some time ago. He said that you were a most promising student, but that you abandoned the career when your father died.'

'And have you passed this information on to the police?' asked Randall.

'No,' said Fielding. 'I did not consider it any business of mine.'

Randall leaned forward, and switched on his engine again. 'Well, you should,' he said. 'Superintendent Hannasyde would love it.'

Fielding shrugged. 'Oh, I've no wish to make mischief,' he said.

Randall gave a little croon of mirth. 'You flatter yourself, my dear doctor, really you do! Pass on your information: it will brighten the Superintendent's dull life, and it won't hurt me.'

'In that case, why should I bother?' said Fielding, and with a nod of farewell turned and walked on to the house.

His errand was to warn its inmates against making any statement to the Press. He had returned from his afternoon round to find his own house besieged with reporters, and in consequence he was in no very pleasant mood. Finding his fiancée inclined to treat the peril of the Press as a minor matter, he said somewhat tartly that he wished she would consider his position a little. Mrs Matthews, wearing a worldly-wise smile, at once assured him that he had nothing to fear. 'I saw one of the reporters myself,' she said gravely. 'And I think I made him understand how we all feel about it. I talked to him – words seemed to be sent to me – and I think he realized, and was ashamed.'

Guy said uneasily: 'I say, mother, you didn't give them any sort of statement, did you?'

'Dear boy, haven't I told you that I didn't?'

Guy said no more, but the doctor, when Stella saw him off, said: 'Really, Stella, I do think you might have prevented your mother seeing that fellow! If you don't object to publicity, I do. This case is doing me quite enough harm as it is.'

'I expect,' said Stella, in a small, very steady voice, 'it does you harm to be known to be engaged to me, doesn't it?'

'It's no use discussing that,' said Fielding. 'I don't suppose it does me much good, but it can't be helped.'

150

'It might be,' said Stella, raising her eyes to his face.

'My dear girl, please don't think I'm trying to back out of it,' he said.

Guy came out into the hall at that moment, so the conversation had to be suspended. Guy was as uneasy as the doctor, and said that he wouldn't mind betting that his mother had talked a lot of ghastly hot air to the reporter.

His mistrust of her was justified. Next morning the *Daily Reflector* carried a fat, black headline on its front page, a photograph of the Poplars, and another (inset) of Mrs Matthews stepping out of the court-room after the Inquest. When Guy came down to breakfast he found his aunt and sister with no less than four picture papers, indignantly reading extracts aloud to each other.

'"Murdered Man's Sister in Suburban Poison Drama Refuses to Discuss Mystery Death,"' read Stella in an awed voice. '"'We think it wiser to say nothing,' says Mrs Zoë Matthews, the graceful fair-haired widow concerned in the mysterious poisoning case at Grinley Heath which is baffling the Scotland Yard experts." Mummy will love that bit. Guy, *look* at the photograph of Mummy! I ask you!'

'Listen to this!' begged Miss Matthews in a trembling voice. 'I never heard anything to equal it, never! "Wearing mourning" – I should like to know what else she would be wearing! – "and with a look of strain in her sad eyes, charming Mrs Zoë Matthews, the widowed sister-in-law of Gregory Matthews, whose death under mysterious circumstances took place at his residence at Grinley Heath a week ago, received me yesterday in her sunny drawing-room." Her drawing-room, indeed! Oh, I've no doubt she told him it belonged to her, but as for it being sunny it never gets a ray of sun all day, as she very well knows!'

Guy, quite pale with dismay, came hurriedly across the

151

room to look over his aunt's shoulder at the offending paragraph. '"One has to remember that life goes on . . . irreparable loss . . . as much a mystery to us as to Scotland Yard . . ." Good God, she *can't* have said all this muck!'

'Of course she said it!' snapped Miss Matthews. 'It's just the sort of rubbish I should expect her to talk. "There was a great bond between my poor brother-in-law and me!" . . . oh, *was* there? And not one word about what my feelings are! . . . "Calm and self-possessed." . . . Self-possessed! Brazen would be nearer the mark! Oh, I've no patience with it!'

Guy rescued the paper, which Miss Matthews seemed to be inclined to rend in pieces, and retired with it to the window. Stella, deep meanwhile in the *Morning Star*, suddenly gave a gasp, and exclaimed: 'Of all the cheek! Aunt Harriet, listen to this! "'Mr Matthews' death was a terrible shock to us all,' pretty, blue-eyed Rose Daventry, the twenty-three-year-old housemaid at the Poplars, informed our representative yesterday." There's miles more of it, and even a bit about Rose's young man. Oh, she says they all feel it as a personal loss!'

'What?' shrieked Miss Matthews.

'There's a photograph too,' said Stella.

Miss Matthews snatched the paper from her. 'She leaves the house today, month or no month!' she declared. 'The impertinence of it! Personal loss! What's more it's a lie, because every servant we ever had hated Gregory! She'd never have dared to do this if she hadn't been under notice!'

Beecher came into the room at this moment, and was promptly glared at by his incensed mistress. 'Do you know anything about this disgraceful affair?' demanded Miss Matthews, striking the paper with her hand.

Beecher coughed. 'Yes, miss. Very reprehensible

indeed. Mrs Beecher has been giving Rose a piece of her mind. Mr Randall is on the phone, miss.'

'What does he want?' growled Guy.

'He did not say, sir.'

'Well, I'm not going to answer it,' said Guy, sitting down at the table. 'Tell him we're out.'

'You go, Stella,' said her aunt. 'Though what he can want I'm sure I don't know.'

Stella sighed, and put down the paper. 'Why it should have to be me I fail to understand,' she remarked, but she went out into the hall and picked up the receiver. 'Hullo?' she said in a discouraging voice. 'Stella speaking. What is it?'

Randall's dulcet voice answered her. 'Good-morning, my sweet. Tell me at once – I am quite breathless with excitement – why have I never been privileged to set eyes on pretty, blue-eyed Rose Daventry?'

'Oh, damn you, shut up!' said Stella crossly. 'What is it you want?'

A laugh floated to her ears. 'Only that, darling.'

'Then go to hell!' said Stella, and slammed the receiver down.

Others beside Randall had seen the picture papers that morning, and it was not long before Mrs Lupton arrived at the Poplars in a state of outraged majesty. She wished to know whether Rose had been turned out of the house, and if not why not; whether Mrs Matthews realized the height of her own folly; what her sister Harriet had been about to let a reporter set foot inside the house; and what steps were being taken by the police to discover Gregory Matthews' murderer. No one was able to give an answer to this last question, and Mrs Lupton, not in any hasty spirit, but as the result of impartial consideration, pronounced her verdict. 'The case is being handled with the grossest incompetence,' she declared. 'I do not find that the police are making the smallest effort to trace my unfortunate brother's assassin.'

This harsh judgement, however, was not quite fair to Superintendent Hannasyde, who at that very moment was seated in Giles Carrington's office with Gregory Matthews' Pass-book open on the desk between them.

'Do you know what connection Matthews had with a man called Hyde?' Hannasyde asked.

Giles shook his head. 'No, I'm afraid I don't. Why do you want to know?'

'I've been going through these Bank accounts,' replied Hannasyde, 'and it appears that a considerable number of the cheques paid into his Bank by Matthews came from this Hyde. Take a look. They're all rather large sums, and seem to have been paid in regularly once a month.'

Giles took the Pass-book, and studied the marked entries. 'Looks as though he were running some sort of business,' he remarked. 'If he was, I never heard of it. Do you suppose he owned a Pawnbroker's, or a Fish-and-Chips shop, and didn't want anyone to know of it?'

'I can't make it out at all. It may be something of that nature. I've had an interview with the Bank Manager, but he doesn't know any more than you do. The cheques were all drawn on the City Branch of Foster's Bank. The Chief Cashier remembered them at once. I'll have to go and see what I can find out there.' He got up, and held out his hand for the Pass-book. 'I came to see you first because it's always a bit of a job getting information out of Banks.'

'Sorry,' said Giles. 'Nothing doing at all. I'll tell you what, though: if anyone knows, Randall Matthews would. It's my belief there's precious little about his uncle that young gentleman doesn't know.'

Hannasyde smiled rather grimly. 'Yes, I had thought of

him. But I haven't found Mr Randall Matthews precisely falling over himself to take me into his confidence. Still, I can try him if all else fails.'

He left Adam Street, and journeyed east, to the City. At Foster's Bank the manager was civil, but by no means friendly. The Bank, he said, was no doubt what Superintendent Hannasyde would consider old-fashioned; they had old-fashioned ways in it; he himself greatly deplored the modern methods of the police in trying to obtain information through Banks. Time was . . . Hannasyde, who never made enemies wantonly, listened, and sympathized, and quite agreed with the manager. In the end he got some information out of him, though not very much. The manager knew very little about John Hyde, who hardly ever came in person to the Bank. He had opened an account a good many years ago now. It was believed that he was an agent for some northern firm of manufacturers; his address was 17 Gadsby Row; the manager regretted he could give Hannasyde no further information.

Gadsby Row, which was a narrow, crowded street in the heart of the City, did not take Hannasyde long to find. He turned down it from the busy thoroughfare which it bisected, and, threading his way between hurrying typists and bare-headed errand-boys, soon arrived at No 17. This was found to be a newsagent's shop, which also sold the cheaper kinds of cigarettes and tobacco. It was a mean little place, with dirty, fly-blown windows, and it bore the name H. Brown on the fascia-board. A couple of steps led up into the interior of the shop, which was dark, and small, and smelled of stale smoke. Hannasyde walked in, and almost at once a door at the back of the shop opened, and a stout woman in an overall came into the shop, and asked him what he wanted.

'I am looking for a Mr John Hyde,' said Hannasyde. 'I understand this is where he lives.'

'He ain't in,' she replied shortly. 'Don't know when he'll be back.'

'Where can I find him, do you know?'

'I couldn't say, I'm sure.'

The door at the back of the shop opened again, and a middle-aged man with a wispy moustache and a pair of watery blue eyes came out in his shirt-sleeves, and said: 'What's the gentleman want, Emma?'

'Someone asking for Mr Hyde,' she answered indifferently.

'You'll have to call back. He's not here.'

'That's what I told him,' corroborated his wife.

'Is this where he lives?' asked Hannasyde.

'No, it isn't,' said Mr Brown, eyeing him with dawning dislike.

'Then perhaps you can tell me where he does live?'

'No, I'm sorry, I can't. Take a message, if you like.'

Hannasyde produced a card, and gave it to him. 'That's my name,' he said. 'It may help your memory a bit.'

Mr Brown read the legend on the card, and shot a swift, lowering look at the Superintendent. His wife craned her neck to see the card, and perceptibly changed colour. She stared at Hannasyde and thrust out her lip a little. 'We don't want no busies here!' she announced. 'What d'you want to know?'

Hannasyde, who was accustomed to being regarded by the Mrs Browns of this world with deep distrust, did not set a great deal of store by her obvious uneasiness, but replied in a business-like voice: 'I've told you what I want to know. Where can I find Mr John Hyde?'

'How can we tell you what we don't know?' she cried. 'He ain't here, that's all.'

Her husband nudged her away. 'That's OK, Emma:

156

you get back to the kitchen.' He put the Superintendent's card down on the counter, and said with a smile that showed a set of discoloured teeth: 'That's right, what she says. We haven't set eyes on Mr Hyde, not since last Tuesday.'

'What does he do here?'

Mr Brown caressed his stubbly chin. 'Well, you see, in a manner of speaking he owns the place.'

Hannasyde frowned. 'You mean he owns this shop?'

'No, not to say the shop, he doesn't. The whole house is his.'

'He's your landlord, in fact?'

'That's it,' agreed Mr Brown. 'He's an agent for one of them big firms up north. I don't know as he's got what you'd call a fixed address, barring this. You see, he travels about a lot in the way of business.'

'Do you mean that he has an office here, or what?'

'That's right. You can see it if you like. There ain't anything there.'

'How long has he been here?'

'Well, I couldn't say offhand,' said Mr Brown vaguely. 'A goodish time. Somewhere round about seven or eight years, I think.'

'What age man is he? What does he look like?'

'He's nothing particular to look at. I don't know as I could hardly describe him. He hasn't got the sort of face you can take hold of. Middle-aged, he is, and keeps himself to himself. What do you want with him?'

'That's my business. How often does he come here?'

'Pretty often,' Mr Brown said sullenly.

'Come along, answer! Does he come here every day?'

'Sometimes. Sometimes not. It ain't nothing to do with me. He comes as he pleases.'

'When did you see him last?'

157

'I told you. It was last Tuesday. I ain't laid eyes on him since.'

'Did he say he was going away?'

'No, he didn't. He didn't say nothing.'

'Didn't give you any address for his letters to be forwarded too?'

Mr Brown shot him another of his lowering glances. 'There hasn't been no letters.'

There was little more to be got out of him. After one or two more questions which were answered in the same grudging manner, Hannasyde left the shop. The personality of Mr John Hyde, about which he had felt, an hour earlier, only a mild curiosity, had suddenly become a problem of unexpected importance. The elusive Mr Hyde would have to be found, and his connection with Gregory Matthews traced to its source. It was a job for the department, but while he was on his way to Scotland Yard Hannasyde all at once changed his mind, and instead of going to Whitehall, got on an omnibus bound for Piccadilly, and went to pay a call on Mr Randall Matthews.

9

It was nearly noon by the time Hannasyde arrived at Randall's flat, but that elegant young gentleman received him in a brocade dressing-gown of gorgeous colouring and design. He seemed, with the exception of his coat, to be fully clad under the glowing robe, so Hannasyde concluded that the wearing of it was due rather to a love of the exotic than to actual sloth. He smiled inwardly at the thought of Sergeant Hemingway's appreciation of the dressing-gown, could he but have seen it, and embarked without preamble on an explanation of his visit.

'Sorry to disturb you, Mr Matthews,' he said, 'but I think you may be able to help me.'

'How gratifying!' said Randall. 'Let me give you a glass of sherry.'

'Thank you, but I won't take anything just now. Does the name of Hyde convey anything to you?'

Randall poured himself out a glass of sherry, and replaced the stopper in the decanter. 'Well – parks,' he said.

'No.'

'Give me time,' said Randall, picking up his wineglass. 'Stevenson?' he suggested.

'Nothing else, Mr Matthews?' Hannasyde asked, watching him closely.

Randall met the steady gaze with one of his blandest looks. 'Well, not just at the moment,' he said. 'Do you want to pursue the subject? Because if so I'm afraid you'll have to explain things to me. I don't seem to be very intelligent this morning.'

'You don't happen to recall having heard your uncle mention that name at any time?' Hannasyde persisted.

Randall continued to look at him over the rim of his wineglass. 'No, I can't say that I do,' he replied. He strolled over to a chair, and sat down on the arm of it. 'Will you have a cigarette, or a nice game of Blind Man's Bluff?' he inquired.

Hannasyde accepted the cigarette. 'I'm disappointed, Mr Matthews. I hoped that you might be able to throw some light on this little problem. I have been going through your uncle's Bank books.' He struck a match, and held it to the end of his cigarette. 'And I find that quite a substantial part of his income has apparently been derived from a person going by the name of John Hyde. Or, possibly, from some business of which Hyde is the representative.'

Randall sipped his sherry. Nothing but a faint interest could be read in his face. He said: 'When you speak of a substantial part, what precisely do you mean, Superintendent?'

'I haven't added all the sums together, but at a guess I should say they must amount to something in the region of twelve or thirteen hundred pounds a year.'

Randall inclined his head with an expression of mild surprise. 'Quite a respectable income,' he remarked. 'May I ask how it was paid into my uncle's account?'

'By cheque,' replied Hannasyde. 'And at regular monthly intervals, though not in regular amounts.' He thrust his hand into his inner coat-pocket, and pulled out Gregory Matthews' Pass-book. 'Perhaps you'd like to see for yourself.'

'I think I should,' said Randall, setting down his wine-glass and taking the book.

Silence reigned while Randall went unhurriedly through the book. Then he gave it back to Hannasyde, and said:

160

'I feel quite unable to throw any of the expected light, Superintendent. What are your views on the matter?'

'I don't know that I have any,' answered Hannasyde. 'You must remember that I was not acquainted with your uncle. That is why I come to you. I suppose you knew him as well as anybody, Mr Matthews?'

'I haven't considered the question,' said Randall. 'Moreover, I believe I told you at the outset of our agreeable dealings with each other that I was not in my uncle's confidence.'

'You did,' agreed Hannasyde. 'But I can't help suspecting that you were over-modest. You were the only member of his family, I believe, to whom he imparted his discovery of Mr Lupton's double life.'

'Do you call that a confidence?' inquired Randall. 'I thought it was a smutty story.'

'Well, let us waive the question of confidences, Mr Matthews, and say that there was a bond of sympathy between you,' suggested Hannasyde.

As he spoke he caught a glimpse of Randall's eyes, and experienced a sensation of shock. What the expression in them meant he had no time to decide: it was gone in a flash, but it left him feeling oddly shaken, and with an impression forcibly stamped on his mind that something very unpleasant had suddenly sprung up and as suddenly vanished again.

Then Randall said in his composed drawl: 'No, I don't think there was any bond of sympathy between us. You have possibly been misled by the fact that alone of my family I didn't quarrel with him.'

'Come, Mr Matthews!' said Hannasyde persuasively. 'Why can't you be frank with me? Whether there was sympathy between you or not, I think you know more of him than you have told me. On the question of these cheques from John Hyde, for instance: do you ask me to believe that you, the heir to your uncle's property, are ignorant of the source of part of his income?'

'No,' said Randall, 'but it is nevertheless true.' He rose and strolled over to the table, and refilled his glass. 'The varying amounts, coupled with the regular appearance of the cheques, would lead one to suppose that my uncle was amusing himself with some business venture which he preferred to keep his name out of. It will probably come to light in due course.'

'In fact, you don't set much store by it, Mr Matthews?'

Randall shrugged. 'No, I can't say that I do. To tell you the truth, I think you are wasting your time in looking for John Hyde. His significance in the case seems to me to be somewhat obscure.'

'Quite so,' replied Hannasyde. 'But when I come across something that calls for an explanation I find it pays to follow it up, however trivial it may appear. I have already made some inquiries into Hyde's identity, both at his Bank and at his only known address.'

'I hope such painstaking industry was suitably rewarded?'

'I think it was,' said Hannasyde imperturbably. 'I find that John Hyde describes himself as an agent, and owns a squalid little house in Gadsby Row, in the City, with a newsagent's shop attached. The property is apparently let to a man called Brown, who owns the shop, but one room has been retained by Hyde for his own use.'

'Indeed?' said Randall.

'The fact that a man who is in a position to make large monetary payments each month should have as his only address an office in a shabby back-street strikes me as being sufficiently unusual to call for further investigation. What do you think, Mr Matthews?'

'That you are wasting your time, my dear Superintendent.'

162

'And when I tell you that John Hyde has not been seen at his office since Tuesday, May 14th?'

Randall had wandered over to where his cigarette-box stood, and his back was momentarily turned to Hannasyde. 'Who says that he has not been seen since May 14th?' he asked.

'The man who runs the shop – and I don't think he was lying.'

'It doesn't seem to me a very valuable piece of information,' Randall remarked, coming back to his chair. 'He may conceivably be ill, or away.'

'Certainly,' said Hannasyde. 'But there is an elusive quality to Mr John Hyde which needs explaining. There is something more than a little odd about a man who has no home address, Mr Matthews.' He got up. 'I'm sorry you can't help me.'

'Looking for mares' nests has never been one of my pastimes, Superintendent. May I know whether you have been favoured with a description of your quarry?'

'A very vague one, which might possibly be false.'

'How useful! And what was it?'

'A middle-aged man, with an ordinary face. That's all so far.'

'I should give it up, if I were you,' said Randall.

'You can hardly expect me to follow that advice,' said Hannasyde rather shortly, and took his leave.

But the quest of John Hyde proved to be a singularly thankless task. No one knew him; nor, when Hannasyde and Sergeant Hemingway, armed with a search warrant, visited his office, could any clue to his identity be discovered. The office, a dingy room above the shop, contained nothing but a table, a chair, a typewriter, and a safe.

'If this bird's an agent, what's become of his sample-goods?' demanded Sergeant Hemingway.

Mr Brown, still in his shirt-sleeves, looked round the bare apartment with vague disquiet. 'I never known him go off like this before, and no word said,' he muttered. 'I seen him Tuesday before last, and I'll take my dying oath he ain't been near the place since.'

This oft-reiterated statement was borne out to a certain extent by Foster's Bank. On the 14th May a cheque of Hyde's for £25 had been presented, made out to Bearer. Questioned, the cashier faithfully described Mr Brown, added that he had been in the habit of cashing cheques made out by Hyde to Bearer. Mr Brown did not deny it. He stated that Mr Hyde had always employed him to cash his cheques for him, and that he had merely collected the money, and handed it over to Hyde. As it further transpired that he had very often paid in moneys for Hyde there seemed to be no reason for doubting this statement, but why he had been so employed or what his connection with Hyde was there was no getting out of him. He persisted in saying that he didn't know, he was sure; and that Mr Hyde never told him nothing. When asked whether Hyde ever had visitors he replied sulkily that Hyde did sometimes see people in the way of business, but who they were or where they came from he couldn't say.

The safe, when opened, disclosed nothing but a half-used cheque-book, with every counterfoil blank, and a bundle of share-certificates.

'Well, this is the queerest turn I ever saw in my life!' said the Sergeant. 'I've heard of people doing a bunk, but I never knew them leave their cheque-books and a tidy Bank balance behind till now. Looks almost as though this bloke had to clear out in the devil's own hurry, Chief. Something happened after he left this place on the 14th which made him scared stiff to come back.'

'But why did he keep his cheque-book in the safe?'

demanded Hannasyde. 'We know from the Bank that it was the only one he possessed. Most men would carry it about with them, if they'd only got one. Or they'd keep it in a desk at home – not in an office they visit at irregular intervals!'

'You can search me,' said the Sergeant. 'The point is, where is his home?'

But this was something that the most rigorous inquiry failed to discover. An advertisement inserted in the papers asking for any information concerning Hyde produced no results, and an attempt to discover documents at his Bank which might give some clue to his identity also failed. He kept no documents at the Bank.

Sergeant Hemingway, who had a genius for making his fellows confide in him, produced in triumph the châtelaine of No 11 Gadsby Row, a corpulent lady with a slight beard, who remembered having seen Mr Hyde once when she had popped into Mr Brown's to buy a paper. She hadn't happened to look at him particular, for she was passing the time of day with Mr Brown, like anyone might, when in he walked, and without a word to no one went straight through the shop into the back-parlour. Well, that had struck her as being a funny thing to do, and she had said to Mr Brown, not thinking: 'Who's that?' And she remembered as well as if it had been yesterday him saying: 'Oh, that's only Mr Hyde, that is!' It was a bit hard to say what he'd looked like, because he'd had his hat on, and a pair of them dark spectacles, but he was dressed very gentlemanly, that she would say.

It was not very helpful, but it was the best Sergeant Hemingway could do. No one else in the Row seemed ever to have noticed Hyde, and no shop in the vicinity had been patronized by him.

A watch was set on No 17 Gadsby Row, and an inquiry made into Mr Brown's past history. It did not surprise

165

either Hannasyde or the Sergeant to discover that Mr Brown was known to the police, and had done time for fraud seven years previously, but it did surprise them to find that since the date of his release from prison he seemed to have kept out of trouble. Mr Brown, searchingly interrogated by the sceptical Sergeant, assumed an air of outraged virtue, and said bitterly that he supposed the police had never heard of a man turning over a new leaf, and running straight.

The plain-clothes detectives on the look-out for a middle-aged gentleman in dark spectacles found their task peculiarly dull, and although several middle-aged men visited the shop none of them wore spectacles, and none of them stayed longer than the time it took them to purchase their morning papers, or their packets of cigarettes. The shop was not patronized by men who dressed 'very gentlemanly', a circumstance which made Mr Peel, the younger of the two detectives, take a good deal of interest in one of its customers, a young man whose attire was very gentlemanly indeed, and who came strolling down the street one early afternoon, and went into Mr Brown's shop.

Mr Brown, who was serving a navvy with a couple of ounces of shag, took a fleeting glance at the newcomer but paid no further heed to him until his first customer had pocketed his change, and was about to leave the shop. Then he leaned his hands on the counter, and asked what he might have the pleasure of doing for the foppish young gentleman.

Mr Randall Matthews watched the navvy go out, and produced a shilling from his pocket. 'Twenty Players, please,' he said.

Mr Brown pushed a packet across the counter, and picked up the shilling.

Randall opened the packet, and drew out one of the

166

cigarettes and lit it. Over the flame of his lighter his eyes sought Mr Brown's. 'Hyde in?' he asked softly.

The guarded look descended like a curtain over Mr Brown's face. 'No,' he replied. 'Nor I don't know when he will be.'

Randall put his lighter away, and drew out an elegant notecase, and in a leisurely fashion extracted a Bank note that rustled agreeably. 'That is a pity,' he remarked. 'It is important that I should see him.'

'I can't tell you what I don't know,' said Mr Brown, impelled by curiosity to try to see whether the note between Randall's long fingers was for ten pounds or only five.

'Perhaps I ought to tell you that I am not a policeman,' sighed Randall. 'Though I believe one of the plain-clothes fraternity is wandering about outside.'

'Think I don't know?' said Mr Brown scornfully. 'I could tell a busy half a mile off.' It dawned on him that his visitor also appeared to possess this useful faculty, and he added with more respect in his voice: 'You'd better clear off out of this. I don't want no more trouble than what I've got already, and I tell you straight Mr Hyde ain't here, nor he hasn't been near the place for ten days.'

'In view of the gentleman outside that hardly surprises me,' said Randall. 'But I feel sure you could direct me to him – for a consideration.'

'Well, I couldn't,' said Mr Brown curtly. 'What do you want with him?'

Randall's slow smile curled his lips. 'Do Hyde's visitors usually confide in you?' he asked.

There was a slight pause. Mr Brown stared frowningly at him, and after a moment said: 'Look here, I don't know no more than you do where Mr Hyde is, and what's more I've had enough of him and his games! You clear off out of this before that busy outside starts smelling round after you, that's my advice!'

Randall regarded him thoughtfully. 'Perhaps,' he said, 'if I were to leave a letter for him in your charge it would be delivered? Oh, for a consideration, of course!'

Mr Brown cast a hasty glance towards the door of the shop, and said loudly: 'Well, it wouldn't then, because I don't know where to deliver it! What do you want? What's your blooming hurry to get hold of Mr Hyde?'

'Oh, I don't think it's necessary for you to know that,' said Randall. 'I just have business with him – ah, somewhat, important business. I wonder if you could use ten pounds?'

'It's no good, I tell you!' said Mr Brown roughly. 'He's gone – vanished!'

'Yes. Yes, I had grasped that,' said Randall. 'But you might still be able to use ten pounds.'

'How?' demanded Mr Brown involuntarily.

'Oh, quite easily!' said Randall in his nonchalant way. 'You can tell me where Hyde keeps his papers.'

Mr Brown shook his head with some vigour. 'Not me. Besides I don't know.'

Randall dropped his half-smoked cigarette on the floor, and set his heel on it. 'How disappointing!' he remarked. 'The information would have been worth quite a lot – in hard cash, you understand. While if you happened to be holding any correspondence addressed to Hyde that too would be worth ten pounds, or even more.'

'I ain't got no correspondence,' muttered Mr Brown. 'You don't think I'd keep any letters here with them busies nosing around, do you? Any letters that came – and I don't say any did, mind you – I burned, and that's Gospel-truth. I tell you, I've had enough of the whole business.' He watched Randall restore the Bank-note to his case. The faint crackle of it caused a regretful, covetous gleam to shine in his eyes. He passed his tongue between his lips, and said angrily: 'How do I know you wouldn't set the cops on to it, supposing there was anything I could tell you?'

'You don't,' said Randall amiably. 'But as you can't tell me anything that I want to know, that needn't worry you.'

The notecase was shut, and the hand that held it in the act of sliding it back into an inner pocket. Mr Brown cast another glance towards the door, and after a moment's hesitation leaned slightly forward across the counter, and said in a quick undertone: 'I could tell you something about his papers, but it won't help you. That's fair warning, ain't it?'

Randall drew out his notecase once more. 'Where are they?' he asked.

'They're where no one can't get at them. Nor I don't know exactly myself, and he may have taken them away with him.'

'I'll risk that,' said Randall.

'Well, he kept them in one of them safe-deposits,' said Mr Brown reluctantly.

'Of course!' said Randall softly. 'Which one?'

'I can't tell you that. He never said, nor I didn't ask. I said it wouldn't do you no good.'

'Where did he keep the key?'

'On his watch-chain. Never off it, it wasn't. I seen it often. That's all I know, and if it ain't enough you can't say I didn't warn you.'

'On his watch-chain,' repeated Randall, the smile fading from his lips.

Mr Brown, watching him, thought the look on his face downright ugly, and said uneasily: 'It ain't my fault if you don't like it. I told you the truth, so help me, and that's

169

more nor what I ought to have done. What's it worth – to stop me telling the same to the police?'

'I hardly think that you are anxious to confide in the police,' said Randall, 'but it is worth – to me – exactly what I said I would pay for it.'

Mr Brown held out an eager hand for the note. A smile stole over his unprepossessing countenance. 'You wanted to know mighty bad, didn't you? I hope you're satisfied, that's all.'

'Quite,' said Randall, and flicked the note into his hand.

After a swift glance at it to make sure that it was correct, Mr Brown thrust it into his pocket and cast another of his puzzled looks at Randall. He watched him put his notecase away and draw on one of his gloves, and suddenly said: 'I ain't seen you before, have I?'

'I should think it very unlikely,' said Randall.

Mr Brown stroked his chin. 'Funny thing, but the minute you come into the shop I got a feeling I had seen you somewhere.'

Randall paused with his hand stretched out to pick up his malacca cane from the counter, and let Mr Brown see his eyes. 'Look again,' he said smoothly. 'Have you seen me before?'

Mr Brown's gaze shifted under that curiously vivid, intent stare. 'No, I don't know as how I have,' he said uncertainly. 'Not to be sure, anyway. Just something in the cut of your jib seemed to strike me as being a bit familiar, that's all. No offence!'

Randall picked up his cane. 'None at all,' he replied. 'But you have not seen me before, Mr Brown, I can assure you. Nor are you very likely to see me again.'

Mr Brown gave him a knowing leer. 'I can keep my mouth shut, don't you worry!' he said.

A smile which Mr Brown liked even less than the

expression he had found ugly a few minutes before flitted across Randall's face. 'No, I shan't worry,' he said, and walked with his graceful, untroubled gait out of the shop.

Detective Peel, observing him from the opposite side of the road, thought it worth his while to follow him at a discreet distance.

His report, made to Superintendent Hannasyde later in the day, interested the Superintendent considerably.

'Mr Randall Matthews,' he said slowly. 'Yes, you did quite right to follow him. How long was he in the shop?'

'Matter of twenty-five minutes,' replied Peel. 'Came walking down the street as though he didn't give a damn for anyone.'

'Yes, I think he would do that,' said Hannasyde. 'It may, of course, have failed to dawn on him that the place was being watched.' He tapped the pencil he was holding on his desk. 'I think we might keep Mr Randall Matthews under observation,' he said. 'You couldn't hear what was said in the shop, I suppose?'

'No, I couldn't, Superintendent. It's a bit difficult, hanging round the entrance with so many people about,' replied Peel apologetically.

Hannasyde nodded. 'Yes, I know. It doesn't matter. But I shall be interested to see what Mr Randall Matthews' next move is.'

However Randall Matthews' next move was an unexceptionable one. On the following afternoon, arrayed in all the sombre elegance of a morning-coat, with a sleek top-hat set at an unsuitably rakish angle on his still sleeker black head, he motored down to Grinley Heath in a hired limousine to attend his uncle's funeral.

The service was held at the Parish Church, and there were very few mourners. Apart from the dead Man's relatives, only the Rumbolds, Dr Fielding, and Mr Nigel Brooke, who was Guy's partner, attended it. Nigel

171

Brooke, a tall young man with curly yellow hair and a profile which, because some misguided person had once told him it was Grecian, he was rather too much inclined to present to the world, explained confidentially to Dr Fielding that he had only put in an appearance because one liked to do the proper thing. 'Speaking for myself,' said Mr Brooke, 'I regard funerals as pure relics of barbarism. I daresay you feel the same.'

'I have never thought it worth while to consider the matter,' replied Fielding.

This was not encouraging, but Mr Brooke said in a thoughtful voice: 'I am inclined to think that that point of view is extraordinarily indicative of the spirit of the age.'

'I shouldn't be at all surprised,' said Fielding.

'I am afraid,' said Mr Brooke, starting a fresh topic, 'that dear old Guy feels all this very much.'

'It is hardly surprising that he should.'

Mr Brooke put his head on one side. 'One is inclined to ascribe it more to an inherently artistic temperament though, than to any profound feeling of sorrow in his uncle's death.'

'I daresay.'

'After all, old Matthews was a pretty good stinker, wasn't he?' said Mr Brooke, momentarily abandoning his affectations.

The doctor made no reply to this, and after a slight pause, Mr Brooke suddenly remarked: 'There is a woman here whose setting should be a mixture of horsehair and tubular steel.'

'What?'

'Ah, you think that a little too daring, I expect,' said Mr Brooke with a smile of superiority. 'One ought never to be afraid of contrasts, however. I learned that lesson very early in my career, and believe me, I have often used the most startling anachronisms to obtain amazingly successful results.'

'I haven't the slightest idea what you're talking about,' said Fielding.

Mr Brooke's gaze rested dreamily on Mrs Lupton, who was just about to enter her car. 'That woman,' he said simply. 'Don't you feel it? One would resist the obvious temptation of red plush, of course.'

The doctor gave him a look of contemptuous dislike, and moved away.

The Matthews family were drifting out of the Churchyard to seek their various cars by this time, and Owen Crewe was anxiously trying to convey to his wife through the medium of silent grimace that he did not desire to accompany her to her father's house for tea. Unfortunately Agnes was not very susceptible to messages thus conveyed, and instead of discovering an urgent need for their immediate return to town, she accepted Mrs Lupton's invitation, and said that she knew Owen would love to come. The scowl with which Owen greeted this interpretation of his wishes could not have been misread by the blindest wife, and Agnes at once said: 'You don't mind, do you, darling? You did say you were going to take the rest of the day off, didn't you?'

'I want to get out of these clothes,' said Owen, with the air of one who has been taken against his will to a fancy-dress party.

'Oh no, you look so nice in them!' said his wife fondly.

'Well, I'm not like your pansy little cousin Randall, and I feel a fool in them,' said Owen Crewe.

Randall, who had succeeded in annoying both Mrs Lupton and Miss Matthews by pressing his Aunt Zoë's hand feelingly, and remarking in a voice of concern that he feared the painful nature of the occasion would prove too much for her nerves, had moved away to where the

Rumbolds were waiting for their car to drive up. 'How do you do?' he said. 'An impressive sight, is it not?'

'Why, whatever do you mean?' said Mrs Rumbold, who thought him a very smart, witty young man, and was prepared to be entertained.

'Merely the spectacle of my relatives assuming expressions of decent grief,' said Randall.

'What things you do say, Mr Matthews! I'm sure they must feel it. I mean, it stands to reason, doesn't it, Ned?'

'Yes, I think it's rather unfair to assume that they none of them feel any regret,' replied Rumbold.

Randall raised his brows. 'How long have you known my affectionate family?' he drawled.

Rumbold laughed. 'Three years,' he answered.

'And your simple faith survives! I suppose you would be shocked if I ventured to ask which of my uncle's loving relatives is, in your mature judgement, the likeliest suspect?'

'Yes, I should,' said Rumbold sternly. 'Nor do I think it's a question you ought even to ask yourself.'

Mrs Rumbold, lest Randall should feel snubbed, said hastily: 'Well, I'm sure anyone might be forgiven for wondering, considering the way they were all at daggers drawn, half the time. I know one oughtn't to speak ill of the dead, but really, I do think that Mr Matthews was the limit! Talk about rude, overbearing people! Well, he fairly took the cake! And quarrelsome!'

'My dear, you had no reason to say so.'

'No, but I've heard him with his family, and what I say is, If you can be civil to strangers you can be civil in your own home, too. Not that he was always civil to strangers either, because everyone knows he was shockingly rude to the Rector, not to mention the way he behaved to Dr Fielding. And it's no credit to him that he liked you, Ned, because everybody likes you.'

'Rubbish!' said her husband. 'He liked me because I could give him a game of chess.' A gleam of amusement crept into his eyes. 'And because he thought he could always beat me,' he added.

'Yes, I always suspected you were the soul of tact in your dealings with my uncle,' said Randall pensively. 'So was I. It saved trouble.'

Mrs Rumbold gave a giggle. 'Oh, Mr Matthews, as though you'd ever bothered to be tactful in all your life!'

'I ought perhaps to explain that tact from nephew to uncle consisted in this case of refraining from asking him for money,' said Randall.

'Well, they say virtue brings its own reward, don't they?' observed Mrs Rumbold. 'I wish someone would leave me a fortune, just for being what you call tactful!'

'It has certain disadvantages,' said Randall in his bored voice. 'It puts strange ideas into the heads of policemen, for one thing, and that, though amusing up to a point, is apt to become a nuisance.'

'I'm sure that's all nonsense,' said Mrs Rumbold, reddening. 'No one really thinks you had anything to do with it, do they, Ned?'

'What you really mean,' corrected Randall gently, 'is that everyone is afraid that I couldn't have had anything to do with it.'

Mrs Rumbold did not know what to say in answer to this, and merely looked rather uncomfortable. Her husband said bluntly: 'In face of your own remarks you can hardly object to your relations speculating on whether *you* might not be the guilty party.'

'Oh, I don't!' said Randall, with all his accustomed urbanity. 'I regard it as a tribute.' He perceived a speck of dust on his sleeve, and carefully flicked it away with the glove he was holding. 'Which reminds me,' he said, 'that I quite forgot to congratulate my clever Aunt Zoë on the beautiful words she gave to the world through the medium of the Press. I shall have to go to the Poplars, after all.'

Rumbold's lips twitched in spite of himself, but he only said: 'Why bother?'

'Oh, I never neglect little acts of courtesy,' said Randall.

Mrs Rumbold watched him stroll away towards his hired car, and remarked that he was a caution.

'Queer chap,' Rumbold said, looking after him. 'I've never known what to make of him. Is it all pose, or is he as malicious as he seems to want us to think?'

Randall's relatives entertained no doubts on this point. His arrival at the Poplars was greeted by only one member of the family with any sort of acclaim, and that one, surprisingly enough, was Stella, who, from the window in the library, saw him alight from his car, and exclaimed: 'Oh, good! Here's Randall!'

Mrs Matthews, rudely interrupted in the middle of the soulful lecture she was delivering on Death, Human Frailty, and her own thoughts during the Burial Service, sighed, and said that it made her doubly sad to think that her own daughter should have so little interest in Serious Things. Miss Matthews, sniffing into a damp handker-chief, said that it only needed *that*, and in any case she would like to know what Zoë thought poor Gregory's death had to do with her; and Guy, staring at his sister, ejaculated: '*Good*? Have you gone batty, or something?'

'No,' snapped Stella, 'I haven't! I'd sooner have Ran-dall being waspish than this – this atmosphere of faked-up emotion! At least he's normal, but you and Mother and Aunt Harriet are like people out of a Russian play!'

'I hope,' said Mrs Matthews, a quiver of anger in her voice, 'that you are overwrought, Stella. That could be

176

the only possible excuse for you. You grieve me more than I can say.'

Randall had entered the room at the beginning of this speech, and stood on the threshold, regarding his aunt with anxious concern. 'No, no, we can't believe that!' he said soothingly. 'You are bereft of the power of self-expression for the moment, perhaps, but you will find words, my dear aunt, if you give yourself time. After all, when have you ever failed to find words suitable to any occasion?'

Stella turned away hurriedly, and stared out of the window, biting her lip. Even Miss Matthews stopped sniffing, and permitted herself to indulge in a somewhat sour smile. Mrs Matthews begged Randall to remember that he stood in a house of mourning, to which Randall replied: 'My dear aunt, have you no message of cheer to give us, no elevating thought to carry us through this sad day?'

'Is nothing sacred to you, Randall?' asked Mrs Matthews tragically.

'Certainly,' he replied. 'My personal appearance is quite sacred to me. I am shocked at being asked such a question. Surely you must have realized that so perfect a result could not be attained without solemn prayer?'

Stella gave a gasp. '*Randall*!' she said in a choking voice.

'You are an ass!' remarked Guy.

'You wrong me, little cousin. Dear Aunt Zoë, do not look so outraged! I have come especially to compliment you on your Message to the Public. It was only equalled by pretty, blue-eyed Rose Daventry's affecting words.' His mocking glance fell on Miss Matthews. 'Aunt Harriet, I must warn you that I have every intention of staying to tea. I am aware that there will not be enough cake to go round, but I am hoping that neither you nor my poor

177

dear Aunt Zoë will have the heart to eat anything. I am going upstairs to wash my hands now, and that will give you all time to think out a crushing reply to me.' He opened the door as he spoke, and with an encouraging smile bestowed on both his aunts, walked out of the room.

He left behind him an atmosphere tense with hostility. His aunts joined in condemning his manners, morals, and total lack of proper feeling; Guy said that what he chiefly objected to was the damned side the fellow put on; and Stella sat and frowned at the shut door. Observing this, Guy said: 'What's eating you, sister? I thought you were glad to see the little ray of sunshine?'

'I don't mind him,' said Stella impatiently. 'In fact, I'm grateful to him for creating a diversion. But I don't believe his hands wanted washing.'

'What on earth are you drivelling about?' demanded Guy.

Stella looked at him for a moment, and then said curtly: 'Oh, nothing!' and got up, and went quickly out of the room, and ran upstairs.

Before she had reached the landing Randall was on his way down again. She stopped and looked up at him, her hand on the banisters.

Randall smiled, and came lightly down and flicked her cheek with one careless finger. 'Suspicious little Stella!' he said softly. 'You would like to know what I've been up to, my pet, wouldn't you?'

'Yes, I would,' said Stella slowly.

'Just washing my hands, darling, just washing my hands!' said Randall.

An hour later he was back in his own flat, telephoning to Superintendent Hannasyde. 'Oh – er, Superintendent!' he said apologetically. 'Something I feel I must say to you. I'm so glad I caught you in.'

'What is it?' Hannasyde asked.

'The detective shadowing me,' said Randall plaintively. 'Could he be told not to wear brown boots with a blue suit, do you think?'

10

'Well, I'll be damned!' said Sergeant Hemingway.

'Exactly,' said Hannasyde dryly, and picked up the paper, and once more read the notice on the front page.

HYDE – *On May 22nd, 1935, at a nursing-home, suddenly, JOHN HYDE, of 17 Gadsby Row, in his 50th year. No flowers by request.*

The Sergeant scratched his nose. 'And what's more, it may be true, Chief,' he pronounced. 'What does it say? – *suddenly*? There you are then. All the time we've been chasing round after him the poor fellow's been lying in hospital with appendicitis. No wonder we couldn't find him! Well, well, and now where are we?'

'Get on to the office of the paper, and find out who sent in that notice,' commanded Hannasyde rather irritably. 'And do try and keep your infernal imagination within bounds!'

The Sergeant shook his head sadly. 'Yes, I thought this case would get on our nerves before we were through with it,' he remarked, and went out before his superior had time to reply.

He came back some little time later, and said: 'Well, now I am going to surprise you, Super. That notice was sent in by General Sir Montague Hyde, of Crayly Court, Herts.'

'*What*?' exclaimed Hannasyde.

'Didn't know he'd got such classy relations, did we?' said the Sergeant cheerfully.

'Who is General Sir Montague Hyde?' demanded Hannasyde.

The Sergeant consulted the slip of paper in his hand. 'Born 1871 . . . eldest son of Sir Montague Hyde, 5th baronet . . . Educated Eton and Sand – '

'I don't want to know where he was educated, and you can cut out the Boer War, and the Great War, and his decorations, if any!' said Hannasyde. 'What are his clubs? Has he a town address?'

'Green Street, Mayfair,' said the Sergeant. 'Clubs, Boodle's and the Cavalry.'

Hannasyde glanced at his watch. 'If he's in town I may catch him at his house, then,' he said, and got up, and reached for his hat and for the copy of the newspaper.

The General was in town, but an austere butler, looking down his nose at Superintendent Hannasyde, said frigidly that the General was still at his breakfast. Hannasyde expressed his willingness to await the General's pleasure, and sent in his card. He was ushered into a room at the back of the house, and informed presently by the butler that the General would see him in a few minutes.

A quarter of an hour later the General, a fine-looking old man with iron-grey hair, and a beak-like nose, entered the sombre room, nodded to Hannasyde, and with a glance at the card in his hand said, in the voice of one who commanded whole armies: 'Well, Superintendent? What's all this?'

'I must apologize calling on you at such an early hour, sir,' said Hannasyde, 'but my attention has been drawn to a certain notice appearing in today's paper for which I understand you are responsible.'

The General looked at him somewhat glassily. 'What the deuce are you talking about, my good man?' he said. 'What notice in what paper?'

Hannasyde produced the paper, and pointed out the fatal entry. The General, after a very sharp glance cast at him, got out a pair of spectacles, and held them over the

181

bridge of his nose, and peered through them at the notice of John Hyde's death. He then lowered the paper, removed the spectacles from his nose, and desired to be told what this fellow (whoever he might be) had to do with him.

'I am informed, sir, that the notice was inserted by you,' replied Hannasyde.

'You are informed!' said the General. '*Who informed you*?'

'The office of the paper in question, sir,' said Hannasyde.

'Then let me tell you, Superintendent, that you have been misinformed!' said the General. 'John Hyde? Never heard of the feller in my life!'

It was apparent to Superintendent Hannasyde that the General was displeased. He was required instantly to explain to the General what Scotland Yard meant by it. He did explain, as briefly as he was able, but the General, stating that he had no interest in Scotland Yard's damned activities and didn't want to hear about them, demanded to know who was the impudent scoundrel who had dared to make use of his name? When he found that Hannasyde could give him no information on this point he said, upon his word, he wondered what Scotland Yard was doing. He made it abundantly plain to the Superintendent that he expected him immediately to trace the perpetrator of this impudent hoax. He himself had every intention of getting to the bottom of the matter.

Hannasyde left him, twenty minutes later, breathing vengeance, and felt sorry for the hapless editor who was shortly to receive a call from him. He himself visited the offices of the newspaper, but could discover little there. The notice had been typewritten, enclosed in a half-sheet of Cavalry Club writing-paper with the name and address of General Sir Montague Hyde also typed on it.

'Then it wasn't Brown,' said the Sergeant decidedly. 'He's got a nerve all right, but not enough nerve to go waltzing into the Cavalry Club and asking for a bit of notepaper. Why, I wouldn't have myself! Come to think of it, whoever pulled this one must have got nerve enough for a rhinoceros.'

'Yes,' said Hannasyde, and added with a reluctant smile: 'Also a certain sense of humour. And I took Ferguson off!'

'You did?' said the Sergeant. 'I suppose he hadn't got any black boots?'

Hannasyde ignored this heavy sarcasm, and replied: 'It was no use having Matthews watched if he knew of it. He succeeded in giving Ferguson the slip three times, you know.'

'If you ask me,' said the Sergeant severely, 'he complained about the boots just on purpose to get you to take Ferguson off.'

'He complained about the boots to annoy me,' said Hannasyde. 'He could have shaken him off at any time he pleased. If you know you're being followed it's child's play to get clear in London.' He thought for a moment. 'If it was he who put that notice in the paper what was his object?'

'Bit of comic relief,' suggested the Sergeant.

Hannasyde looked at him frowningly. 'Hyde's papers,' he said abruptly. 'Somebody wants to get hold of them.'

'Well, we shouldn't mind having a squint at them ourselves,' agreed the Sergeant. 'But if young Matthews got the name of Hyde's lawyer out of Brown he's cleverer than I am, that's all I can say. Unless he knew all along, which somehow I don't think.'

'Not a lawyer,' Hannasyde said. 'Matthews couldn't get papers out of a lawyer on the strength of that notice. And if the papers aren't – Good God, why didn't I think of it? A safe-deposit, Sergeant! Get me the names of all the big safe-deposits in London: there aren't many of them. We've got to stop anyone getting hold of those papers – if we're in time.'

But they were not in time. The first safe-depository Hannasyde rang up stated that Mr John Hyde's papers had been removed an hour ago by his brother, Mr Samuel Hyde, who had signed a receipt for them. Hannasyde, suppressing a desire to swear, made the rest of his way to the City, and presented himself in person at the Safe-Depository. The receipt for the contents of John Hyde's safe was signed in a sloping, copybook handwriting. Mr Samuel Hyde, said the official who had attended to him, had produced the notice of Mr Hyde's sudden death, together with a copy of his will, wherein his own name appeared as sole executor. Mr Samuel Hyde was in possession of Mr John Hyde's keys: everything had seemed to be perfectly in order.

'What did he look like?' Hannasyde asked. 'Was he a young man, smartly dressed?'

'Oh no, not at all,' replied the official. 'Really, I didn't study him very closely, but he had grey hair, I'm sure. What I should call a very sallow complexion, as though he'd been in the East. I don't remember him being smartly dressed. He wore an overcoat – quite an old-looking overcoat. In fact, he was very like his brother, very.'

'If he was the man I suspect,' said Hannasyde, 'there is one thing about him you could not fail to have noticed. Had he very vivid blue eyes, and extremely long eyelashes?'

'Well, I'm afraid I couldn't say,' was the apologetic answer. 'He was wearing smoked spectacles, you see.'

'My lord!' exclaimed the Sergeant involuntarily. A few minutes later, when they had left the building, he said:

184

'It's the man himself, Chief. Somehow or other Brown managed to tip him off. And if you want to know what I think, when we've laid our hands on Mr Vanishing Hyde we'll have got Gregory Matthews' murderer. You think it over: first, there's – '

'Thanks, I am thinking it over,' said Hannasyde. 'I can see that Hyde's the likeliest person to have inserted the notice of his own death – if he wanted to disappear. I can see that there would have been nothing easier for him to have done than to have made a Will appointing a fictitious person as his executor. But what I do not see is why it should have been necessary to darken his face, and pretend to be someone else merely to get his own papers out of his own safe. If you've got an answer to that, let me have it!'

'Well, I have,' said the Sergeant briskly. 'The notice of his death wasn't meant for the safe-deposit people, Super. It was meant for us. He wants us to think he's dead, and we wouldn't be very likely to do that if we found he'd walked into that place and taken out his papers with his own hands, would we? He's got brains, this bird, that I will say. When you asked them at the safe-depository to describe John Hyde they didn't say one word about any sun-glasses. Seems as though he only wore them in Gadsby Row. All you got out of those fellows was that Hyde was a middle-aged man, and nothing particular to look at. Now how I look at it is this: in case you hit on the notion of a safe-deposit Hyde wanted to have it on record that it wasn't him who'd taken the stuff out of his safe. But though I wouldn't call those blokes we've been talking to an observant lot, it stands to reason they'd know John Hyde if they saw him. So he provides for that by putting on his spectacles, darkening his skin, and calling himself Hyde's brother. Neat, I call it.'

Hannasyde said nothing for a few minutes, but walked

on beside the Sergeant, frowning. 'You may be right,' he said at last. 'But I can't see my way. Look here, Hemingway! Go and see Brown, and try and scare him into telling you what Randall Matthews wanted that day. I'm going to see Randall himself.'

'I might scare Brown,' said the Sergeant, 'but it's my belief that it would take a herd of wild elephants to scare young Randall. What's more, I can't make out what he wants with Hyde anyway. Or his blooming papers, if it comes to that. You can't have it both ways, Chief. Seems to me that's what we're trying to do.'

'If you mean that the case is in a muddle, I know that,' said Hannasyde bitterly.

'It always was in a muddle,' replied the Sergeant. 'The trouble is the more we go into it the worse the muddle grows. Proper mess, that's what it is. But what I mean is, if Hyde's the man we're after – for reasons at present unknown – Randall's out of it. If Randall pulled the murder, Hyde's out of it.'

'Somewhere there's a connection between them,' Hannasyde said. 'There must be. I don't pretend to know what it is, but I've got to find out.'

The Sergeant scratched his nose. 'Well, I'm bound to say I don't see it,' he confessed. 'Friend Randall's motive for doing his uncle in is as plain as a pikestaff. We don't know what Hyde's motive may have been, but how it can have had anything to do with helping Randall to a nice little fortune has me beat. It don't make any kind of sense, Super.'

'I know, I know, but I've got to follow up the clues I've got. Randall didn't want me to pursue investigations into Hyde. He talked about mares' nests, and tried to make me believe he was not interested in Hyde. But he was sufficiently interested to pay a call on Brown, and to stay for nearly half an hour in his shop.'

'Yes,' admitted the Sergeant. 'And I wouldn't wonder but what he knows one or two members of the Cavalry Club.'

'Nothing more likely,' said Hannasyde. 'I've got to try and rattle him.'

'It's him that'll do the rattling,' said the Sergeant darkly. 'He's the nearest thing to a snake I've seen outside of the Zoo.'

On this pronouncement they parted, the Sergeant boarding an omnibus bound for the Bank, and Hannasyde making his way westwards to St James's Street.

He found Randall at home, writing letters at his desk. Randall, as Benson ushered the Superintendent into the room, said without looking up from his task: 'Do come in, and make yourself quite at home, my dear Superintendent. We are becoming almost boon companions, I feel. You will find cigarettes on the table by the sofa. Forgive me if I finish this letter, won't you?'

'Please do finish it,' said Hannasyde. 'For I want your undivided attention, Mr Matthews!'

'You shall certainly have it,' replied Randall, his hand continuing to travel across the paper. He signed his name, enclosed the letter in an envelope, and sealed it. Then he took the telephone receiver off its hook, and dialled a number, and while waiting for an answer wrote the direction on the envelope. After that he picked up a newspaper, folded open at the racing news, and spoke into the telephone. Having placed three bets with his bookmaker he laid down the receiver, and got up. 'The more arduous of the day's tasks being accomplished, I am now almost entirely at your disposal, Superintendent,' he said. 'Which reminds me that I have to thank you for the removal of the brown-booted gentleman. That was most considerate of you, but you need only have given him a pair of black boots. I had no personal feeling

187

against him, I assure you. In fact, I thought he had a nice, kind face.'

'He would no doubt be flattered to hear you say so,' replied Hannasyde. 'I am sorry if his presence hampered your movements in any way. That was not my intention.'

'Of course it wasn't,' agreed Randall affably.

Hannasyde looked directly across at him. 'Perhaps you have guessed why I have come here today, Mr Matthews?'

'Well, no, I don't think I have,' said Randall. 'Unless, of course, it is to ask me what I was able to discover from the unsavoury gentleman in Gadsby Row?'

Hannasyde felt all at once a strong desire to take Mr Randall Matthews by the throat and choke him. Instead he answered in his most even tones: 'Yes, it is to ask you that, Mr Matthews.'

'Delighted,' murmured Randall. 'But I'm afraid I didn't discover anything of very much importance.'

'My information,' said Hannasyde, 'is that you asked Brown if he knew where Hyde kept his papers.'

It was a bold stroke, but if its design was to make Randall betray the least sign of uneasiness it failed. 'And does your information include Brown's answer?' inquired Randall politely.

'I am waiting for you to tell me what that was, Mr Matthews. And I think you would be wise to do so.'

'My dear Superintendent, you mustn't – you really mustn't utter veiled threats to me,' said Randall with gentle reproach. 'They are quite unnecessary, believe me. If you don't know where Hyde's papers are – but I find that almost incredible – I will tell you. They are in a safe-deposit. Now, isn't that disheartening? I paid ten pounds for the knowledge, too.'

'Why didn't you bring this news to me, Mr Matthews?'

'But why should I?' asked Randall, very bland. 'Surely if I could discover it, you clever experts could do so too?'

'We experts,' said Hannasyde, nettled, 'are not allowed to resort to bribery!'

'Ah, I daresay that hinders you considerably,' nodded Randall.

'What made you take so sudden an interest in Hyde?' asked Hannasyde. 'When last I saw you you were at pains to convince me that you had no interest in him.'

'You infected me with some of your own enthusiasm, Superintendent,' said Randall, with a graceful bow.

'Did I indeed?' said Hannasyde grimly. 'And was it my enthusiasm which made you anxious to find out where Hyde's papers were kept?'

'Strictly speaking,' said Randall, 'I wasn't anxious about his papers. But it is my business as executor to my late uncle to wind up his estate. I think Mr Hyde wants winding up with the rest, don't you?'

'You know very well that I do, Mr Matthews. But if you think that, I don't understand why you refused to co-operate with me in any way when I called on you before.'

Randall regarded him with an expression of courteous surprise. 'My dear Superintendent, my recollection of your call is that you came to ask me what I knew of one John Hyde. I knew nothing of him, and I told you so. I don't remember being asked to co-operate with you?'

'You were aware that I attached importance to him, however. Why did you choose to visit Brown without telling me?'

'For very much the same reason that I chose to have my hair cut yesterday without telling you,' drawled Randall. 'And – er – would not my telling you have been a little superfluous? I felt quite sure that the myrmidon on duty in Gadsby Row would tell you all about my visit.'

'He could not tell me what you had discovered, Mr Matthews, and you made no attempt to. How am I to take that?'

189

'Exactly as you please, of course,' replied Randall. 'But I should like to remind you that I am not – ah, employed by Scotland Yard to gather information, and to assure you that if you imagine it has ever been my practice gratuitously to help policemen, or, in fact, anyone else, you have a singularly erroneous idea of my character.'

'Mr Matthews,' said Hannasyde bluntly, 'I tell you frankly that the attitude you have chosen to adopt will do you no good. It leads me to suspect very strongly that for some reason best known to yourself you do not want your uncle's murderer to be discovered.'

Randall's expressive black brows rose. 'You should not give way to mere prejudice, Superintendent,' he said. 'Are you accusing me of suppressing valuable evidence? I would point out to you that when you asked me if I had elicited from Brown where Hyde had kept his papers I told you with the utmost readiness.'

'With the utmost readiness when it was too late to be of use!' Hannasyde said sternly.

'Now you are talking in riddles,' sighed Randall. 'If you want me to understand you you will have to be more intelligible.'

'Would it surprise you to learn that John Hyde's safe was visited early this morning, and its entire contents removed?' asked Hannasyde.

Randall's brow wrinkled slightly. 'No, I don't know that I think it would,' he replied, after a pause for consideration. 'Perhaps he was aware of the interest you take in him.'

Hannasyde pulled the folded newspaper out of his pocket, and handed it to Randall. 'Take a look at the announcements of deaths, Mr Matthews!' he said.

Randall glanced down the column, and said placidly: 'Well, well! How very disconcerting! Does it happen to be true?'

190

'I have every reason to believe that it is entirely false,' answered Hannasyde. 'But it enabled some person calling himself Hyde's brother to get at the safe, and to walk off with the contents.'

'I don't wonder that you are out of humour,' said Randall sympathetically. 'Can't you trace this person? And did the officials in charge of the safe-depository just break open the safe, or use a skeleton key, or what? It all sounds most irregular.'

'That wasn't necessary,' said Hannasyde. 'The so-called brother had Hyde's key in his possession.'

Randall laid down the paper. 'Had he indeed? Well, that puts me in mind of a piece of information which I think might be really useful to you. Brown told me that Hyde always carried that key on his watch-chain.'

There was a pause. Hannasyde still stood looking at Randall from under heavy brows, and at last he said slowly: 'Did he?'

'Yes,' said Randall, putting a cigarette between his lips, and feeling in his pocket for his lighter. It was not there; he glanced round the room, saw it lying on his desk, and strolled over to get it. 'Which, when one comes to think about it (but I admit I haven't thought very deeply) would seem to imply that either John Hyde is dead, or that the person calling himself his brother was in reality Hyde himself.' He lit his cigarette, and slid the lighter into his pocket. 'Or,' he continued reflectively, 'it might, of course, mean several other things.'

'As what?' Hannasyde asked.

Randall exhaled two spirals of smoke down his thin nostrils. 'As, for instance, that he has been robbed of his key by some person unknown, or even murdered. I should look for an unidentified corpse if I were you, Superintendent. Failing that, why not find out who put that notice in the paper?'

'I mean to,' said Hannasyde. He added with startling abruptness: 'Do you ever visit the Cavalry Club, Mr Matthews?'

'Frequently,' replied Randall. 'Why?'

'Have you been there recently, may I ask?'

'Yes, I lunched there a couple of days ago,' replied Randall without the least hesitation. 'Have you any objection?'

'None at all, Mr Matthews. And do you ever write letters on the club notepaper?'

'Certainly not,' replied Randall rather haughtily. 'I am not a member of the club. Are there any other little things you would like me to tell you?'

'There are many things I should like you to tell me, Mr Matthews, but I think I will not trouble you with them today.' He picked up the newspaper, and restored it to his pocket.

'I believe,' said Randall, faintly smiling, 'that for some obscure reason of your own, you connect me with the disappearance of Hyde, or his papers, or both. Would you like to search my flat?'

Somewhat taken aback Hannasyde said shortly: 'No, Mr Matthews, I should not. I have no warrant to search your flat, nor do I suppose that I should find anything if I had. I will wish you good-morning.'

Randall opened the door for him, and followed him out into the hall. 'Good-bye, my dear Superintendent,' he said, with his hand on the latch of the front door. 'Or shall I say *au revoir?* Come in any time you're passing: I am always pleased to see you.'

'You are too kind!' said Hannasyde. 'Good-bye, Mr Matthews!'

He went out, just as Stella Matthews came up the stairs on to the landing.

'Why, if it is not my beloved little cousin Stella!' said

192

Randall, an inflexion of surprise in his voice. 'My sweet, is it possible that you have come to call on me, or have you merely got into the wrong house?'

Stella murmured good-morning to the Superintendent, and waited until he had disappeared round a bend in the staircase. 'No, I've come to see you – on business,' she replied. 'I tried Mr Carrington's office, but he was out, so I thought I might as well come here, and sound you.' She walked into the dove-grey hall, and looked critically about her. 'What a weird-looking room!' she remarked. 'Like some of Guy's efforts.'

'My God!' said Randall in a failing voice. 'My poor ignorant child, have you *no* discrimination?'

'I don't like rooms to be affected,' replied Stella. 'I call this damned affected.'

Randall said lovingly: 'Shall I now tell you what I think of that hat you are wearing, my precious?'

'As a matter of fact, I know it isn't one of my better-efforts,' admitted Stella candidly. 'So you needn't trouble. Where can we talk?'

'In here,' said Randall, leading the way to the library. 'Don't hesitate to say what you think of this room, will you? Your opinion is entirely valueless, but I shouldn't like you to feel constrained to keep it to yourself.'

'Well, I don't mind this room,' said Stella. 'A bit opulent, perhaps, but that's your affair.' She walked over to the fireplace, inspected a bronze figure on the mantelpiece, and said rather haltingly: 'Look here – I – you're probably wondering what on earth I've come here for.'

'Oh no!' said Randall, setting his finger on the bell. 'You have come here because you want me to do something for you. I have few illusions, my pet.'

'No, I don't. Not exactly. At least – Well, I'd better explain.'

'Reserve your explanations until you have removed that hat and powdered your nose,' said Randall.

'I'm not going to remove it. I've only come for a minute.'

'Whether you have come for a minute or for an hour, I decline to sit looking at that utterly discordant atrocity. I did not invite you to my flat, and if you do not care to make yourself presentable you may go away again,' said Randall coolly.

Stella flushed, but took off the offending hat and threw it aside. 'All right, then. You don't lose many opportunities of making yourself objectionable, do you?'

'I endeavour to live up to your expectations, my love,' said Randall. He turned, as Benson came into the room. 'The sherry, Benson. Or do you prefer a cocktail, Stella?'

'I don't want either, thanks.'

'Bring the sherry, Benson. And lay for Miss Matthews.'

'Oh, I haven't come to lunch!' said Stella hurriedly.

'Lay for Miss Matthews,' repeated Randall. He picked up the cigarette-box, and offered it to Stella. 'Must you oppose my every suggestion, darling? Or are you afraid of poison?'

'Shut up!' Stella said fiercely. 'We've had enough of that subject! I wish now I hadn't come.'

'Why did you?' he inquired.

She suddenly looked rather forlorn, and said in an undecided voice: 'I don't know. I mean, I had to see either you or Mr Carrington. It's about the money uncle left me.'

'Which you wouldn't touch if you were starving,' said Randall. 'What do you want me to do with it? Found a home for lost cats?'

'No, I don't. I know I said I wouldn't touch it, but I've changed my mind.'

'You've plenty of time to change it again before you're twenty-five,' said Randall.

'Yes, but that's the whole point. I – ' She broke off, for Benson had come back into the room with the sherry. When he had set the tray on the table and gone away again, she took a firm grip on her handbag, and said: 'What I want to know is this: if I – if I signed a paper saying I wouldn't marry Deryk Fielding, ever, could I possibly have the money now?'

Randall paused in the act of pouring out the sherry, and raised his head. 'Don't tell me you've quarrelled with the boy friend?' he said.

'No, we haven't quarrelled, but I've decided not to marry him, that's all,' replied Stella curtly.

Randall went on pouring out the sherry. 'I expect you would rather I didn't ask you why,' he remarked. 'But you can't have everything you want, my pet. Why have you come to this momentous decision?'

'Various reasons. For one thing I find I'm – not really – in love with him.'

'And for another you've discovered that he isn't really in love with you. It's nice to see glimmerings of intelligence in you, darling.'

'You're perfectly right,' said Stella, keeping her voice rigidly under control. 'He thought I was going to inherit a lot of money, and when I didn't he cooled off. Have a good laugh: I don't mind. I think it's rather funny myself. Anyway, I'm not breaking my heart over it.'

'Why should you?' said Randall, handing her a glass. 'Are you expecting me to ooze sympathy?'

'No, I'm not. I didn't come here to talk about Deryk, only to tell you that the engagement's off, and to ask if I can have the money uncle left me.'

'When you're twenty-five, certainly.'

'The whole point is that I want it now,' said Stella.

'Why this sudden need?'

'Because I'm frightfully hard-up, and I want to share a flat with a girl I was at school with, and get something to do. Only I shall probably have to learn shorthand or something first, and if I'm not earning anything I don't quite see how I'm to live. Mother says she can't afford to increase my allowance – besides, she's dead against the idea, anyway – and I haven't got any money of my own, except what uncle left me. Of course, I know the Will said not till I'm twenty-five, but I thought if I signed a paper promising not to marry Deryk, and you and Mr Carrington agreed – because if both the trustees agree you can sort of wangle things, can't you?'

'Not to my knowledge. As I haven't the remotest intention of agreeing, the point doesn't arise.'

'Why not?' Stella demanded. 'As long as I sign a paper, what difference can it possibly make? I don't mean I want to blue the capital. All I want is the income from it.'

'You won't get it, my love.'

Stella put down her glass, and rose. 'Thanks so much!' she said. 'I was a fool to come. I might have known you'd put a spoke in my wheel if you could. But considering what you've inherited, I think you might have been willing to let me have my rotten two thousand!'

'Dear cousin,' said Randall, 'until after Probate I have inherited nothing, and nor have you. After Probate the first charity that meets my eye will get the lot.'

Stella was so surprised that for a moment she could only stare at him. Then she said: 'Rot! I don't believe you!'

Randall laughed. 'I don't suppose you do, my sweet.'

'But why?' she demanded. 'What's the idea?'

He shrugged. 'Oh, I already have enough for my – er – simple needs,' he said.

'Either you're mad or you're up to something,' said

Stella with conviction. 'Whoever heard of giving away a whole fortune?'

'Yes, I feel that there's a certain pleasing originality about it,' agreed Randall. 'Have some more sherry?'

She shook her head. 'No thanks. Even you wouldn't do a thing like that for a gesture. Is it to stop people saying that you probably killed uncle because you were hard-up?'

'Do they say so?' inquired Randall. 'I thought that particular theory was confined to the members of my affectionate family. Moreover, I'm not hard-up.'

She said shrewdly: 'It's my belief you know something about uncle's death that we don't.'

'If by that ambiguous remark you mean that you believe I had something to do with uncle's death, I would point out to you, my sweet one, that the last time I saw him was on Sunday, May 12th.'

'I know. And I didn't mean that. I don't see how you could have done it. What does that Superintendent think?'

'He, like you, sweetheart, doesn't see how I could have done it. It disheartens him, I'm afraid.'

'Randall, will they ever find out who did it?'

'Why ask me?' he countered.

'Because you know something. It's no good saying you don't. I don't see how you could have murdered uncle, but I'm certain you're hiding some fact, or clue, or something which you don't want anyone to get hold of. I haven't forgotten that I saw you coming out of uncle's room that day. You were looking for something.'

'I was,' said Randall imperturbably. 'But I didn't find it.'

'What was it?' she asked.

'I don't know.'

'Don't *know*?'

197

'Not yet. I was looking for something that might have contained the poison. I admit it was a forlorn hope.'

'I don't think I altogether believe you,' said Stella.

'Well, that doesn't surprise me,' he replied, quite unmoved. 'Shall we talk of something else for a change? I find these eternal and barren discussions on uncle's death begin to pall on one after a time.'

'Mr Rumbold thinks it will fizzle out for want of evidence.'

'Mr Rumbold is probably right. Does he continue to sustain my afflicted aunts in their more anguished moments?'

'He does manage to soothe them,' admitted Stella, with a smile. 'All the same, you needn't sneer at him, Randall: he's been most frightfully decent to us all.'

'I regard him with profound respect,' said Randall.

'I suppose that means you don't.'

'Why you should suppose anything of the sort is quite beyond my comprehension,' said Randall wearily.

'Well, whenever you say something nice about anybody it generally means the reverse,' said Stella.

'Ah, that is only when I am talking about my relations, or other persons of sub-normal intelligence,' said Randall. 'I always respect brain when I meet it.'

'Thanks very much!' said Stella warmly. 'I suppose you would class me as a sort of moron?'

'Oh no, not quite,' said Randall. 'I have several times known you actually to think before you spoke. Occasionally you even show signs of a certain quickness of intellect. I admit that during your adolescence I had no hope of you at all, but you've improved a lot, my precious.'

'I *am* glad,' said Stella. 'Of course, you've taken such an interest in my progress, haven't you? I expect, if I only knew it, all your visits to the Poplars this last year have been really to see me.'

'Well, I imagine you don't suppose I came to see your mother, do you?'

Stella blinked at him. 'You came to see uncle!'

'Good God!' said Randall. He took her arm above the elbow, and propelled her towards the door. 'Not one of your intellectual days, my love. Let us go in to lunch.'

11

Stella drove herself home to Grinley Heath, profoundly meditating on her cousin Randall's astonishing words. She had received them with surprise and suspicion, and had consequently assumed a defensive, unapproachable attitude. Randall had made no attempt to pursue the subject, but had taken her in to luncheon, and regaled her on lobster à la Newburgh, and an excellent Chablis. Stella, who had eaten no meals away from the Poplars since her uncle's death, frankly enjoyed herself, and managed to forget the troubles clustering about the family until coffee was brought into the room. Some chance words of Randall's recalled them to her then, and her face clouded, and she said with a sigh that it was beastly having murders in the family, because it was like a black cloud hanging over one.

'Everybody suspects everybody else,' she said. 'And though uncle was horrid to people, it isn't any better in any way now that he's dead. I mean, take me, for instance. Uncle made it practically impossible for me to marry Deryk while he was alive, and that was beastly, but as soon as he died and I could marry Deryk, it all started to go wrong.'

'Now please don't fall into a sickening mood of self-pity,' said Randall dampingly. 'You have been a charming companion during lunch, and not one thought of your late swain has crossed your head. You are not in the least heartbroken, so it is no use trying to get me to utter facile expressions of sympathy. I am not even remotely sorry for you.'

200

'I have eaten your salt,' said Stella with dignity, 'so I can't say what I should like to.'

'Don't let that deter you, my love. I have eaten salt – and very little else – at the Poplars, but it has not so far affected my power of speech.'

Stella watched him make the coffee, and said: 'Well, I wasn't pitying myself, if you want to know. All the same, it gives one a jolt to discover that a person you – you thought you could utterly depend on has – well, feet of clay.'

Randall removed the spirit-lamp from under the machine, and transferred his gaze to Stella's face for a moment. 'Did you really think your amorous doctor would prove a tower of strength in adversity? How trusting girls are!'

'The trouble is there isn't anyone we can turn to,' Stella said. 'Uncle Henry is no use, and Guy isn't old enough, besides being – well, anyway, he's not the type. And Mr Rumbold's all very well, but he isn't like someone in the family; and Owen thinks the whole thing is bad form, and doesn't want to be mixed up in it.'

'And Randall is a snake in the grass, and would only sneer at you,' said Randall, stirring the coffee in the top of the machine.

Stella looked faintly startled. 'You would too,' she said. 'I wasn't thinking about you, though.'

'Another of your little errors, darling. You had better start thinking about me. I am now the head of this lamentable family.'

'What's that got to do with it?'

'Oh, quite a lot,' said Randall. 'As head of the family I propose to see this thing through.'

'How nice of you!' said Stella. 'That ought to help a lot. I expect if the police take it into their heads to arrest

201

any of us you'll float in like a fairy godmother and clear up the whole case?'

'Not if they arrest Aunt Gertrude,' said Randall. He poured out the coffee, and handed one cup to Stella. 'For you I might.'

'Give yourself up as the murderer, I should think,' said Stella scornfully.

'Who knows?' said Randall. 'But don't you worry, my sweet: I shan't have to. This little murder-case isn't going to be solved.'

'But I want it to be solved!' Stella said.

'Possibly,' replied Randall. 'But I don't.'

More he refused to say, but quite firmly turned the subject. Stella left his flat shortly after two o'clock, and drove home, pondering his words. She refrained from telling anyone at the Poplars what her errand to town had been; in fact, when closely interrogated by Miss Matthews in a spirit of rampant curiosity, she said unblushingly that she had lunched with a school-friend. Miss Matthews, sniffing, said that she should have thought Stella might have refrained from gallivanting up to town the very day after her uncle's funeral.

Dinner was enlivened by the presence of Mrs Lupton who, as her husband was detained in town, announced her intention of coming to the Poplars, and arrived at a quarter-to-eight in a dress of rustling black silk, and found fault with every course that was set before her. She had some justification, since Miss Matthews, now that her brother's wrath could no longer descend on her, had embarked on a campaign of the most ruthless economy.

'Let me tell you, Harriet,' said Mrs Lupton, 'that if you think to deceive me by covering things up with a thick sauce you are mistaken. This fish is Cod.'

Mrs Matthews sighed, and remarked in a reminiscent

voice: 'I must say, when one remembers how particular dear Gregory was about what he ate – '

'Instead of remembering Gregory's tastes you would be better employed, my dear Zoë, in doing your share of the housekeeping,' interrupted Mrs Lupton. 'Harriet never could order a meal.'

By the time Mrs Matthews had regretted that her wretched health prevented her from undertaking such an arduous duty, and Miss Matthews had declared that nothing would induce her to hand the reins over to her sister-in-law, the next course had arrived, a leg of lamb, which Mrs Lupton at once detected to be foreign. The sweet escaped criticism, but some sardines served up on toast as a savoury called forth a severe rebuke. Mrs Lupton after one mouthful, pushed her plate away and said that it was a false economy to buy cheap brands of sardines. Miss Matthews, seeing the savoury declined by the rest of the family, fiercely attacked her own, and said that there was nothing wrong with it at all.

In the drawing-room after dinner the three elder ladies maintained a sort of guerrilla warfare. Guy escaped to the library and Stella went early to bed, wondering whether, if she sold it, her car would realize enough money to enable her to leave the Poplars.

At breakfast next morning Guy was more cheerful than he had been since his uncle's death, and to his sister's relief announced his intention of resuming work on Monday. 'Because it's obvious to me,' he said, 'that nothing more is going to happen. It's just going to fizzle out.'

'I can't make out what the police are doing,' remarked Stella. 'They seem to have stopped haunting the house. You don't suppose they've given it up, do you?'

'I shouldn't be surprised,' said Guy. 'I don't blame them, either.'

'Somehow I don't think we're through with it,' Stella said. 'There's one thing that rather puts the wind up me. Randall knows something.'

'Knows what?' Guy said, looking quickly up from the newspaper.

'He didn't say. But – ' She broke off. 'I rather think the police have got their eye on him.'

'How do you know? Who told you?'

'No one. I just do know.' She heard her aunt's step in the hall, and frowned at Guy, who had opened his mouth to question her further. 'Not now! Aunt Harriet's coming.'

Miss Matthews entered the room with a complaint on her lips. Someone had forgotten to open the bathroom window after having a bath, and the room reeked of scent.

'Sorry: my new bath-salts, I expect,' said Stella.

'It is to be hoped you don't marry a poor man,' said Miss Matthews. 'I must say, I should have thought you could have found something better to squander your allowance on than your personal appearance. However, no doubt I am wrong. I'm sure I never expect anyone to listen to what I have to say.'

'Will you have grape-fruit?' said Stella, from the side-table.

'All I want is a cup of tea, and some toast,' said Miss Matthews. 'I am not feeling at all well this morning, which is not surprising when one thinks of what I have been through. And Guy home for lunch every day, too! Not that I grudge it, but it all makes more work. And why your Aunt Gertrude should elect to come here to dinner simply to make a lot of unkind remarks about my catering – '

'It's probably that sardine which is making you feel queasy now,' said Guy.

Miss Matthews was so incensed by this malicious suggestion that she could only glare at him; and by way of demonstrating that the sardine had in no way upset her digestion she got up, and in awful silence helped herself to a slice of bacon, and resolutely ate it.

This apparently was ill-judged, for when Stella went upstairs half-an-hour later she found her mother, swathed in a lilac-coloured wrapper, coming out of Miss Matthews' room with an empty medicine-glass in her hand, and an expression on her face of pious resignation.

'Hullo!' said Stella. 'Aunt Harriet worse?'

Mrs Matthews, who regarded the right to be ill as her sole prerogative, said: 'I don't know what you mean by worse, darling. There's nothing whatever the matter with her beyond a slight bilious attack.'

'She said she felt seedy at breakfast. Guy suggested that the sardine she ate last night might be disagreeing. *Not* well-received. Have you given her some dope?'

'Some of that wonderful medicine Dr Martin prescribed for me,' said Mrs Matthews. 'Not that I think it necessary. But poor Harriet was always one to make a fuss over the slightest ailment. I sometimes wonder what she would do if she had as much ill-health to bear as I have. I've put her to bed with a hot-water bottle, but I could wish that she had chosen some other day to be ill on. The strain of this past week has been too much for my nerves, and I'm feeling far from well myself. I'm afraid, darling, that you will have to do the shopping. I really don't feel up to it.'

'All right,' said Stella obligingly. 'Shall I go and talk to Mrs Beecher?'

'Yes, dearest, do. And, Stella! Tell her to cook a very light lunch. Soles, perhaps, with a *soufflé* to follow.'

Stella grinned. 'I bet Aunt Harriet was going to condemn us to cold mutton.'

'Yes, dear, but if she is feeling seedy it is much wiser

for her to keep off meat,' said Mrs Matthews, with an air of the purest altruism.

'Of course,' agreed Stella solemnly. 'Shall I take that glass down with me?'

'No, this is my own glass, and I always prefer to wash it myself. Tell Mrs Beecher that your aunt is lying down, and is not to be disturbed, and ask her to order a chicken for dinner. Something really digestible.'

'I should think Aunt Harriet'll pass out when she sees it,' commented Stella.

Mrs Beecher received her in the kitchen with an indulgent smile, tut-tutted when she heard of her mistress's indisposition, and said that she was not surprised. 'That joint we had last night was downright wicked,' she said. 'And as for the fish, well, I was ashamed to send it to table! Enough to make the Master turn in his grave, was what I said to Beecher. And so you're going to do the ordering today, are you, miss? Well, it'll be good practice against the time when you have your own house, won't it?'

Stella, who recognized in this sally an attempt to find out whether she was going to marry Dr Fielding or not, merely smiled and agreed, and firmly turned the conversation on to Poultry. She sallied forth presently in her car to do the marketing, and returned shortly before noon to find her mother just coming downstairs from her room. 'How's the invalid?' Stella inquired.

'Asleep,' Mrs Matthews replied. 'I peeped in a moment ago, but she was sound, so I didn't disturb her.'

Miss Matthews did not come down to luncheon, so Mrs Matthews, who with the passing of every hour her sister-in-law had spent in bed had become more martyr-like, sighed, and told Stella to run up and ask her aunt if she was going to get up, or if she would like a tray sent to her room. 'I must say, I do think it's just a little inconsiderate of Harriet to elect to be ill at a moment when she must know that it's all I can do to keep going without having all her work thrust on to my shoulders,' she said.

Stella, who knew the processes of her mother's mind too well to waste her breath in pointing out that it was she, and not Mrs Matthews, who had performed Harriet's duties that morning, merely winked at Guy, and went off to visit her aunt.

There was no answer to her gentle tap on the door, so after waiting for a moment Stella softly turned the handle, and went in.

The curtains had been drawn across the windows to shut out the light, and the room was dim. Miss Matthews was lying on her side with her eyes closed, and did not stir. Stella went to the bedside, wondering whether to wake her or not. It struck her all at once that Miss Matthews looked very ill; she bent over her, laying her hand cautiously on the slack one that rested on the sheet.

It was not hot with fever, but on the contrary oddly chilly. Stella recoiled with a sobbing gasp of fright and shock. With her eyes fixed on her aunt's motionless form she backed to the door, her knees shaking under her, and pulled it open, and called: 'Mother! Guy! Oh, come here, quickly! *Quickly*!'

Terror vibrated in her voice; it brought Guy up the stairs two at a time. 'What's up?' he demanded. 'Good God, what's the matter?'

'Aunt Harriet!' Stella managed to say. 'Aunt Harriet . . . !'

He stared at her white face for an instant, and then thrust past her into Miss Matthews' room.

Stella tried to pull herself together, but she could not bring herself to go farther into the room than the doorway, where she stayed, leaning against the wall, her handkerchief pressed to her mouth. She saw Guy put his hand on Miss Matthews' shoulder, and shake it, and heard him say in a voice sharp with alarm: 'Aunt Harriet, wake up! Aunt Harriet!'

'Oh don't!' Stella whispered. 'Can't you see?'

He strode to the window, and wrenched the curtains back, with a clatter of rings along the brass rod. Across the room his eyes met Stella's. 'Stella . . .' he said. 'Stella . . . What are we going to do?'

She looked back at him, her own eyes widening as she read the thought in his. Then, before either of them could speak, Mrs Matthews came into the room. 'Well, Harriet, how are you feeling?' she said. 'My dear child, what in the world is the matter?'

Stella said baldly: 'Mother, Aunt Harriet is dead.'

'Dead?' repeated Mrs Matthews. 'Nonsense! You don't know what you're talking about! Let me pass at once! Really, your love of the dramatic – ' She broke off, feeling Miss Matthews' hand as Stella had done. Her make-up was too perfect to allow of her changing colour, but her children saw her stiffen. One swift glance she shot at them, then she said in a carefully controlled voice: 'Your aunt must have had a stroke. We must send for a doctor. Guy, go at once and ring up Dr Fielding. Now please don't stand there in that silly way, Stella dear! Of course it's only a stroke!'

'She's dead,' Stella repeated. 'Like uncle. You know she's dead.'

Mrs Matthews went to her, and took her hand. 'Darling, you've had a shock, and you're a little overwrought. You mustn't say things like that. Now, the best thing you can do is to go to your own room, and lie down for a bit. You can't do anything for your aunt till Dr – '

'No one can. Oh, why didn't you send for Deryk when she said she felt ill? Why didn't you, mother?'

'My dear little Stella, there was no question of sending

for a doctor. You must try and pull yourself together, my pet. No one could have foreseen this. It was nothing but a slight stomach-upset; in fact, your aunt said herself that all she wanted was to lie down and keep quiet for a while. Now I am going to give you a little sal volatile to pull you round, and then you shall go to your own room till you are more yourself.'

Stella allowed herself to be led away to her mother's room, and she obediently swallowed the dose poured out for her, but she would not go to her own room. She sat down in a chair on the landing and gritted her chattering teeth together.

Dr Fielding had come home to lunch, and within five minutes he was at the Poplars, following Guy upstairs to Miss Matthews' room. Mrs Matthews was standing at the foot of the bed, and greeted him with composure, but in a hushed voice. 'I think my sister-in-law must have had a stroke, doctor. I haven't tried to do anything for her, as I thought it would be wiser to wait until you came. I have thought for some little while that she wasn't quite herself, but of course I never dreamed of anything like this happening. Poor Harriet! I'm afraid my brother-in-law's death was – '

Dr Fielding straightened himself. 'Mrs Matthews, your sister-in-law is dead,' he said harshly. 'She has been dead for as much as two hours, I should say. Why was I not called in before?'

'Dead!' Mrs Matthews repeated, and bowed her head slightly, covering her eyes with one hand.

Guy said: 'We'd no idea! How could we have had? She said she felt seedy. We thought she'd eaten something that had disagreed with her. I tell you, there didn't seem to be anything the matter with her, did there, mother?'

'Nothing,' Mrs Matthews said in a low voice. 'A trifle

bilious. I gave her some of my own medicine, and put her to bed. She just wanted to be quiet.'

'What did she complain of?' Fielding asked.

'Nothing that could lead one to suppose – She said she felt giddy, and that her head ached.'

'Any sickness?'

'She had a slight feeling of sickness, which was why I gave her my medicine. It is an excellent prescription – '

'Did she complain of any sensation of cramp? Any shivering in the extremities, or creeping in the arms? Did she seem to you to have difficulty in breathing?'

Mrs Matthews shook her head. 'Oh, no, no! If there had been anything like that I should have sent for you at once! She seemed better after taking the medicine. She was drowsy, and I tucked her up, and left her to have a sleep. I am such a firm believer in the healing qualities of – '

'Fielding, what did she die of?' Guy demanded.

The doctor looked from one to the other of them, his own face set into hard lines. 'It is impossible for me to answer that question without performing a post-mortem examination.'

Mrs Matthews laid her hands on the bed-rail, and grasped it nervously. 'Surely that cannot be necessary!' she said. 'It is so obvious to me that she must have had a stroke! The shock of her brother's death – '

'It is not obvious to me, Mrs Matthews. I am sorry, but I cannot undertake to sign a certificate. This is a case for the Coroner.'

'Oh, my God!' groaned Guy.

Mrs Matthews said in a shaking voice: 'It's absurd! My sister-in-law has been through a great deal, and she was not a young woman. Moreover, I myself have noticed signs of failing health in her for some time past.'

'Look here, you've got to tell us!' said Guy, taking a step towards the doctor. 'What do you suspect?'

Fielding met his angry stare with cold severity. 'I suspect that Miss Matthews has been poisoned,' he replied.

'It's a damned lie!' said Guy.

'Hush, Guy!' Mrs Matthews said mechanically. 'It is ridiculous, of course, quite ridiculous. Who could have wanted to poison poor Harriet? If it were not so terrible it would be almost laughable! But to subject us all to the horror of another inquest – really, doctor, don't you think you are letting yourself – '

'Mrs Matthews, I must decline to discuss it with you. I was not attending your sister-in-law at the time of her death; I was not called in when she was first taken ill. I could not reconcile it with my conscience to sign a certificate under such circumstances. Now, if you will please go downstairs, both of you, I will lock this room up until the police come to take charge.'

'You cannot have thought what this will mean to us,' Mrs Matthews said. 'The scandal – so unnecessary, so dreadful for everybody concerned! You can't seriously think that anyone would dream of poisoning Harriet! Good heavens, what possible object could anybody have for doing such a thing?'

The doctor shrugged. 'That is not a question for me, Mrs Matthews. I can only tell you that I am very far from satisfied that Miss Matthews died a natural death.'

Guy took his mother's arm. 'Come downstairs, mother. It's no use arguing. If he's not satisfied, it's got to go to the police,' he said.

She let him lead her out of the room, and down the stairs; the doctor locked the door on the outside, and withdrew the key, and would have followed Mrs Matthews at once had not Stella got up from the chair

211

on the landing where all the time she had been sitting. She said: 'Deryk, for God's sake tell me! You don't really think that? I didn't come in, but I heard all you said. She can't have been poisoned!'

'I'm sorry,' he answered in his professional voice. 'But I can't help it, you know.'

'If it hadn't been for uncle's death you'd never have suspected poison!' Stella said.

'The cases are not the same,' he replied. 'Your uncle was already suffering from heart-trouble. Miss Matthews, when last I was called in to attend her, had nothing wrong with her heart or her blood-pressure. If your uncle were alive today I should still consider Miss Matthews' death extraordinary.'

'But, Deryk, Aunt Harriet! Who could want to kill her? Deryk, are you sure you aren't making a mistake?'

'Stella, I've told you I'm very sorry, but I can't help you. The matter must be reported to the Coroner immediately. My duty is perfectly clear.'

'But what are we going to do?' Stella said, wringing her hands together.

He said uncomfortably: 'No one will think you had anything to do with it. Look here, I've got to go and report this. Try not to worry!' He added again: 'I'm awfully sorry!' and hurried away downstairs.

Mrs Matthews had gone into the library, and was sitting on the sofa there, one hand fidgeting nervously with the pleats of her frock, the other gripping her handkerchief. Guy had gone over to the window, and was looking out. He heard Dr Fielding speak to Beecher in the hall, and then pick up the telephone-receiver, and he stole a glance at his mother. She did not seem to be attending; her mouth was folded tightly, her eyes were fixed on the opposite wall.

The doctor went away, and presently Beecher came in,

looking pale and shocked. In a low voice, and keeping his eyes downcast, he wanted to know whether Mrs Matthews desired her lunch.

She did not move or answer. Guy said: 'Mother!'

She was recalled to her surroundings with a slight start, and looked blankly from Guy to the butler. 'Lunch?' she repeated. 'Oh! No, I don't think I could swallow anything. You and Stella go, dear.'

'I don't want any either,' said Guy. 'And I don't suppose Stella does.'

The butler bowed, and withdrew again. Mrs Matthews dabbed at the corners of her eyes. 'I don't seem able to realize it,' she said. 'Harriet gone! I shall miss her terribly.'

Guy turned a shade paler, and said: 'For God's sake, mother, don't!'

'Of course, I know she was often very, very tiresome,' Mrs Matthews continued, 'but one gets used to people, somehow. I can't imagine this house without her. I feel dreadfully upset.'

'Mother, what's the use of talking like that? Don't you realize? The police will be here at any minute! What are we going to tell them?'

Mrs Matthews looked at him in silence for a moment, and then said, more in her normal manner: 'Dear boy, we shall tell them exactly what happened. We did everything we could, and you must remember that it is by no means proved that poor Harriet was poisoned. Personally I feel sure she had a stroke.'

Stella came into the room, still rather white, but quite calm. She stood on the threshold, and said: 'Aunt Gertrude ought to be told. Shall I ring her up?'

'Darling, if only you would allow me to be quiet for just a little time!' her mother said. 'You neither of you seem to think of what I must be feeling. We did not always agree, but Harriet and I – '

'Aunt Gertrude's her sister. She ought to be told,' Stella repeated.

Mrs Matthews made a gesture of resignation. 'Tell anyone you please, only don't keep on worrying me when you can see how upset I am.'

Stella went out again. Mrs Matthews leaned her head in her hand and murmured: 'I really don't think I feel up to seeing Gertrude. I believe I'll go to my room, and lie down.'

'You'll have to see her,' Guy answered. 'She'll insist – she's bound to.'

Stella came back in a few moments, and said curtly that Mrs Lupton was coming at once.

'What did she say?' Guy asked.

'Nothing much. Utterly taken aback at first. Then she just said she'd come round. She'll be here in about ten minutes.'

They sat down to wait. After what seemed an age they heard the hush of tyres on the gravel-drive, and in another minute or two Mrs Lupton walked into the room.

It was a relief to find, in a world become suddenly distorted, that Mrs Lupton was still herself. She swept a glance round the room, and said in a voice of outraged majesty: 'What is all this nonsense Stella tried to tell me?'

'It's true,' Guy said. 'Aunt Harriet's dead.'

Mrs Lupton said: 'Impossible! I don't believe it!' Then, as though the inutility of these words dawned on her, she added: 'It is incredible! I hardly know what I am saying. How did it happen? She was well enough last night!'

'It must have been a stroke,' Mrs Matthews answered. 'I said so the instant I saw her. The worry of Gregory's death – it was all too much for her.'

214

'A stroke! Harriet?' Mrs Lupton looked from her sister-in-law to her nephew. She moved towards a chair, and sat down in it. 'Kindly tell me at once what has happened here!' she commanded.

'She said she felt seedy at breakfast,' Guy said jerkily. 'We thought she'd eaten something that disagreed with her.'

'Very likely,' said his aunt. 'But I have yet to learn that indigestion can be the cause of death. Go on!'

'She went up to her room, to lie down. Stella found her at lunch-time.'

'Dead?' Mrs Lupton asked on a note of horror.

'Yes.'

Mrs Lupton put up a hand to her eyes. 'This is terrible!' she announced. 'First Gregory, then Harriet! I do not know what to say. I am completely bowled over. My poor sister! I do not seem able to grasp it. Did you say she had a stroke?'

'We think it must have been that,' Mrs Matthews replied. 'And I suppose we should be thankful the end was so quick and painless.'

'The end!' Mrs Lupton exclaimed indignantly. 'Good heavens, Zoë, you talk as though my unfortunate sister had been a hopeless invalid! She was perfectly healthy! She should have had many years to live!'

Stella blurted out: 'There's going to be a post-mortem. Deryk thinks she was poisoned.'

There was a defensive note in her voice, but Mrs Lupton rather surprisingly said after a moment's blank silence: 'Rubbish!'

A little sigh broke from Mrs Matthews. She said: 'Of course it is rubbish. But it is very, very painful for all of us, none the less.'

'I have no opinion of Dr Fielding,' pronounced Mrs Lupton. 'Pray, how does he presume to diagnose a case of poisoning when he was totally unable to detect it in Gregory's death? And who wanted to poison poor Harriet, I should like to know? I am not aware of anyone, except you, Zoë, having the least motive for doing such a thing.'

'That'll do, thanks!' Guy said harshly. 'Mother had no motive, none that would satisfy any jury in the world!'

'I can respect your championship of your mother,' replied Mrs Lupton with a certain grimness, 'but you would be better employed in facing the facts as they are. Your mother had a certain motive for poisoning my poor sister – not that I accuse her of having done it, for I cannot suppose that she would have been fool enough to take such a risk while the police are still investigating your uncle's death. But if you think that the police will not make very particular inquiries into her movements today you are living in a fool's paradise, my dear Guy, and the sooner you cease to do so the better it will be for you!'

Mrs Matthews arose from the sofa, and said tragically: 'I can only hope, Gertrude, that you don't realize what you are saying. I don't think you know how deeply you have wounded me. I am going to my room now. Somehow I don't feel I can bear any more.'

Mrs Lupton made no effort to detain her. She watched her go out of the room, and then herself rose, and announced that she wished to see her sister's body.

'Fielding's locked the room up,' Guy said briefly.

Mrs Lupton's bosom swelled. 'Dr Fielding takes a great deal upon himself!' she said. 'In my opinion he is an officious and incompetent young jackanapes!'

That seemed to dispose of Dr Fielding. Mrs Lupton, promising to give him a piece of her mind at the first opportunity, laid a strict charge on her nephew to notify her by telephone of whatever should happen next, and left the Poplars.

Not until Miss Matthews' body had been removed did Mrs Matthews come downstairs again. As though by tacit consent, neither Stella nor Guy, alone in the library, made any attempt to discuss the cause of their aunt's death, but when Mrs Matthews reappeared she opened the subject by saying, as she entered the room: 'I have been thinking about it all very deeply, and I feel more than ever convinced that poor Harriet had a stroke. You know, she has not been herself ever since Gregory was taken from us. When the police come we must tell them the truth just as simply as possible. We have none of us anything to hide, and I do so want you, my dears, to be your natural selves, and not to behave in any silly, exaggerated way that might make anyone who didn't know you as I do think that you were afraid of something coming out.'

Stella raised her eyes. 'What are we to say, mother?'

Mrs Matthews returned the look with one of her limpid gazes. 'Dearest, Stella, I don't understand you. You must just tell the police exactly what you know.'

'And the medicine you gave her? You told Deryk, mother.'

'Naturally I told him, dear, and it goes without saying that I shall tell the police, and let them see the bottle for themselves.'

Guy turned his head. 'It hasn't come to that yet. We don't know that this is a matter for the police until after the post-mortem. Fielding was wrong before, and he may be wrong now.'

'Of course,' Mrs Matthews agreed. 'I was only thinking of what we should do if the worst happened. Please don't run away with the idea that I believe your aunt was poisoned!'

217

Beecher came into the room. He still looked rather shaken, and he spoke in an expressionless voice which made Stella think, He's going to give notice: They all will. 'Mr Rumbold has called, madam, and would like to see you.'

'Show him in,' said Mrs Matthews.

It was evident that Rumbold had heard the news. He looked even more shocked than Beecher. He said, not in his usual calm way, but with a note of horror in his voice: 'Mrs Matthews, I have just heard – It can't be true!'

Mrs Matthews held out her hand, but turned her face away. 'Yes, my dear friend, it is true,' she said. 'We can scarcely believe it ourselves. My poor, poor sister-in-law!'

He clasped her hand, and continued to hold it, half-unconsciously. 'Your housemaid told our cook – but I couldn't think it possible! I don't know what to say. That poor, unfortunate woman – '

Guy wheeled round to face him. 'Mr Rumbold, we think there can be no doubt that my aunt had a stroke!' he said.

Rumbold looked quickly across at him. 'A stroke! Is that Fielding's verdict?'

'Fielding's a fool. He doesn't know what caused my aunt's death, but we are quite sure it must have been a stroke.'

Rumbold released Mrs Matthews' hand, glancing down at her with an expression of foreboding in his face. 'What did Fielding say?' he asked. 'Tell me, Mrs Matthews!'

They had none of them heard him speak so sternly before. Mrs Matthews answered: 'It is all too dreadful, Mr Rumbold! Dr Fielding thinks that Harriet was poisoned.'

'Did you ever hear of anything so far-fetched, sir?' demanded Guy.

Rumbold looked at him for a moment, but he did not speak.

'Mr Rumbold, no one could have wanted to poison her!' Stella said urgently. 'You can't think that one of us – one of us – '

At that he said quickly: 'No, no, my dear child, of course not! Good God, no! But if Fielding suspects poison – It is too appalling!'

Guy, still standing by the window, said suddenly: 'Superintendent Hannasyde and that Sergeant-fellow are coming up the drive now.'

Mrs Matthews gave a start. 'Oh, Guy, no! Not yet!'

He moved across the room to her side. 'It's all right, Mummy,' he said. 'I expect it's only to make inquiries. They can't do anything – I mean, they don't know yet that Aunt Harriet was poisoned.'

'Don't keep on saying that she was poisoned!' Mrs Matthews cried, as though her nerves were snapping. 'She wasn't! She couldn't have been!' She turned with an effort to Edward Rumbold. 'Please don't go!' she said faintly. 'I have no one to advise me – I feel quite shattered!'

'I'll do anything I can to help you,' he answered. 'You must be perfectly open with the Superintendent – I'm sure you will be. There's nothing to be afraid of.'

The door opened. 'The police are here, madam,' said Beecher, in a voice of doom.

12

Mrs Matthews saw that both her children were watching her. She straightened in her chair, smiled, and turned her head to speak to the butler. 'Very well, Beecher,' she said, her voice once more smooth and controlled. 'Show them in here, please.'

A moment later Hannasyde came into the room.

Mrs Matthews bowed slightly. 'Good-afternoon, Superintendent. You wish to see me?'

'I wish to ask you some questions, Mrs Matthews, about Miss Harriet Matthews' death.'

She raised her brows. 'Surely you are a little premature in assuming that my sister-in-law's death is a case for the police?'

Hannasyde looked steadily down at her, and replied: 'Have you any objections to answering my questions, Mrs Matthews?'

'It is very painful to me to have to discuss it,' said Mrs Matthews with sorrowful dignity.

'I quite appreciate that it must be,' said Hannasyde. 'I am sorry to intrude on you at such a moment, but I am sure you will realize that in the circumstances my department is bound to investigate the matter.'

'I suppose so,' sighed Mrs Matthews. 'But one cannot help feeling that Dr Fielding's conduct has been extraordinary. We ourselves believe that my sister-in-law had a stroke.'

'That is a point which the medical authorities must determine,' said Hannasyde. 'When was Miss Matthews first taken ill?'

'I am afraid you will have to ask my son or my daughter that question,' replied Mrs Matthews. 'You see, I never come down to breakfast, so I don't know what happened until my poor sister-in-law came upstairs.'

Hannasyde turned towards Stella, who answered at once: 'My aunt said that she didn't feel very well when she came down to breakfast. It was a little before nine o'clock, I think.'

'Did your aunt say when she first began to feel ill?'

'N-no. No, I'm nearly sure she didn't. She just said, "I don't feel very well this morning," or something like that.'

'Did she ever take anything before breakfast? Early tea, for instance?'

'Yes, she always had early tea.'

'Who took that to her?'

'Oh, the under-housemaid! Usually the upper-house-maid, but we haven't got one at the moment.'

'Does she also prepare the tea?'

'I don't know. She or the cook, I suppose.'

'Did Miss Matthews take anything else? Any medicine, perhaps?'

Stella looked questioningly at her mother, but Mrs Matthews shook her head. 'Really, Superintendent, I've no idea what my sister-in-law may or may not have taken.'

Hannasyde did not pursue this. Instead he asked Stella what her aunt had eaten for breakfast. When he heard that Miss Matthews had had only tea and one slice of bacon, he said: 'Was it the same tea which you and your brother drank, Miss Matthews?'

'Well, I had coffee,' replied Stella. 'Guy, you had the tea, didn't you?'

'Yes,' said Guy. 'Same pot, too.'

'And after breakfast, what did your aunt do?'

221

'Ah, there I can help you,' intervened Mrs Matthews. 'I was just going to have my bath when my sister-in-law came upstairs, and told me that she felt sick and rather giddy. Nothing to alarm one. Indeed, I thought it no more than a slight bilious attack, but I always feel that one can't be too careful, especially when one is getting on in years as my sister-in-law was. So I made her go to bed with a hot-water bottle.'

'Did you give her anything for this sickness, Mrs Matthews?'

'Yes, I gave her a dose of some very excellent medicine which I have made up for indigestion. My own doctor – Dr Herbert Martin of Harley Street – prescribed it for me, and I know from my own experience – '

'I should like to see both the medicine and the glass it was given in,' said Hannasyde.

'Certainly,' said Mrs Matthews, as one humouring a child's whim. 'But naturally the glass has been washed, and put away.'

'Are you sure of that?' Hannasyde asked. 'Was the glass removed from Miss Matthews' bedroom?'

'Oh, surely!' Mrs Matthews said, wrinkling her brow. 'I should never have left it there. It was my own medicine-glass, and I'm afraid I'm very fussy about things like that. I always like to be sure that they are properly washed, and put away.'

'Did you perhaps wash the glass yourself?'

Mrs Matthews put a hand to her brow. 'I don't think I remember. I may have, or it may simply have gone down to the pantry.'

'Well, I can find that out by asking the servants,' Hannasyde said cheerfully. 'You did not think to ask your doctor to call and see Miss Matthews?'

'Oh no!' Mrs Matthews said. 'My sister-in-law did not

222

want a doctor to be called in, and really I could not see that it was at all necessary.'

'Did your sister-in-law say that she didn't want a doctor?'

'I don't know that she actually said those words, but she was not a person who ever consulted doctors very willingly. I am very sorry that she didn't, for if only she had been under some good man I feel that whatever it was that was wrong with her might have been treated, and she would have been with us now. Undoubtedly there must have been some trouble which we none of us knew about – '

'Then when you put your sister-in-law to bed you saw no cause for alarm?'

'Absolutely none!' replied Mrs Matthews earnestly.

'And later, when she grew worse, did you still feel no anxiety?'

'But you see I had no idea!' Mrs Matthews said. 'I did not go into her room again until about twelve o'clock – '

Hannasyde interrupted: 'One moment, Mrs Matthews. You say you did not go to her again until about twelve. When was it that you left Miss Matthews?'

Mrs Matthews smoothed the pleats of her frock rather nervously. 'I really don't think I can tell you. I didn't look at the time. After all, why should I?'

'What time do you usually get up, Mrs Matthews?'

'Oh, when I have had my breakfast! I never take anything but tea, and a little toast, so – '

'Quite. But I want to know when you get up in the morning, please.'

'Really, Superintendent, you cannot expect me to keep a detailed timetable of my – '

Edward Rumbold spoke for the first time. 'I think you always get up at about the same time, don't you, Mrs

Matthews? Somewhere between half-past nine and ten, isn't it?'

'Yes, generally,' she said reluctantly. 'Oh – this is Mr Rumbold, Superintendent, a very great friend of ours. He has been most kind – '

'You know, I don't think the Superintendent wants to hear about my so-called kindness, dear Mrs Matthews,' said Rumbold. 'Stella, can you perhaps help over this question of time?'

She said hesitatingly: 'You mean – when Mummy put Aunt Harriet to bed?'

'Yes. Your mother is feeling too upset to remember very clearly, but naturally the Superintendent must know when it was,' he said reassuringly. 'If you know, tell him.'

She looked at him in rather a frightened way, but he repeated calmly: 'Do you know, Stella?'

'Well, yes. I know it was just ten when I went upstairs, because the grandfather clock in the hall was striking. Mummy was just coming out of Aunt Harriet's room with a – ' She saw her mother's eyes fixed on her, and broke off.

'With what, Miss Matthews?'

Stella gave a little laugh. 'Well, I was going to say, with her dressing-gown on, but I suppose that's irrelevant.' She found that the Superintendent was steadily regarding her, and with a slightly heightened colour she added: 'And I asked if Aunt Harriet was worse, and my mother said she didn't think it was anything much, but that she'd put her to bed, and – and given her some stuff to take. Then I went down to the kitchen, and afterwards out to the shops.'

'Thank you.' Hannasyde turned towards Mrs Matthews again. 'It seems then that you left your sister-in-law at ten o'clock. Did you go out after that?'

'Out?' repeated Mrs Matthews. 'No, I had many little duties to perform about the house.'

'And between ten and twelve you did not go into Miss Matthews' room?'

'No. I wrote letters, and then I had to do the flowers.'

'You did not think it advisable to look in on your sister-in-law, if only to see whether she wanted anything?'

Mrs Matthews replied with dignity: 'No, Superintendent, I did not. When I left her my sister-in-law was drowsy. I thought it far better that she should have a good sleep.'

He accepted this without comment, and asked: 'At twelve o'clock, when you did go into her room, did there not seem to you to be anything amiss?'

'I thought she was still asleep. I opened the door very quietly, and just peeped in. She was lying on her side – she seemed asleep. The curtains were drawn, so naturally I could not see very clearly. I went away again, and it was not until lunch-time when I sent my daughter to see how she was feeling, that I had the least suspicion of what had happened. Even then I could not believe that she was dead. My son rang up the doctor immediately. It was he who broke the terrible news to us.'

'Thank you,' said Hannasyde. 'Mr Matthews, were you at home this morning?'

'Yes,' replied Guy.

'All the morning?'

'Yes, I was working in this very room. Anything else I can tell you?'

'Nothing, thank you. I should like, however, to interview the housemaid who took up Miss Matthews' early tea.'

'All right, I'll ring for her,' said Guy, moving towards the bell.

'Perhaps,' said Hannasyde, 'it would be possible for me to see her in some other room?'

Guy flushed. 'Oh, certainly! See her anywhere you like!'

'I should very much prefer you to wait until you have proof that my sister-in-law was poisoned,' said Mrs Matthews stiffly. 'All this is very upsetting to the servants, and we are already short-handed. Moreover, Mary cannot possibly tell you any more than we have, for she doesn't know anything.'

'In that case I shan't keep her long from her work, Mrs Matthews.'

Beecher came into the room. Guy said: 'Yes, I rang, Beecher. Take the Superintendent to the morning-room, will you, and send Mary to him there.'

'Very good, sir.' Beecher held the door open for Hannasyde, and ushered him out into the hall, and across it to the morning-room.

In a few minutes Mary appeared, round-eyed and scared, and stood just inside the door, with her hands behind her back. 'Yes, sir?' she said in a frightened whisper.

Hannasyde bade her good-afternoon, and asked her what her name was. She told him, and he said: 'I shan't keep you long. I just want you to tell me who made Miss Matthews' early tea this morning, and who took it up to her.'

'Mrs Beecher, she made the tea, sir. It was me carried the trays up – me and the kitchenmaid.'

'Which of you took Miss Matthews' tray?'

'I don't rightly know, sir. The kitchenmaid, she only took two trays up the stairs and put them down on the table on the landing. I can't exactly remember which they was.'

'Did the kitchenmaid go downstairs again once she had put the trays down on the table?'

'Oh yes, sir! She only carried them up to oblige. She doesn't go into any of the bedrooms.'

'No, I see. And whose tray did you take in first?'

Mary blushed, and stood on one leg. 'Well, Mr Guy's, sir. He does like his tea so hot!'

'Were you long in his room?'

'Oh no, sir!' said Mary, shocked. 'I only put the tray down by the bed, and drew the curtains back, and things like that.'

'Things like what?'

'Well, straightening the room, sir, and putting his shaving-water on the washstand, and waking him up.'

'So you might have been there about five minutes or so?'

'Yes, I expect it would be about that,' Mary agreed.

'When you came out again was anyone on the landing?'

'Oh no!' Mary said. 'Whatever would anyone be out there for at that hour?'

'I just wanted to know. Whose was the next tray you took in?'

'I took Mrs Matthews' hot water in, sir. She doesn't have tea.'

'Did you have to wake her, too?'

Mary shook her head. 'Mrs Matthews is always awake in the mornings. She doesn't never sleep after six, so she told me.'

'Doesn't she? Whose tray was the next?'

'Miss Harriet's, sir. She was awake, too.'

'Did she seem quite well then, or did she complain of feeling ill?'

'No, sir, she didn't say nothing about feeling ill. She was just like she always was.'

227

'Did you go into her room again at any time during the morning?'

'No, I never saw her again,' replied Mary, ready tears springing to her eyes. 'Mrs Matthews gave orders no one wasn't to disturb her.'

Hannasyde asked her no more questions, but sent her away to find the butler, in whose charge Dr Fielding had left the key of Miss Matthews' bedroom. The Sergeant, who had been pursuing investigations in the servants' hall, joined him, and escorted by Beecher they went upstairs together.

Miss Matthews' room, at first glance, told them nothing. The Superintendent got rid of Beecher, and shut the door. 'If she was poisoned the stuff may have been put into her early-morning tea,' he said. 'Apparently the tray was left on that table outside for a few minutes while the housemaid took young Matthews' tray to his room. Or it may have been given in the medicine Mrs Matthews gave the unfortunate woman. That presupposes that she felt unwell this morning from purely natural causes, of course.'

The Sergeant pursed his mouth. 'It's what I'd call an audacious sort of a crime, Chief. If it's more of this nicotine it looks like the same person at work. Well, I have known people get away with one clever murder, and think themselves so smart they can get away with another, but to go and commit the second murder before the police have finished with the first strikes me as being fair madness! What's more, if this turns out to be murder there's only Mrs Matthews could have done it, as far as I can see. How's she taking it?'

'She's upset. But the woman's such a mass of insincerity it's very hard to know what to make of her.'

'That's where psychology comes in,' said the Sergeant.

'I'm looking for motive, thanks. She had one for

murdering Gregory Matthews, but to poison a woman because you want her share of the house seems too thin.'

'I don't know,' said the Sergeant ruminatingly. 'Some of the nastiest murders we've handled were committed because of some reason no one in their senses would think big enough. But what I'd like to know, Chief, is where our precious Hyde fits in now?'

Hannasyde shook his head. 'It's beyond me. Perhaps he doesn't; perhaps we've been wasting our time looking for him.' He glanced round the room. 'Hemingway, I want every conceivable thing poison could have been put into. Collect them, will you? Pills, and medicines, and face-creams, and lotions.'

'Right!' said the Sergeant briskly. 'But we don't know that it was poison yet, do we?'

'You heard what Fielding had to say. He's seen one case of nicotine poisoning, and he thinks this is another.'

'Well, if he's right there's someone pretty ruthless at work,' remarked the Sergeant. 'And what's more it hasn't made the case any easier. Of course, if it was Mrs Matthews the thing straightens out at once, but it knocks out Hyde, and it knocks out young Randall. And somehow, Chief, that doesn't satisfy me. Hyde's a blinking mystery, and I'm naturally suspicious of mysteries; and young Randall's hiding something.' He had walked over to the washstand, and was inspecting a bottle of mouthwash. 'But why did either of them want to do in a harmless old body like Miss Matthews? It doesn't make sense. What about this gargle? Do you want it?'

'Yes, and that tube of ointment.'

'It isn't ointment,' said the Sergeant. 'It's toothpaste. There's another one here too, but that's empty.'

'Take it, anyway. I'm not leaving anything to chance this time.'

'Just as you say, Super,' said the Sergeant. 'But if you

ask me the likeliest place for poison was in the tea, or in that medicine you say Mrs Matthews gave the old girl.'

'Yes,' agreed Hannasyde, 'but we've got to try every-thing. The tea-things were washed up hours ago, and so was the medicine-glass.' He stopped, and then said suddenly: 'Aren't tea-leaves kept sometimes to lay the dust when the floors are swept?'

'That's right,' said the Sergeant, and put down the tin of cough-lozenges he had picked up. 'I'll see if I can get hold of today's little lot.'

But he came back presently, and shook his head. 'They don't hold with it,' he said shortly. 'Mostly use an Electrolux. You know, you can begin to understand why people talk about the curse of the machine-age, can't you? Tea-leaves burned with all the other rubbish.' He began to pack into his attaché-case all the pots and the bottles which Hannasyde had collected. 'Lot of talk going on in the servants' quarters,' he said. 'They don't like Mrs Matthews. Seems to have been a fair amount of what you might call friction going on ever since the old man died. They say Miss Stella's clearing out because she wouldn't live with her aunt. The cook can't stand Mrs M., but at the same time she says that Harriet M. has been carrying on like a lunatic this last week. Gone potty on economy. I think there's a case against Mrs M. all right.'

On their way downstairs again they met Edward Rum-bold, who was awaiting them in the hall. He said: 'You're leaving now, Superintendent? Mrs Matthews would rather like to know when you expect to hear the result of the post-mortem.'

'I'm afraid I can't tell you that,' replied Hannasyde. 'Not very long, I think.' He looked Rumbold over, and asked: 'Are you a close friend of the family, Mr Rumbold?'

'I live next door,' Rumbold answered. 'I think I may say that I am a fairly close friend.'

'Did you know the late Mr Matthews well?'

Rumbold smiled faintly. 'I doubt whether anyone did, Superintendent. I certainly knew him.'

'Perhaps you can help me over a small matter,' Hannasyde said. 'Did Mr Matthews ever make any mention to you of any business in which he was interested?'

Rumbold frowned. 'I don't think I quite understand. Do you mean some speculative venture? He did once or twice ask my opinion of investments he thought of making.'

'No, that wasn't what I meant. You don't know whether he was engaged in any business which his family didn't know about?'

'He never mentioned it to me if he was,' answered Rumbold. 'What sort of a business?'

'That I can't tell you. I thought it possible Mr Matthews might have confided in you.'

Rumbold shook his head. 'No, he never spoke of anything like that.'

Hannasyde sighed, and said: 'He seems to have been very reticent. Tell me, did you happen to see him on the day he died?'

'No, I was away. I only got back last week.'

'Oh, I see!' Hannasyde said. 'Never mind, then: it doesn't much matter.'

Edward Rumbold, rejoining the family in the library, made no mention of his conversation with the Superintendent, but merely said that Hannasyde had not told him when he expected to receive the analyst's report.

'What does it matter?' Stella said impatiently. 'What's the use of blinking facts? We know she was poisoned!'

'My dear child, we do not know anything of the sort,' said Mrs Matthews. 'Please try to control yourself!'

'Why did you pretend you couldn't remember who had washed that medicine-glass?' Stella demanded. 'Mother, why?'

Mrs Matthews arranged her pleats again. 'Really, Stella!' she protested. 'I should have thought you must have known that my memory is not my strongest point. I have had far more important things to think about today than who washed up a glass.'

'You always do it yourself! You told me so!'

'Very well, dear, no doubt I did wash it, then. It is not a very vital matter, after all.'

Stella was silenced, and turned away. Guy said, as though he had been rehearsing it: 'I suppose you know that Aunt Harriet's money comes to me?'

'Money!' said Mrs Matthews sharply. 'She had none to speak of. Don't be so foolish, Guy! And I don't think it's quite nice of you, dear boy, to think about what poor Harriet may or may not have left you when she's only been dead – '

'There's about four thousand,' Guy interrupted. 'God knows I could do with it, too!'

Stella made a choking sound, and went hastily out of the room. The telephone on the hall-table caught her eye. She stood still, looking at it, and then, as though of impulse, picked up the receiver, and gave a number.

In a little while a precise voice answered her. Stella asked if she could speak to Mr Matthews.

'Mr Matthews is not at home, madam,' answered the precise voice.

'Oh!' said Stella. 'When do you expect him back?'

'I couldn't say, madam. Can I take a message?'

'No, it doesn't – Yes! Ask him to ring Miss Stella Matthews up as soon as he comes in, will you, please?'

She put the receiver down again, and turned to find

that Guy had followed her out of the library, and was standing staring at her.

'What on earth do you want with Randall?' Guy demanded.

Stella flushed. 'He's the head of the family, and he said he was going to see this through. Besides, he knows something.'

'He'd like us to think he does,' said Guy scornfully. 'And if you can tell me what the devil could make him want to dispose of Aunt Harriet you're darned clever. I thought he might have had a hand in uncle's death, though I still can't see how, but setting aside the fact that he wasn't here when aunt died, why should he do it?'

'I don't know. I mean, I don't think he did do it. But everything's like a nightmare, and at least he's sane.' She gripped her hands together nervously. 'Why did you come out with all that rubbish about Aunt Harriet's money?'

Guy laughed. 'Well, it's perfectly true, and it's bound to come out, so why should I try and conceal it?'

'Guy you won't do anything silly, will you?' she asked anxiously.

'I'm not likely to. You keep your hair on,' he said, and walked away towards the morning-room.

'It was not until after dinner that Randall rang up. As soon as she heard his soft voice Stella said: 'Oh, it's you at last! Where have you been? I – '

'At the races, sweetheart. And what do you want with my unworthy self?'

'Randall, the most ghastly thing's happened. Aunt Harriet's dead!'

There was a slight pause. 'Aunt Harriet is what?' asked Randall.

'Dead,' Stella repeated. 'This morning. And they think it's poison.' The silence that greeted this pronouncement was so prolonged that she said: 'Are you there? They think she was poisoned, I tell you!'

'I heard you,' said Randall. 'I am somewhat taken aback. Who are "they", may I ask?'

'Deryk Fielding, and of course the police. I can't tell you it all over the phone. There's a post-mortem being done.'

'And what, my lamb, do you expect me to do?' inquired Randall.

'You said you were going to see the thing through!'

'What a rash statement!'

'Couldn't you come down?' Stella said impatiently.

'I could, but I'm not going to. Tomorrow I might. Do you want me?'

'I want you to clear it up. You said – '

'My sweet, you can forget what I said. If Aunt Harriet has been poisoned, nothing I said is of any value. I will come down and see you tomorrow.'

With this she had to be content. She did not tell her mother that Randall was coming, and she hoped that his visit might take place whilst Mrs Matthews was at Church. But Mrs Matthews returned from Church, bringing Edward Rumbold with her before any sign of Randall had been seen, and it was not until nearly half-past twelve that the Mercédès swung into the drive and Randall came into the house.

Mrs Matthews, who did not look as though she had slept much during the night, was describing to Mr Rumbold the atmosphere of peace which she said had descended on her in Church, but she broke off as Randall entered the room, and looked anything but peaceful. 'Randall!' she said. 'I suppose one might have expected you.'

'One might, but apparently one didn't,' said Randall.

234

'Do not let me interrupt you, my dear aunt. I am always interested in your spiritual experiences.'

'Matthews, your aunt has had a great shock,' Rumbold said quietly.

'We have all had a great shock,' agreed Randall. 'Are you very much upset, my dear Aunt Zoë? I am sure that well-meaning Superintendent is.'

'What makes you think that?' inquired Rumbold.

'Well,' said Randall, critically surveying his own tie in the mirror over the mantelpiece, 'when last I saw him he was busily concocting a case against a person unknown.'

'What do you mean?' Stella asked. 'Are you just trying to be funny?'

'My precious! At this solemn hour?' Randall met her eyes in the mirror, and looked beyond her reflection to where he could see Mrs Matthews, seated beside Rumbold on the sofa.

'Then what – who is the unknown person?'

'Don't be silly, darling,' said Randall, still not satisfied with the set of his tie. 'Naturally, no one knows. His name is Hyde – John Hyde. Do you know a John Hyde, Aunt Zoë?'

'No, Randall, I do not, nor do I pretend to know what you are talking about.'

'What has this John Hyde of yours to do with Miss Matthews' death?' asked Rumbold. 'Who is he? I mean – '

'That is what the police want to know,' said Randall. 'They have been hunting for him high and low. Not that he had anything to do with my poor Aunt Harriet's untimely end. He's dead, you know.'

'He's dead?' repeated Rumbold.

'Or, rather,' pursued Randall, 'a notice of his death appeared in the paper several days ago.'

Rumbold stared at him. 'A notice of his death appeared

in the paper?' he said. 'But – My dear Matthews, what are you talking about? First you say the police are hunting for this person called Hyde, and then you say that a notice of his death has been published. Which do you mean?'

'Oh, both!' said Randall, turning away from the mirror and facing him. 'The police are so disbelieving. They don't think Hyde is dead. In fact, unless I am much mistaken they suspect him of having murdered Uncle Gregory and gone into hiding. So you see, Aunt Harriet's death must be very upsetting to them. It abolishes Hyde.'

Stella, who had been following this dialogue in some bewilderment, said: 'But what has someone we've never even heard of got to do with it? I mean, what had he to do with uncle, and why should he have murdered him?'

'Why, indeed?' said Randall.

'Yes, but what makes the police suspect him?'

'Well, he's vanished, you see.'

'Yes, but – '

'Darling, don't keep on saying "yes, but." Use your intelligence. The police don't like people to vanish. It isn't seemly.'

'That's all very well,' said Rumbold, 'but the police must have had some reason for suspecting him other than his disappearance – or death, whichever it was.'

'Oh, they had,' agreed Randall. 'They discovered that uncle had had dealings with him. So they went to call on him, and he wasn't there. Then they went to look for his papers, and they weren't there either.'

'Weren't where?' asked Rumbold.

'In a safe-deposit. All very mysterious. You ask the Superintendent.'

Mrs Matthews heaved a weary sigh. 'I can't see what any of this rigmarole has to do with your aunt's death, Randall.'

236

'As usual, my dear Aunt Zoë, you hit the nail on the head. It has nothing whatsoever to do with it.'

'Then why do you waste time discussing it?' she said. 'Surely – '

'Just to create a diversion,' said Randall sweetly. 'But I'll discuss Aunt Harriet's death instead if you prefer it. When and how did she die?'

Mrs Matthews shuddered. 'I am sorry, Randall. I am afraid I can't bring myself to talk about it.'

'Then my little cousin Stella shall tell me all about it,' said Randall, and turned to her. 'Would you like to drive slowly round the heath, my pet, and unburden yourself to me?'

'All right,' Stella said, after a moment's hesitation. 'You've got to know, anyway. I'll go and put a hat on.'

Guy looked up quickly. 'Look here, Stella – ' he began, and then stopped, uncertain how to proceed.

Randall said kindly: 'You mustn't be shy of me, little cousin. Naturally you want to warn her not to say anything indiscreet.'

This left Guy without a word to say. He glared at Randall, who smiled and opened the door for Stella to pass out.

She did not keep him waiting long while she put on her hat, but soon came out to the car, and got in beside him. 'Thank God to be out of it for half-an-hour!' she said. 'It's absolutely awful, Randall.'

'Yes, I didn't flatter myself you came for the pleasure of my company,' he returned, letting in the clutch.

'Sorry. I didn't mean to be rude.'

'My sweet, you're not yourself. You mustn't let it get on your nerves, you know.'

She gave a reluctant laugh. 'Well, it is on them. You've got to help, Randall.'

He did not answer for a moment, and then he said with

237

a marked drawl: 'What leads you to suppose that I can help?'

'You did. You practically said you knew something.'

'Your imagination runs away with you, my pet. I said I didn't want the mystery to be solved.'

'Well, it's got to be!' said Stella fiercely.

'I'm very much afraid that it may be,' said Randall.

'Randall, what is it you know? Why do you say you're afraid it may be? You didn't kill Aunt Harriet!'

'Certainly not,' he replied calmly. 'In fact, I regard Aunt Harriet's death as an entirely needless complication. You had better tell me how it happened.'

'Well, she said she didn't feel well at breakfast. Dinner the evening before had been about the worst ever, and Guy suggested it might have something to do with it.'

'By way of being helpful, or mere airy persiflage?' inquired Randall.

'Airy persiflage. Your style,' said Stella.

'You must learn to appreciate me better, darling. My style is unique.'

'All right. Just as well if it is. Anyway, aunt was annoyed and she ate some bacon, by way of proving that the sardine hadn't upset her.'

'One moment,' interposed Randall. 'I like to have things clear. Does the sardine play a major part in the story? Because if so I should wish to have its rôle carefully explained to me.'

'No, it was the savoury at dinner, that's all.'

'If it was really all, Aunt Harriet's economy must have reached a staggering pitch,' commented Randall.

Stella gave a spurt of laughter, but became instantly sober again. 'Randall, you mustn't joke. It isn't funny. And it's beastly of you to laugh at – at a thing like this.'

'Acquit me, darling. I only wanted to raise a laugh out of you.'

She turned her head to look at him. 'Why?'

He smiled. 'Such a solemn Stella. I don't like it. But go on with this entrancing story.'

'Well, there isn't much more. Apparently she felt worse after breakfast, and went up to tell Mummy she wasn't well. Mummy put her back to bed, and gave her some dope, and – and she felt sleepy. And Mummy looked into her room about twelve o'clock, only she seemed to be fast asleep, so Mummy didn't disturb her, and at lunch-time I went up to her, and – and she was dead.'

Randall shot the car forward past a lorry, and slackened speed again. 'And now tell me all the bits you've left out,' he said.

'I – I haven't, really. Except that I can't help feeling that the police – think Mummy had something to do with it.'

'They do not seem to be alone in that belief,' remarked Randall.

'What do you mean?' said Stella.

'If you are not afraid that your sainted parent had a hand in this, what are you worrying about, my love? Tell me the whole truth!'

'I'm not afraid she did it! I'm not, I tell you! I'm only afraid that it's going to look black against her, and I don't know what to do. She washed up the glass she gave the medicine in, and she gave orders no one was to go into aunt's room. It was what anyone would have done, Randall! but the police – made it sound fishy, and Mummy – I think Mummy saw that it did, because she said that she couldn't remember who'd washed the glass, and it was obvious that she did remember. And she kept on saying she was sure aunt had had a stroke, and – and finding reasons for it. She was worst with Deryk, but – but I don't trust him, and I'm afraid he may have told the

239

police how she fought against having a post-mortem. Supposing they arrest her?'

'Supposing we wait and see whether Aunt Harriet was poisoned or not?' countered Randall.

'Randall, why won't you tell what you know?' said Stella imploringly. 'Deryk wouldn't have said that if he hadn't been pretty sure. And if she was poisoned, don't you see that Mummy, or Guy (or me, I suppose), are the only people who had any motive at all?'

'I do,' said Randall. 'But if you would all of you contrive to keep your heads, you may yet escape the gallows.'

'Don't!' she said sharply. 'I thought at first you were going to be decent, and take it seriously. I might have known you'd only sneer!'

'Strange as it may seem to you, my love, I am taking it extremely seriously.'

She looked curiously at him. 'Were you fond of Aunt Harriet?'

'Not in the least. But I infinitely preferred her alive to dead.'

'Why do you say it like that?'

'Because, my dear Stella, by dying Aunt Harriet has created a damnably awkward situation!' he answered.

13

The rest of Sunday passed uncomfortably. Randall left the Poplars soon after lunch, Mrs Matthews retired to rest, and her children, finding it impossible to occupy themselves indoors, went for a walk. Mrs Matthews remarked three times during the course of the evening that she felt quite lost without her sister-in-law, and when Guy, whose nerves were badly frayed, said caustically that he had been under the impression that life under the same roof with Harriet had become insupportable to her, she read him a lecture on the folly of exaggeration, and went to bed proclaiming herself not angry, but merely hurt. Stella then took her brother to task for having started a quarrel, and Guy, announcing that a little more from her (or anyone else) would be productive of the direst results, slammed out of the room. After that Stella too went to bed, and was troubled with bad dreams till morning.

Guy's praiseworthy resolve to go to work as usual had, he felt, to be abandoned. He came down to breakfast looking pale and heavy-eyed, drank a great deal of rather strong tea, and crumbled a piece of toast. His answers to Stella's remarks were monosyllabic, so she presently gave up trying to talk to him, finished her breakfast, and went off to interview the cook.

Mrs Beecher added her mite to the day's ills by greeting her with a month's notice. She and Beecher, she said, were very sorry, but they were feeling Unsettled.

'Well, I can't say I'm surprised,' replied Stella candidly.

'No, miss, and I'm sure it's not your fault. But one's

got to think of oneself, when all's said and done, and right or wrong, we don't neither of us care to stay in a house where people drop down dead with poison six days out of the seven. 'Tisn't natural.'

'No,' agreed Stella, too dispirited to point out a somewhat gross overstatement. 'Is anything wanted in the town?'

Mrs Beecher thereupon produced a sheet of paper, which seemed to be entirely covered with writing, and said there were just one or two little things she needed.

Stella took the list, and went upstairs to consult her mother.

Mrs Matthews was just about to get up when her daughter entered the room. She, like Guy, looked rather heavy-eyed. She said that she had had a bad night, and upon being shown Mrs Beecher's shopping list, moaned faintly, and implored Stella not to worry her with that.

'There's worse than this,' said Stella, pocketing the list. 'The Beechers have given notice. Leaving at the end of the month. Shall I call in at the Registry Office?'

Mrs Matthews said that it made her sad to think of all the people in the world who never gave a thought to anyone but themselves. However, after moralizing in this strain for about five minutes, she remembered that she had always meant to get rid of the Beechers if Gregory had left the house to her, so really it was a blessing in disguise. Stella left her planning the new staff, and went off to do the shopping.

When she returned, nearly an hour later, she found Guy pacing up and down the hall. She commented unfavourably on this, but he turned a strained, pale face towards her, and said abruptly: 'The police are here. She was poisoned.'

Stella put her parcels rather carefully down on the

242

table, and replied after a slight pause: 'Well, we practically knew that. What was it?'

'Nicotine. Same as uncle.'

She nodded. 'Bound to be. Where are the police?'

'In the library, with mother. They wouldn't let me stay.'

'Have they found out what the poison was put into?'

'No. At least, I don't think so. They took away a lot of medicines and things from Aunt Harriet's room on Saturday. I suppose there hasn't been time to analyse them yet.'

Stella slowly pulled off her gloves, and smoothed out the fingers. 'As long as they don't know how the stuff was given, there's no need for us to panic,' she said.

'No one's panicking,' he answered irritably. 'But they'll go on motive. I tell you, I've thought it all out from A to Z. It was all right when uncle died. Anybody might have done it. But Aunt Harriet's death has narrowed the field down to two: myself and Mother. And the serious part of it is that we had motives for both murders. No one else had the slightest motive for murdering Aunt Harriet. It's no use blinking facts: one or other of us is going to be arrested – perhaps both of us.'

'Don't be such an ass!' said Stella. 'They can't prove anything against either of you – can they?'

Guy stopped pacing up and down, and came to a halt by the table, and stood facing his sister across it. 'If you'll take the trouble to look at it fair and square you'll see they've got a nasty-looking case against us,' he said forcibly. 'I was in a jam, and nothing would induce me to go to South America, so I poisoned uncle. Then I found that Aunt Harriet had left her money to me, and because I'm hard-up, I poisoned her, too.'

'No one would commit a murder for £4,000,' said Stella.

'Wouldn't they just? Don't you believe it, my girl! People commit murders for much less.'

'At that rate, I might have murdered her because she made the house unbearable.'

'I don't think so. Of course, you might have murdered uncle because he threatened to ruin Fielding, but that isn't likely either, especially now it's all off between you. It's Mother the police suspect. She was dressing when they turned up, and I interviewed them first. The Superintendent asked me a whole lot of questions – damned awkward ones! Those blasted servants must have been talking. If you think it over, you can see for yourself how suspicious things must look. You remember the row Mother had with Uncle Gregory about me going to Brazil? Well, naturally, you do: it's the only real quarrel she ever had with him, and the whole household knows of it. But as I see it, it wouldn't matter so much about that if she hadn't so suddenly stopped having a row, and gone all honey-sweet to uncle.'

'Oh, that's just Mummy!' Stella said quickly. 'Partly remembering she was a Christian, and partly hoping to coax uncle. Anyone who knows Mummy would recognize that act.'

'The point is the police don't know her. Why, good Lord, even I was surprised at her giving in so soon! And apparently she told the police she never took uncle seriously over the Brazilian business, and that's an obvious lie. I don't mind betting the servants are ready to swear she was more serious than she's ever been before. And you know what she is! She always believes things happened in exactly the way she wants to think they did, and consequently she comes out with the most idiotic fibs, which a babe in arms could see through.'

'Yes, but surely the police can't think that she'd murder

Aunt Harriet simply for the sake of getting this house to herself?'

Guy brought his open palm down on the table. 'Don't be such a thick-headed little fool! Don't you realize that uncle left a trust of £2,000 a year for the upkeep of this place? Well, as things were, not only did Aunt Harriet run the show, but £2,000 was just about enough. With Aunt Harriet dead it's a good deal more than enough! Now do you see?'

'No, I don't,' said Stella stoutly. 'The money wasn't going to be given to Aunt to spend as she liked.'

'Thanks, I know exactly how it was left. The trustees have to pay the rates and taxes, and that kind of thing, but the balance is paid into the Bank quarterly, and as long as it isn't overstepped, who's to say how it shall be spent?'

'Yes, I see that,' admitted Stella. 'At the same time, it's a bit thick to think a thing like that about Mummy, whatever her faults may be.'

'It isn't what I think. It's what the police are going to think,' said Guy.

'Well, I should imagine they'd think twice before arresting her,' replied Stella. 'If she'd wanted to murder Aunt Harriet she could surely have waited till uncle's death blew over. I mean, to do it now is absolutely asking for trouble!'

'No, I don't agree with you,' said Guy instantly. 'If she did it, she probably thought it would be safer while the police were in a complete fog over uncle's death. Lots of people to suspect. If she'd waited she'd probably have been the only suspect. Something like that might have gone on in her mind.'

Stella gave a shiver. 'It's too beastly. Shut up about it, for God's sake! What about the man Randall spoke of – I can't remember his name?'

245

'What man? Oh, that rubbish! I don't know: it sounded to me like Randall trying to be funny.'

'No, it wasn't. He meant it.'

'Well, if he did I can't see what it can have to do with Aunt Harriet's death.'

'No,' said Stella heavily. 'Randall said that too.' She glanced towards the library-door. 'How long has Mother been shut up with the police?'

'About twenty minutes.' Guy began to walk up and down again. 'I can't make Mother out!' he said. 'Generally she doesn't give away much. She didn't when uncle died. But this time she seems – badly rattled.'

'It's enough to rattle anybody.'

'Well, I wish to God she'd stop telling everybody how much she's going to miss Aunt, and how heartbroken she is!' said Guy explosively. 'It rings so dam' false!'

Stella considered this. 'Do you know, I'm not so sure of that? It's quite possible she does miss her.'

Guy stared at her. 'They fought like cats!'

'Yes, I know, but – but they were awfully used to each other, and they often joined forces against uncle, or Aunt Gertrude, and if ever one of them was ill the other always rallied round at once.'

'Better if they hadn't!' Guy said significantly. 'Oh, hell, why did Mother give Aunt a medicine of her own instead of sending for the doctor? And what possessed her to forbid anyone to go into Aunt's room? The servants all say that she impressed it on them that they weren't to disturb Aunt, and it came out today that she even forbade Mary to sweep the landing that morning.'

'Anyone would have done the same,' insisted Stella. 'Aunt said she was sleepy, so naturally Mummy wouldn't let Mary fidget about outside her room.'

Guy started to reply, but broke off as the library-door was opened, and looked quickly round. Mrs Matthews stood holding the door-handle, and said in a faint voice: 'Stella, I want you.'

Both her children at once went towards her. Stella slipped a sustaining arm round her waist, and said: 'It's all right, Mummy; I'm here. What is it?'

Mrs Matthews led her into the library. 'Darling child, I want you to think back carefully, and tell the Superintendent. Do you remember when poor Aunt Harriet was taken ill how you and I discussed whether we should send for Dr Fielding or not?'

'Yes, of course,' responded Stella, whose only recollection was of her mother stating that a doctor was quite unnecessary. She looked across the room to where Hannasyde stood, and met his searching gaze unflinchingly. 'I didn't think it was in the least called-for.'

Hannasyde did not reply to her, but instead addressed her mother. 'Mrs Matthews, this is quite useless. The fact remains that you did not send for a doctor, though it must surely have been obvious to a woman of your experience that your sister-in-law was very unwell indeed.'

Stella felt her mother's fingers tighten unconsciously on her own arm. 'But it was not obvious!' Mrs Matthews said, in a low, unsteady voice. 'I knew she felt sick, and I saw that she was a bad colour, but I put that down to acute indigestion. She never had what I call a really healthy colour, never!'

'Mrs Matthews, your sister-in-law must have felt other symptoms than these. Did she not complain to you of cramp, or a creeping in her arms, or even of extreme cold in her feet and hands?'

'I can't remember her mentioning anything beyond sickness and giddiness. She may have said she felt chilly, but I should expect that. I gave her a hot-water bottle.'

'And yet,' said Hannasyde, 'when Miss Matthews

passed the butler in the hall, on her way up to her room, he was struck by her appearance, and thought that she seemed to be out of breath, as though she had been running.'

'So he says!' Guy interpolated scornfully. 'Servants will make up any tale to create a sensation!'

'If he made it up, Mr Matthews, it is an odd coincidence that the shortness of breath which he described should be one of the symptoms of nicotine poisoning. Did you not notice it, Mrs Matthews?'

'If I did I should only have thought it due to faintness,' replied Mrs Matthews.

'Your sister-in-law did not complain to you of feeling very ill?'

Mrs Matthews gave a little tinkling laugh. 'Poor Harriet was never one to minimize her own ailments,' she said. 'I daresay that she may have said that she felt very bad, but I was so accustomed to her habit of exaggerating the least disorder, that I am afraid I didn't set a great deal of store by what she said. It seemed obvious to me that her stomach was thoroughly upset, and I did exactly what I should have done for one of my own children.'

The Superintendent's calm voice, with its undercurrent of implacability, broke in on this. 'Yet Mrs Beecher, who had known Miss Matthews for seven and a half years, states that she was never one to give way easily.'

Mrs Matthews' eyes snapped. 'Mrs Beecher knows nothing about it! It was hardly to be expected that my sister-in-law would confide in the cook. Stella, you know what an absurd fuss your aunt used to make if she had as much as a cold in her head, don't you?'

'Mrs Matthews, I am sure your daughter will corroborate any statement you ask her to, but you should realize that her testimony when prompted in that manner, is not likely to weigh with me.'

248

'It comes to this, Superintendent: you prefer to believe the servants' words sooner than mine!' said Mrs Matthews.

'It comes to this, Mrs Matthews: you have not been frank with me; you are still not being frank. It is only fair to tell you that I am not satisfied with your evidence. I must warn you that your continued refusal to remember circumstances which I am convinced cannot have slipped your memory may have very serious consequences.'

Guy, who had been standing quite still, with his back to the door, suddenly walked forward into the middle of the room, and said: 'Stella, let mother sit down. Look here, Superintendent, my mother had nothing whatsoever to do with either of these murders, and I'm not going to stand by and see her bullied by you, or anyone else! What the Beechers say is utterly beside the point. They neither of them like my mother, and they're under notice to leave. My aunt didn't complain of any of the things you've mentioned to my sister and me at breakfast, and we neither of us thought that she looked particularly ill.'

'That is quite possible,' said Hannasyde. 'Some little time elapsed between your seeing your aunt at breakfast and the butler's meeting her in the hall. I appreciate your feelings in the matter, Mr Matthews, but you are doing no good by this sort of interruption.'

'There's one thing you seem to be leaving out of account,' said Guy, disregarding this warning. 'Both my sister and I can certify that my aunt complained of feeling ill at breakfast, before ever she had seen my mother. If you imagine there was nicotine in the medicine my mother gave her, I would remind you that it was given at least an hour after she began to feel ill – and, since you set so much store by what Beecher says – after he had met her in the hall, and been struck by her appearance.'

'I am quite aware of that, Mr Matthews.'

'It is utterly absurd,' said Mrs Matthews, pressing her handkerchief to her lips, 'but the Superintendent seems to think that I could have put that dreadful poison into your aunt's early-morning teapot.' She gave a wan smile, and added: 'If it were not such a painful thought, so wounding to one's feelings, I could laugh at it! I haven't the least idea what was done with the early tea-trays, and I didn't wake until the housemaid came into my room, so how I could have tampered with your aunt's teapot, I entirely fail to see.'

'You say that you only awoke when the maid came into your room, Mrs Matthews, but she states that you were already awake when she went in. Are you quite sure that you are telling me the truth?'

'I suppose,' said Mrs Matthews tragically, 'that you are at liberty to insult me as much as you choose. It only remains for you to arrest me. Indeed, I am astonished that you haven't done so already.'

Hannasyde did not answer immediately, and Guy, who at the mention of the early tea had shot one swift, horrified look at his sister, now removed his hand from the back of his mother's chair, and said jerkily: 'Nobody's going to arrest you, mother, I can assure you. You're very clever, Superintendent, but it was I who poisoned my aunt, not my mother.'

'Guy, you fool!' Stella cried.

He paid no attention to her, but looked squarely at Hannasyde. Mrs Matthews said tensely: 'That's not true! Don't listen to him! I know it's not true!'

Hannasyde met Guy's bright, defiant eyes with an enigmatical look in his own. 'How did you poison your aunt, Mr Matthews?'

'In her tea,' replied Guy. 'The tea she had at breakfast. I was down first. I knew my sister always has coffee.

When I told you I drank tea that day, I lied. I didn't. I drank coffee.'

'No, Guy, no!' said his mother. 'You don't know what you're saying! Superintendent, my son is only trying to shield me! There's not a word of truth in what he says! You can see for yourself – '

'Did you also poison your uncle, Mr Matthews?' inquired Hannasyde.

'Yes, in the whiskey-and-soda,' replied Guy recklessly.

'Stop being theatrical!' Stella said angrily. 'What good do you think you're doing, making dramatic gestures? You did not drink coffee that morning, or any other morning! You don't like coffee! You're behaving like someone in a penny novelette!'

Guy paid no heed to this, but continued to address the Superintendent. 'Well, have you got a warrant for my arrest?' he demanded.

'No, I'm afraid I haven't,' replied Hannasyde.

'Then you'd better go and apply for one!' said Guy.

'When I am satisfied that I have sufficient grounds for doing so, I will,' promised Hannasyde.

'I don't know what more you want!' said Guy, in a somewhat flattened voice.

Sergeant Hemingway came into the room at that moment, and handed his superior a sealed envelope.

'Excuse me, please,' Hannasyde said formally, and tore open the envelope, and spread open the single sheet it contained. He ran his eye down the typewritten lines, and then looked up, and at Guy, who said at once: 'You're wasting your time trying to badger my mother. I've told you what happened. Now get on with it, and arrest me!'

'I am sorry, Mr Matthews, but you have not shown me sufficient grounds for applying for a warrant for your arrest. You have stated that you put the poison in your aunt's tea, but Miss Matthews did not swallow the nicotine which killed her.'

These words produced a sudden, surprised silence. Guy broke it. 'What do you mean, she didn't swallow it? She must have swallowed it!'

'Yes, I thought you didn't know quite as much about it as you pretended, Mr Matthews,' said Hannasyde. 'The nicotine did not pass through the stomach. It was absorbed through the tissues of the mouth.' He held up the paper in his hand. 'This is the analyst's report, which I've been waiting for. The medium through which your aunt was poisoned was a tube of toothpaste.'

'A-tube-of-toothpaste?' Guy repeated, blankly, and then was silent.

Hannasyde folded the report again, and put it away in his pocketbook. The deliberation of his movements seemed to fascinate Stella; her eyes followed them in a kind of numb bewilderment while a jumble of thoughts chased one another through her brain. These found expression presently in one sentence, blurted out unwarily. 'Then anyone might have done it!'

'I don't think so, Miss Matthews.'

Mrs Matthews said with something of her usual smoothness: 'Stella darling, just sit down and be quiet. You don't know anything about this, my dear child, and you must not keep on interrupting.' She turned towards Hannasyde, and said graciously: 'You see, now how absurd your suspicions were, Superintendent. We won't say any more about it, however. Naturally I understand that your duty compels you to suspect everybody. But this is most amazing news! A tube of toothpaste! You mean, I suppose, that the poison was injected into it. A hypodermic syringe, no doubt. I don't think that anyone in this house owns such a thing. It is a very, very terrible thought that my poor sister-in-law should have – '

Guy made an impatient gesture, as though to silence her. 'How was it done?' he asked. 'Are you at liberty to tell us that?'

'Certainly,' said Hannasyde. 'The poison was in all probability injected, as your mother seems to have realized, by means of a hypodermic syringe, and inserted into the bottom end of the tube, and driven up a little way through the paste. The paste at the bottom of the tube is untainted, and it is obvious that the paste at the top end must also have been free from poison.'

Guy said softly: 'By Jove, that's clever! It might have been done at any time, then. Aunt Harriet has been working her way down the tube for days, till at last she reached the poison! Gosh!'

'It's awful!' Stella said. 'It's *devilish*!'

'One can only be thankful poor Harriet knew nothing about it,' remarked Mrs Matthews in a saintly voice.

'For God's sake don't talk as though she were a sheep being driven to the slaughter-house!' exclaimed Stella, quite pale with disgust.

'Stella dear, you forget yourself,' said Mrs Matthews repressively. She transferred her attention to the Superintendent. 'One is terribly shocked, of course, but what my son says is right. This appalling thing may have been done at any time.'

'But not, Mrs Matthews, by any person,' replied Hannasyde.

She spread out her hands. 'Anyone who was familiar with this house could have found the opportunity to do it, Superintendent.'

'Possibly,' agreed Hannasyde. 'But few people can have had any motive for killing Miss Matthews.'

Guy muttered: 'O God, we're just where we were before!'

'Ah, Superintendent,' said Mrs Matthews, sadly shaking her head. 'What, after all, do we know of each other's lives? Even I who was so close to my poor sister-in-law would hesitate to say that she had no enemies of whom I knew nothing. She was a strange, eccentric woman! I have sometimes wondered whether there might not have been something in the past to account for many of her oddities. So often an apparently warped nature – '

'If you, who were so close to her, do not know of anything sinister in her past, I think we may assume that there was nothing,' interrupted Hannasyde, with an inflection of contempt in his voice. 'The discovery of the medium through which the poison was administered has not enlarged the field of suspects, as a moment's reflection will, I think, show you.'

Stella grasped a chairback, and said desperately: 'But not one of us three had a motive for killing Aunt Harriet! Not a real motive! This is like a nightmare! Things don't happen like this! Leave me alone, mother: I won't be quiet!' She shook off her mother's hand, laid warningly on her arm, and said, trembling: 'I don't pretend to know who did it. Perhaps she knew something that – that made her dangerous. Supposing it were something about that man you're looking for – the one who disappeared?'

'Well?' said Hannasyde.

'Oh, I don't know!' she said wretchedly. 'How can I know? But why don't you try and find out? My cousin told us about that man, and how you believe he had something to do with my uncle's death. Perhaps Aunt knew something about him. After all, we haven't always lived here; we don't know what may have happened in the past. My mother is quite right! You didn't know my uncle, or how Aunt Harriet hated him. Perhaps she was in a plot to murder him, and then – oh, I know this sounds far-fetched, but it isn't as far-fetched as thinking that my mother could murder aunt in that awful, cold-blooded way just to get this house to herself!' Her voice broke, but she controlled it and added: 'I had as strong a motive as my mother!'

'So had I,' said Guy. 'A much stronger one than either of yours, too.'

'No, that isn't true,' Stella answered. 'You were the only one who really liked Aunt Harriet! You always stood up for her when Mummy and I ran her down. And she didn't interfere with you. She was awfully fond of you!'

'So much so that she left me her money. Don't forget that bit,' interrupted Guy.

'You didn't want her money! Superintendent, it's all rubbish about my aunt's money! She only had quite a little, and now that Uncle Gregory's dead my brother can do what he likes with his own capital!' She stopped short, aware of the implication of her own words, and grew whiter than ever. 'No. I don't mean – I didn't – '

The door opened. 'What a charming reunion!' remarked a mellifluous voice. 'I'm so glad I'm not too late to join in. I should not have liked to have missed the dear Superintendent.'

'Oh, Randall!' gasped Stella, and released the chair-back, and fled towards him, and clung to his arm.

He looked down at her with a curious lift to his brows. Guy, staring in astonishment at his sister's behaviour, saw a gleam in the blue eyes, hard to interpret.

Randall laid his hand on Stella's, but only to remove it from his sleeve. 'My precious, you really must have some regard for my clothes,' he said with gentle reproach. 'Much as I love you, I cannot permit you to maul this particular coat.' He drew her hand through his arm, and walked forward with her, his fingers still lightly clasping hers. 'Now what has been happening to upset my little cousin Stella?' he inquired of the room at large. 'Have you been accusing her of murdering my late aunt, Superintendent?'

'No,' said Hannasyde, 'I have not.'

'You had better tell me all about it,' said Randall amiably. 'I can see that you are all of you – ah, pregnant with news.'

'Really, Randall!' protested Mrs Matthews.

'They've found out what the poison was put into,' said Guy.

'Have they indeed? Well, that's very nice,' said Randall. 'And what was it put into?'

'A tube of toothpaste,' answered Guy.

Randall had led Stella to a chair, and seemed to be more interested in seeing her comfortably settled into it than in Guy's disclosure. It was just a moment before he spoke, and then he merely said: 'Really? Some ingenious brain at work, apparently.'

'That's exactly what I was thinking,' said Guy. 'Damned ingenious!'

Randall turned away from Stella, and regarded Guy with veiled amusement. 'Well, don't stop,' he said encouragingly. 'What else were you thinking?'

'I don't know that I was thinking of anything else,' said Guy slowly.

'Physical disability, or cousinly forbearance?' inquired Randall, taking a cigarette out of his case and setting it between his lips.

'Neither. But Stella was saying just as you came in that perhaps Aunt Harriet was mixed up in some way with that missing fellow you told us about. Perhaps she knew too much, and that was why she was poisoned.'

Randall lit his cigarette. 'On no account miss tomorrow's instalment of this thrilling story,' he murmured. 'What do you call it, sweetheart? *The Hand of Death*? I can see that the Superintendent is positively spellbound. And so Aunt Harriet carried her secret with her to the grave! Well, well!'

'It isn't funny!' snapped Guy.

'Not in the least; it's maudlin,' said Randall crushingly.

'I don't see why there shouldn't be something in it. After all – '

Randall moaned, and covered his eyes with his hand. 'My poor little cousin, have you *no* sense of the ludicrous?'

'Randall, there might have been something we didn't know about,' Stella said in a low voice.

He glanced down at her. 'In Aunt Harriet's life? Pull yourself together, darling.'

It was at this moment that Mrs Lupton sailed into the room, swept a look round, and said in a portentous voice: 'I thought as much!'

'That's very interesting,' said Randall, turning towards her immediately. 'As much as what?'

'I have not come here to bandy words with you, Randall, but to find out what has been going on in this house. From the presence of these two gentlemen I deduce that my unfortunate sister, incredible as it may seem, was indeed poisoned. I demand to be told exactly what has happened!'

'Well, at the moment,' said Randall, 'we are discussing an entrancing theory that your unfortunate sister was murdered because she was in possession of some hideous secret.'

Mrs Lupton cast a withering glance upon him. 'Harriet was never able to keep a secret in her life,' she said. 'I do not know who was responsible for this piece of nonsense, but I may say that I strongly object to it.' She glared at Hannasyde. 'Have you found out how my sister was

257

poisoned, or are you going to tell me that you are still in the dark?'

'Your sister was poisoned through the medium of a tube of toothpaste,' answered Hannasyde, who had drawn a little way back from the group, and had been silently watching and listening.

Mrs Lupton repeated: 'A tube of toothpaste? I never heard of such a thing!'

'What a valuable contribution to our symposium!' remarked Randall.

'Who did it?' demanded Mrs Lupton sternly. 'That is what I wish to know! That is what has got to be found out! Good heavens, do you realize that not one but two murders have been committed, and not one thing has been done about it?'

'My dear aunt, "them," not "it,"' corrected Randall in a pained voice.

'I am forced to look the facts in the face,' continued Mrs Lupton, disregarding this interruption, 'and disagreeable though it may be, I am not one to shirk the truth. My brother and my sister have been murdered in cold blood, and I know of only one person who could have done it, or who had a motive for doing it!'

Mrs Matthews rose to her feet. 'If you mean me, Gertrude, pray do not hesitate to say so!' she begged. 'I am becoming quite accustomed to having the most heartless and wicked accusations made against me! But I should very much like to know how I am supposed to have got hold of any nicotine!'

'We all know how morbidly interested you are in anything to do with illness or medicine,' returned Mrs Lupton. 'No doubt you could have found out, had you wanted to, where to obtain nicotine.'

Stella sat up suddenly. 'You don't buy nicotine,' she

said. 'You extract it from tobacco. Deryk Fielding told me so. Mother wouldn't have known how to do that.'

'If it comes to that,' said Guy, 'who would know, except Fielding himself?' He looked quickly up, and across the room at his cousin, his eyes narrow all at once. 'Or – you, Randall!'

Randall was unperturbed by this attack. He merely tipped the ash off the end of his cigarette, and said: 'Somehow I thought it wouldn't be long before I was identified with the mysterious killer of Stella's little bed-time story.'

Mrs Lupton fixed him with a cold, appraising stare. 'Yes,' she said slowly, 'that is perfectly true, though what reasons you could have had for poisoning your Aunt Harriet I fail to see. But perhaps the Superintendent is not aware that you were training to be a doctor when your father died?'

'Yes, Mrs Lupton, I am aware of that,' Hannasyde replied.

'I do not say that it has necessarily any bearing on this case,' said Mrs Lupton fairly. 'But the fact remains that you have a certain medical knowledge. You had also the strongest motive of anyone for murdering your uncle Gregory.'

Stella said, grasping the arms of her chair: 'No! No, he hasn't. He doesn't want uncle's money. He told me himself he was going to get rid of it.'

An astonished silence greeted her words. Hannasyde, closely watching Randall, saw a flicker of annoyance in his face, and caught the gleam of warning in the look he flashed at Stella.

Guy broke the silence. 'You – don't – *want* – uncle's – money?' he repeated. 'What rot! I never heard such a tale!'

He burst out laughing, but Hannasyde's voice cut

through his laughter. 'That is very interesting, Mr Matthews. May I know why you don't want your inheritance?'

'It's as plain as a pikestaff!' said Guy scornfully. 'He said it so that no one should suspect him of having poisoned uncle.'

'Thank you,' said Hannasyde. 'But I spoke to your cousin, Mr Matthews, not to you.'

Randall was frowningly regarding the tip of his cigarette. He raised his eyes when Hannasyde spoke, and answered pensively: 'Well, do you know, I like to shock my family now and then, my dear Superintendent.'

'You did not by any chance mean what you said to Miss Stella Matthews?'

Randall's lip curled sardonically. 'Is it possible that anyone could wish to be rid of a large fortune?' he said mockingly. 'The answer is to be read in my relatives' expressive countenances. They are more profoundly shocked than if it had been proved to them that I murdered my uncle and my aunt.' He moved towards the table and put his cigarette out in the ashtray that stood on it. 'However, what I mean to do with my inheritance is not in the least relevant to the matter on hand. You mustn't think that I don't know how much you would like my deplorable relatives to continue their artless and revealing discussions, but – I think not, Superintendent: I think not! Let us stick to my aunt's death, shall we? You do not really believe that I had any hand in that – ah, setting aside my cousin Stella's engaging theory, of course. You suspect, and so does my dear Aunt Gertrude, that my clever Aunt Zoë, is the guilty party. I don't blame you in the least. I will even go so far as to say that I don't blame my dear Aunt Gertrude either. With her own fair hands my clever aunt built up the case against herself, and I must say it does her credit. It worries you, doesn't it, Superintendent? My Aunt Harriet's death has upset a cherished theory of your own; in fact, it is quite out of order.'

He paused, but Hannasyde only said: 'Go on, Mr Matthews.'

'It worried me too,' Randall said. 'But I have slightly the advantage of you. I know more about the eccentricities of my family. I admit, I was quite at sea until I heard how the poison had been administered. But an idea has occurred to me.' He looked round the room. 'Do any of you know what became of Uncle Gregory's tube of toothpaste?' he inquired.

No one answered for a moment; blank faces stared at him. Then Stella's chair rasped on the polished floor as she suddenly sprang up.

'Randall!' she gasped. 'You're perfectly right! Aunt Harriet took it!'

'I thought as much,' said Randall.

Mrs Matthews said in a stupefied way: 'Harriet took Gregory's toothpaste? To *use*? Well, really! How very distasteful!'

'Are you sure of this, Miss Matthews?' Hannasyde asked.

'Yes. Oh, perfectly sure! I'd forgotten all about it until my cousin asked that question. Then I remembered at once. It was the very day we found uncle's body. My aunt had his room turned out, and I met her on the landing, carrying all sorts of oddments she'd collected. I can't remember what they were – I know she had uncle's face-flannel, which she said would do for a cleaning rag, and I distinctly remember her showing me a tube of toothpaste. It was half-used, and she said she saw no reason to waste it, and was going to use it herself when she'd finished her own.'

Sergeant Hemingway, who had been till now a silent

but an intensely interested auditor, said: 'That accounts for the empty tube we found, Superintendent. She'd only just come to the end of it. It puzzled me a bit, that empty one being left on the washstand when it looked as though she'd been using the other for several days.'

Hannasyde nodded. Guy blurted out: 'Then – then Aunt Harriet's death was a pure accident?'

Mrs Lupton drew a deep breath. 'If this story is true, I can only say that it is a judgement on Harriet!' she announced. 'I warned her that her exaggerated economies would come to no good. She would not listen to me, and here is the result! It puts me out of all patience. I am utterly disgusted!'

'Gertrude dear, remember that you are speaking of the dead,' said Mrs Matthews reproachfully.

Hannasyde was still looking at Stella. 'Miss Matthews, can you remember what time it was when you met your aunt on the landing?'

Stella thought for a minute. 'Well, I don't think I can, quite. I know it was before lunch. Somewhere about twelve – but I wouldn't swear to it. It might have been later.'

'Not earlier?'

'No, I'm sure it wasn't earlier.'

'Until your aunt went to turn it out, was your uncle's bathroom locked?'

She shook her head. 'Oh, no! His bedroom wasn't either.'

'Could anyone have gone into the bathroom without being seen, do you think?'

'Yes, easily, I should imagine. Why should – oh! To take that tube away, and burn it!' She looked round, puzzled. 'But no one did. Then – then it looks as though it wasn't anyone living in the house, doesn't it?'

'We don't know that Fielding didn't try,' said Guy.

'But he didn't get the chance, because Beecher went up to uncle's room with him.'

'I'm sure it wasn't Deryk,' answered Stella shortly.

'Well, what about Randall?' said Guy. 'Just as a matter of interest, dear cousin Randall, what were you doing on the landing that day I found you talking to Stella at the top of the stairs?'

'Just talking to Stella at the top of the stairs, dear cousin Guy,' replied Randall blandly.

'Stella, what had he been up to?'

Stella glanced fleetingly at Randall, and saw that he was watching her with a faint smile. 'I don't know,' she said. 'You had better ask him. Anyway, Randall hadn't been near the house for days – ' She stopped, and her eyes widened.

'Exactly!' said Guy triumphantly. 'Randall hadn't been near the house for days, and therefore Randall never even came under suspicion. But the poison could have been put into the toothpaste at any time, and none of Randall's perfect alibis exist any longer. He hasn't got an alibi!'

14

Everyone but Stella looked at Randall. Stella cried hotly: 'You're a rotten little cad, Guy! Randall never tried to cast suspicion on to you!'

'Randall's said every spiteful, low-down thing – '

'Yes, because half the time we asked for it! But he didn't try and do the dirty on you, and you know it!'

'What the devil's the matter with you?' demanded Guy, surprised into forgetfulness of his surroundings. 'You yourself said he was an amiable snake!'

A low laugh escaped the subject of this argument. 'My sweet, did you really?' said Randall. 'What a classic phrase!'

'I daresay I did once, but – '

'Oh, don't take it back!' said Randall. 'I like it. And don't bite your little brother's head off either. That isn't a bit necessary. It is perfectly true – one might say obvious – that I have no alibi, but then Superintendent Hannasyde, who is quite as quick in the uptake as Guy, if not quicker, probably realized that for himself some time ago. If you look carefully at him you will observe a slight hint of annoyance – one might almost say chagrin – in his face. That is because he, unlike Guy, has also realized that my entry into the ranks of suspects hasn't eliminated all other suspects, but has merely enlarged the field.'

Hannasyde had listened to this with an unmoved countenance. He said in his impersonal way: 'That is quite true, Mr Matthews. But at the same time – '

'Moreover,' continued Randall, lighting another cigarette, 'you have no better case against me than you have against anyone else. It is true that I have inherited quite a lot of money, but the most cursory investigation into my affairs will convince you (in spite of the belief current amongst my relations that I have run through a fortune) that I stand in no need of my uncle's money.'

'That may also be true,' said Hannasyde. 'Nor do I propose to go into the matter with you at this particular moment.'

Randall looked round the room. 'No, there is rather a crowd,' he agreed. 'Stella, my lamb, let us withdraw, and perhaps that will put it into Aunt Gertrude's head that she is not really wanted here.'

He clasped his fingers round her wrist as he spoke, and drew her towards the door. Sergeant Hemingway looked quickly at the Superintendent, but Hannasyde made no sign. Mrs Lupton began to say that she expected nothing but rudeness from Randall, but before she could finish her severe and well-worded speech he had gone.

In the hall he paused, and looked down at Stella, the smile lingering about the corners of his mouth. 'Well, my love?' he said. 'Why didn't you tell the police that you found me coming out of uncle's bathroom?'

'I don't know,' said Stella childishly.

'Let us go into the morning-room,' he said. 'I have a much worse question coming.'

Stella allowed herself to be led into the morning-room, but said: 'Well, only for a minute, then. I – I can't stop long.'

Randall paid no heed to this. He shut the door, and said quite gravely: 'Why did you run to me as though I were your one hope of deliverance, Stella?'

She blushed. 'Oh, I didn't! I mean – you told me you'd see the thing through, and – and I thought you might help us. I was a bit upset.' She gave a nervous little laugh. 'Sorry I clutched your beautiful coat!'

The smile had gone; there was not even a gleam of mockery lurking beneath those long lashes. 'My coat did not matter,' said Randall.

'Oh! Well, one wouldn't have said so, considering the way you – '

'My dear, did you think I was going to let you give yourself away with all our relations present?'

'Give myself – !' Stella broke off, choking. 'I don't know what you think you're talking about, but – '

'Don't dither, my sweet. Tell me, is my grey hall an insuperable bar to matrimony?'

'Yes!' said Stella hurriedly. 'I mean – '

'I suppose I shall have to let you redecorate it as you like then,' replied Randall. 'But I do stipulate that Guy shall not be allowed to have a hand in it.'

Stella, whose brain was whirling, said in an uncertain voice: 'I don't call this particularly funny. It may be your idea of a joke, but it isn't mine.'

Randall took her hands. 'I'm not joking, darling. I'm asking you to marry me. Will you?'

'No, of c-course not!' said Stella, wondering why her knees had begun to shake.

Randall held her hands for a minute longer, and then let them go and moved away towards the door. Stella looked after him with deep misgiving. 'Are – are you going?' she faltered.

'As you see.'

'But – but you can't leave me – us – like this!'

'Which do you mean?' asked Randall. 'Me, or us?'

'Us! All of us! You can't surely – '

'Oh yes, I can!' said Randall coolly, and laid his hand on the door-knob.

Stella said in some agitation: 'I'm not going to be blackmailed into marrying you!'

He turned his head, and surveyed her enigmatically.

'What do you want?' he asked. 'If you are worrying about your mother's probable arrest, let me assure you that the police are now far more likely to arrest me.'

'I'm not! I mean, it isn't only that! Oh, Randall, don't be such a vile beast!'

'I don't think much of that,' he said critically. 'Amiable snake was far better.'

Stella hunted for her handkerchief, and said, sniffing: 'Yes, I've no doubt you'll throw that up at me for the rest of my life. I can't imagine what possessed you to propose to me.'

'Well, that will give you something to puzzle over any time you can't sleep,' said Randall.

'You know perfectly well you don't really want to marry me!'

An expression of weary boredom descended on to Randall's face. He leaned his shoulders against the door, and said: 'Do I have to make a reply to that utterly fatuous remark?'

'You think I'm fatuous, and stupid, and haven't any taste, and then you expect me to believe you want to marry me! It doesn't make sense! There's no point in discussing it, even!'

'You may have noticed,' drawled Randall, 'that I am making no attempt to discuss it.'

Stella threw him a goaded look. 'I'm perfectly willing to be friends with you – '

'Yes, I've no doubt,' said Randall, 'but I am not in the least willing to be friends with you.'

'Very well, then, go!' said Stella, turning her back on him, and staring blindly out of the window. 'I don't c-care!'

The door opened, and then shut again. Stella gave a despairing sob, and wept silently into her handkerchief.

'You'd better have mine, darling: it's larger,' said Randall's soft voice just behind her.

Stella jumped, and quavered: '*S-snake!* I loathe and detest you!'

'I know you do,' said Randall, taking her in his arms, and quite firmly possessing himself of her handkerchief.

'You'll be sorry if I cry all over your beautiful c-coat!' said Stella from his shoulder.

'Forget my beautiful coat!' said Randall.

Stella groped for his handkerchief. He gave it her, and she carefully dried her eyes with it. 'If I do marry you it won't be because I'm in love with you, because of course I'm not!' she said.

'Very well, you can marry me for my money,' replied Randall equably.

Stella, having finished with it, savagely thrust his handkerchief back into his breast-pocket. 'You have the foulest tongue of anyone I ever met in all my life!' she said with conviction. 'If I didn't want to get away from this place I wouldn't think of marrying you for a moment! And if I do marry you it'll probably be as bad as living here, or even worse,' she added vindictively.

'Nothing could be as bad as living here,' said Randall reasonably. 'I may be a vile beast, but at least I'm not a bore. By the way, are you going to marry me, or not?'

Stella looked for guidance at the top button of his waistcoat, and discovered that there was a smear of face-powder on the lapel of his coat, and rubbed it away with one finger.

A hand came up and captured hers, and held it. 'You are required to answer, you know,' said Randall.

She raised her eyes rather shyly, and blushed. 'Randall, do you – *truly* want me to?' she asked in a very small voice.

'My dear sweet,' said Randall, and kissed her.

During the next ten minutes Stella made only two remarks, both of which were somewhat breathlessly delivered, and neither of which bore any evidence of intellect. Mr Randall Matthews said 'Darling!' in answer to one, and 'My little idiot!' in answer to the other. Miss Stella Matthews appeared to be perfectly satisfied with both these responses.

'I must have gone suddenly mad,' she said, a little while later. 'I don't even admire your type. And how on earth am I to tell Mummy and Guy about it? They'll never believe I mean it!'

'After this morning's exhibition they are probably prepared for the worst,' replied Randall. 'But I'll break the news for you, my pet.'

'Oh no, you won't!' said Stella with decision. 'I can just picture that scene! You'll absolutely swear to me, darling-serpent-Randall, that you won't say one single thing to annoy either of them.'

'I can't,' said Randall. 'I shall have to leave it to you.' He glanced at his wrist-watch. 'I shall have to go, darling. If I don't we shall have that Superintendent arresting somebody – me in all probability.'

Stella put her hand in his. 'Randall, you didn't – have anything to do with it, did you?'

'No, darling, in spite of every appearance to the contrary, I didn't.'

She looked at him. 'Do you know who did?'

He did not answer immediately. Then his clasp on her hand tightened, and he said: 'Yes. I think so.'

'Is it – going to be beastly?'

'Yes, very. Oh, not Aunt Zoë, sweetheart. But I'm afraid it may upset you.'

'Are you going to tell the police, Randall?'

'I must tell them. I did every mortal thing I could think of to stop them from finding out the truth, and I succeeded

269

so well that we are now most of us in danger of instant arrest. All through Aunt Harriet's accidental death! It is, I suppose, rather delightfully ironic, if you happen to be looking at it from the right angle.'

'Can't you tell me, Randall? I'd rather know.'

'Not now, my sweet. I think it's better kept to myself until I've done what I've got to do.'

'Tell me just one thing,' she said. 'Is it something to do with that man – the one they can't find?'

'Everything,' he answered, and kissed her, and got up from the sofa. 'I'll ring you up tonight, my love. Don't worry!'

'As long as they don't arrest Mummy or Guy while you're gone,' she said doubtfully.

'They won't do that. They'll merely interrogate them in the light of the new discovery, and I don't suppose that even your little brother Guy can compromise himself sufficiently to make Hannasyde apply for a warrant for his arrest. Moreover, Hannasyde is hot on my trail now, and will in all probability put in some hours of research into my immediate past.'

It seemed as though he was right. When Superintendent Hannasyde saw Stella twenty minutes later he asked her if Randall were still in the house. When she shook her head he looked at her (or so she thought) rather intently, and inquired whether she knew where he had gone. She was glad to be able to say that she had no idea, but felt herself blushing. However, the Superintendent either did not notice this, or else he set no store by it, for he merely said that he expected he should find Randall at his flat, and went away with the Sergeant.

The Sergeant was in a thoughtful mood; and while they walked down the drive he did not speak. But at the gate he said: 'Chief, I don't set myself up to know better than

270

you, but when you let him go you could have knocked me down with a feather.'

'You know perfectly well I've no warrant for his arrest,' said Hannasyde.

'You didn't think to put a few questions to him?' ventured the Sergeant.

'Not then, or in that house. I'll see him in his own flat, where I trust we shall not be interrupted either by hysterical young men, or importunate matrons,' said Hannasyde a trifle grimly.

'Do you think he did it, Super?' inquired the Sergeant.

'No, I don't.'

The Sergeant stopped short. 'You don't?' he repeated. 'What about that line of talk he put over about giving away all his uncle's money?'

'He didn't say anything about that to me,' said Hannasyde, with what his subordinate could only feel to be wooden placidity.

'He seems to have said it to the girl all right,' the Sergeant pointed out, once more falling into step beside him.

'That's a very different matter.'

'It is, is it?' said the Sergeant. 'I'm bound to say I don't see it myself, not immediately.'

'Ah, Skipper, that's where psychology comes in!' said Hannasyde maliciously. 'Randall Matthews wasn't pleased with Miss Stella for blurting that out.'

The Sergeant eyed him sideways, and with a good deal of expression, but all he said was: 'Well, bearing his antics in mind, and assuming that he didn't put that murder over, what is his little game, Super?'

'I suspect,' said Hannasyde, 'to prevent us from ever finding out the truth.'

'Chief,' said the Sergeant severely, 'you've got something up your sleeve!'

271

'I think I've got an inkling of the truth,' admitted Hannasyde. 'Which is why I'd rather interview Randall Matthews where I can be sure of getting him quite alone. That young man has got to be made to talk.'

But when they arrived at Randall's flat they found only Benson, who informed them, not without satisfaction, that his master was out, and not expected back until the evening.

The Sergeant, bristling with suspicion, said: 'You don't say! Taken the Merc with him, by any chance?'

'If,' said Benson, with awful dignity, 'you refer to the Mercédès-Benz, no, Sergeant! The car is in the garage.'

'Mr Matthews has been here, then, within the past hour?' interposed Hannasyde.

'Certainly he has,' replied Benson. He added grudgingly: 'What's more, Mr Matthews left a message in case you should call.'

'Well?'

'He will not be at home all day, but if you care to come round at nine o'clock this evening he will be happy to see you,' said Benson.

'Tell him when he comes in that I shall call at that time, then,' said Hannasyde, and moved away towards the stairs.

'And what,' demanded the Sergeant, 'is my lord up to now, if I may ask?'

'You may ask,' said Hannasyde, 'but I'm damned if I can tell you. Unless, for some reason or other, he wants to ward me off for a few hours.'

'We'll look clever if the next we hear of him is on the Continent somewhere,' remarked the Sergeant.

'What's gone wrong with your psychology?' asked Hannasyde solicitously.

'There's nothing gone wrong with it,' said the Sergeant. 'But if you weren't my superior, Chief – I say, *if* you weren't – I should be asking you what had happened to make you lose your grip all of a sudden. The way things are, of course, I can't ask you.'

'Don't worry!' said Hannasyde. 'I haven't lost it yet. You can put a man on to watch that flat, if it will make you feel happier. Tell him to report to the Yard anything that happens – particularly Randall's return.'

'Well, that's better than doing nothing,' said the Sergeant. 'Do you expect to get any good out of it?'

'No, but it's as well to be on the safe side,' answered Hannasyde.

It was not until eight o'clock in the evening that the detective watching the flat got into touch with Sergeant Hemingway at Scotland Yard. He rang up then with the news that Randall had come home five minutes before.

The Sergeant relayed this information, and waited for instructions.

'Just on eight o'clock,' said Hannasyde, glancing at his wristwatch. 'He's come home to dinner, I should say. Tell Jepson to keep a sharp look-out, and if Matthews goes out again to tail him.'

But Randall did not go out again, and when Hannasyde arrived at his flat at nine o'clock he was ushered immediately into the library, and found Randall there, lounging in the depths of a large armchair, with a coffee-tray on a low table beside him.

He was looking tired, and not in the least amiable. There was a crease between his black brows, and a grimness about his mouth which Hannasyde had never seen before. He dragged himself out of the chair when the Superintendent came in, and greeted him for once without the faint, sardonic smile which Hannasyde found so irritating.

'Come in, Superintendent,' he said. 'Where is your satellite?'

273

'I'm alone,' replied Hannasyde.

Randall looked him over. 'How fortunate! I wanted you alone,' he said.

'I thought perhaps you might,' said Hannasyde.

Randall continued to regard him for a moment, and then bent over the table and picked up the coffee-pot. 'Did you?' he said. 'Do you know, I begin to think rather well of your intelligence, Superintendent.'

'I have always thought well of yours, Mr Matthews, though I may not have approved the uses it has been put to,' retorted Hannasyde.

At that the smile did flicker for an instant in Randall's eyes. 'Tut, tut, Superintendent.' He handed a fragile cup and saucer to Hannasyde. 'Brandy, or Benedictine?'

'Thank you; brandy, please.'

'A red-letter day,' remarked Randall, pouring the brandy gently into two big glasses. 'Superintendent Hannasyde for the first time accepts refreshment under my roof.'

Hannasyde took the glass, and said: 'Yes. But I believe it is also a red-letter day in that you are going – at last – to tell me what, up till now, you have been so busily concealing.'

'Cigars at your elbow,' murmured Randall. 'It is a thoroughly nauseating affair, Superintendent, and I may mention in passing that my thoughts of my deceased Aunt Harriet are not loving ones.' He sipped his brandy. 'Do you want me to remember that you are a member of the CID, or would you like me to tell you the unvarnished truth?'

'The unvarnished truth, please.'

'Yes, I daresay,' Randall drawled. 'But it will have to be without prejudice, Superintendent.'

Hannasyde hesitated. 'I can't promise anything, but I'm out to solve a murder-case, not to bring a charge against you for getting hold of Hyde's papers by using a false name and a pair of sun-glasses.'

'It would be rather paltry, wouldn't it?' agreed Randall.

'Worse than that. I rather think you may have been within your rights when you took possession of those papers.'

Randall looked pensively down at him. 'Now, when did you tumble to that, Superintendent?' he asked.

'When your cousin told me that you were going to give away all your uncle's money, Mr Matthews.'

'Ah!' said Randall. 'That was certainly a mistake on my part.' He walked across the room to his desk, and picked up the evening paper that lay there, and came slowly back with it. 'I think that's the most important part of my story – as far as you are concerned,' he said, and handed the paper to Hannasyde. 'The second paragraph,' he said.

Hannasyde shot one quick look at him, and then lowered his gaze to the column just below the fold in the newspaper.

Accident on the Piccadilly Tube was the heading. Underneath was a brief statement that shortly after three o'clock in the afternoon a middle-aged man threw himself in front of an express train at Hyde Park Corner Station. It was understood that the man was a Mr Edward Rumbold, of Holly Lodge, Grinley Heath, well-known in City circles as the head of a firm of wool-exporters.

Hannasyde read it deliberately through, and then laid down the paper. 'I think you have a good deal to explain to me, Mr Matthews,' he said sternly. 'What am I to understand by this?'

Randall finished his brandy, and set the glass down on the mantelpiece behind him. 'Well, there won't be a case, Superintendent,' he answered.

'*He* murdered your uncle?'

'Incredible, isn't it?' said Randall. 'But quite true. Only I think we won't call it murder. My uncle had been blackmailing him for years.'

'Then your uncle *was* John Hyde?' Hannasyde said swiftly.

'Yes, he was. But you'd already guessed that, I think. I hope you appreciate his choice of pseudonym. He had a pretty sense of humour, hadn't he?'

'How long have you known this?' demanded Hannasyde.

'Known for certain? Since the day I visited your friend Brown. He rather thought he had seen me before. I am not at all unlike my uncle.'

'But you suspected before that?'

'Oh yes, some time before.'

Hannasyde brought his hand down on his knee. 'Now I know what it was you saw in that drawer!' he said, annoyance in his voice. 'I ought to have thought of that sooner!'

Randall looked down at him with faint amusement. 'My dear Superintendent! What drawer?'

'In your uncle's desk. There was a pair of sun-glasses, horn-rimmed. I thought at the time that you had expected to see something which *wasn't* there.'

Randall gave a little laugh. 'Oh no! But my uncle not only never wore sun-glasses, but poured scorn on those who did. I merely thought it a little odd when I saw that pair in his desk. I think, you know, that I had better tell you just what happened.'

Hannasyde nodded, and watched him move towards the deep chair, and sit down on one of its arms.

Randall lit a cigarette, and smoked in silence for a minute, frowning. 'Well, to go back to the very beginning, Edward Rumbold had a wife living in Australia. The lady at Holly Lodge isn't aware of this – but as Rumbold was not our friend's real name, I hardly think it will be necessary to tell her that she has been bigamously married for the past ten years, do you?'

'I don't know. Please go on!'

'My uncle, under the name of John Hyde, was, even as far back as that date, carrying on quite a lucrative, though not extensive, business in the blackmailing line. What led him to start it, I can't tell you, nor have I discovered who, or perhaps what, it was that first put him on to Rumbold's track. From indications amongst his papers, I imagine that his methods were painstaking rather than brilliant. He got a lot of information through the usual sources, of course, but this particular information was supplied by a firm of private detectives in Melbourne. The real Mrs Rumbold – but her name is Fletcher – is a Roman Catholic of extreme piety and rigour. Hence the reason Rumbold was not able to get a divorce.' He paused, and flicked the ash from his cigarette on to the floor. 'Well, all that isn't very interesting. We'll go on to my charming uncle's part in the affair. He got together the facts – oh, some time before Rumbold went to live next door to him! – and he applied pressure with the usual results. Only he mistook his man. Rumbold paid all right, and went on paying, but he set himself to discover the identity of his blackmailer. He had never set eyes on my uncle, but he watched that newsagent's shop for weeks – till he was sure that the spectacled man who continually visited it, and stayed so long in it, must be Hyde. Then he shadowed Hyde, and in the end he identified him with Gregory Matthews. That was four years ago. I like to think of that grim, patient determination to kill my uncle. I am only sorry that, in the nature of things, my uncle couldn't know that sooner or later he was going to be killed by one of his own victims. He didn't even suspect that Rumbold knew whom he was. Not even when Rumbold went to live at Holly Lodge. He bought that house, knowing that the existing tenants' lease expired in two years' time. When they left the house he and Mrs Rumbold moved into it. You know, I admire him, don't you? He did nothing in a hurry. He just cultivated his next-door neighbours. He became the ideal Friend of the Family. He even played chess with my uncle – and let him win. I hope you appreciate that situation. My uncle, I am convinced, derived intense amusement from it. So did Rumbold. It took him eighteen months to reach the state of intimacy with my family which would allow him to become a *persona grata* about the house. When he had been at Holly Lodge about two years – long enough for him to be no suspicious newcomer to the district, I hope you realize – he put his four-year-old plan into execution. It isn't a very difficult matter, given a smattering of chemistry, to get nicotine out of tobacco, and it wasn't difficult to find an opportunity to substitute his poisoned tube of toothpaste for the one my uncle was using. He effected the exchange on the day he and his wife called at the Poplars to take leave of my aunts before going for a week or ten days to the sea. Then he went away with Mrs Rumbold, and stayed away until after my uncle's death.' Again he paused, and glanced at Hannasyde. 'It is rather staggering, isn't it? Nothing left to chance, nothing done in a hurry. The idea was that no one but himself would ever know that my uncle had been poisoned, but he provided himself with an unshakable alibi in case of accidents. And there were two accidents. First, that damnable aunt of mine demanded a post-mortem. Why she did, what prompted her, God alone knows! And second, my deplorable Aunt Harriet's magpie-instincts caused her to walk off with that tube of poisoned tooth-paste. When Rumbold returned to Holly Lodge his first care was to find and dispose of that tube. He and his wife went to condole with my aunts, and he contrived, with my Aunt Harriet's unwitting help, to dirty his hands among the flower-pots in the conservatory. He went upstairs to wash them in my uncle's bathroom, and he found it swept bare. That was the first hint he had that things were going wrong. He was worried, but a casual question put to my Aunt Harriet – actually in my presence – brought forth the information that she had burned such of my uncle's possessions as were of no use to anybody. He not unnaturally assumed that the toothpaste must have been among them. Well, he went on being the perfect Friend of the Family. He was indeed genuinely sorry for the unpleasantness the family was going through, and he did what he could to smooth things, and to keep my somewhat excitable relatives moderately calm. What he did not bargain for was to find Fielding with a motive for having committed the murder. He knew that Guy was bound to be a suspect, but he credited you with sufficient intelligence, Superintendent, to doubt Guy's capability. Which I think you did.'

'Yes, from the first,' Hannasyde said curtly. 'Not the type to use a rare poison. But go on, please.'

'Fielding,' Randall said. 'Well, Fielding looked like becoming a complication. Rumbold didn't want anyone to suffer the consequences of his crime. If the worst came to the worst, he was prepared to clear up the mess. But he kept his head, and waited. Things looked like blowing over. That was thanks to me, but he didn't know that. Then an entirely unforeseen disaster occurred in the death of my Aunt Harriet. Rumbold was not only horrified on his own account; he was profoundly upset on hers. When he heard what sort of a case my clever Aunt Zoë had built up against herself, he realized that he might have to intervene to save her from arrest at any moment. When I came down, and dropped some of my more airy remarks on the subject of Hyde he guessed that I should probably save him the trouble of telling you the truth. By that time it looked to me as though I should have to. Partly owing to fright and partly to innate hypocrisy, my Aunt Zoë, was queering her own pitch by telling you improbable lies, while Guy, from what I was able to gather, had thought it the moment to make a grand gesture with the noble intention of saving his mother from the scaffold, and the quite opposite effect of making you suspect her rather more strongly than before. But the worst was that you had discovered the medium through which the poison was administered. Once you had that you weren't likely to let up on the case. It was entirely obvious to me that I was, with the destruction of my alibi, the hottest candidate for arrest. Well, Superintendent, Rumbold had my approval, but I can't say that I felt the least inclination to perish without a cry either to protect him or the family honour. Obviously, I should have to cry extremely loudly, whether you arrested me, or my Aunt Zoë, or my irrelevant cousin, Guy. Well, I have a rooted objection to loud noises. That is why Rumbold has committed suicide – in a fit of temporary insanity, shall we say? – and why you are here, listening to me without prejudice.'

Hannasyde got up. 'Mr Matthews, do you realize the part you've played in this?' he demanded.

'None better,' said Randall. 'I rather think I must be an accessory after the fact.'

'Do you imagine that I can possibly hush this up?'

'Well, what do you propose to do about it?' Randall inquired amiably. 'Are you going to get the Public Prosecutor to bring a case against a dead man?'

'Have you any proof of what you've told me?'

'There will be Rumbold's written statement, and I have preserved for your perusal the evidence culled from my

Uncle Hyde's papers. In my character of executor I burned everything but the documents that dealt with Rumbold's case. I think your department will keep it as quiet as possible, Superintendent. Cases of the murder of blackmailers are rather ticklish, aren't they? So few people have any sympathy with the victim. You can, of course, bring a case against me for suppressing evidence, but under the circumstances, I'm inclined to think that might be a bit ticklish, too. You would merely stir up a great deal of mud for nothing. May I offer you a whiskey-and-soda?'

'Yes, you may!' said Hannasyde, with something of a snap.

Randall gave his soft laugh, and went over to a table against the wall where the whiskey decanter stood, and mixed two drinks. He came back with them, and gave one to Hannasyde. 'Well, Superintendent?' he said.

Hannasyde sat down again. 'You had better tell me the rest of it. If I choose to bring it up against you at a prosecution, it will only be my word against yours,' he added sarcastically.

'I shouldn't dream of contradicting you,' said Randall in his most dulcet voice.

'When did you see Rumbold?'

'Today, when I left Grinley Heath.'

'Where? Not at his home?'

'No, certainly not. At his office. He was quite prepared for my visit. We went out to lunch together, and over lunch he told me what I have told you, and I described to him my part in the affair, and gave him my word that I would do what lay in my power to keep the truth from Mrs Rumbold.'

There was not a trace of expression in Randall's voice, but Hannasyde cast one shrewd glance at him, and said

281

in a softer tone: 'Not – a very pleasant lunch, Mr Matthews.'

Randall said dryly: 'That, Superintendent, is putting it mildly.'

Hannasyde nodded. 'I can guess how you must feel about it.'

'Let's leave it at that, shall we?' suggested Randall, with an edge to his voice.

Hannasyde sipped his drink for a while in silence. Presently he said: 'And that's why you so carefully stayed away from here all day? To give Rumbold time to do away with himself?'

'You will have a great deal of difficulty in proving that, my dear Superintendent.'

Hannasyde smiled somewhat wryly, but all he said was: 'Did you expect to find some of the Hyde-papers in your uncle's desk that day you went down to the Poplars with Mr Carrington and me?'

'No, it hadn't dawned on me then. I expected to find what we did find – letters relating to my Uncle Henry's affair. Luckily, not as bad as they might have been.'

Hannasyde could not forbear a grin. 'You behaved atrociously over that, Mr Matthews.'

'At least I not only got rid of my dear Aunt Gertrude for you, but quite effectually stopped her smelling any rat.'

'Well, yes,' admitted Hannasyde. 'Still – ! Was it the sun-glasses that gave it to you?'

'Not immediately. I don't think I can tell you when I first began to suspect. It was the quite freely-expressed opinion of my late father that my uncle was a bad hat, so that I started with an advantage over you in that I was prejudiced against him. Then, too, I had been privileged to observe his handling of my Uncle Henry, and of Dr Fielding. Probably that modified form of blackmail may have put the idea into my head. It – ah, burst into flower when you came to see me one day, and asked me what the name of Hyde conveyed to me. I rather think that I may have been a trifle flippant with you, Superintendent.'

'Very,' said Hannasyde emphatically. 'You suggested first Parks, and then Stevenson.'

'And no sooner was the word out of my mouth,' said Randall, 'than the idea of a dual personality flashed into my head. Not altogether unnaturally. You told me where Hyde lived, and I paid a call on his friend Brown, which I told you all about.'

'Oh, not quite all, Mr Matthews!'

Randall smiled. 'Well, let us say all that it was desirable you should know. When he was induced to divulge where Hyde had kept the key of his safe, I had no doubt that Hyde was none other than my uncle. A pleasing discovery, I can assure you.'

'That was why you looked as though you were ripe for murder when I suggested there had been a bond of sympathy between you?' said Hannasyde.

'Did I? I was certainly not flattered.'

'When did you get the key of that safe?'

'On the day of my uncle's funeral. His watch-chain, with the trinkets that hung on it, were in the drawer of his dressing-table.'

'After which,' said Hannasyde heavily, 'you got me to remove the detective who was watching you, so that you could visit that safe-deposit.'

Randall's eyes gleamed. 'My dear Superintendent, how can you say so? All I did was to complain of his boots.'

'Well, let that go,' said Hannasyde. 'You put that notice in the paper so that you could get to Hyde's paper's.'

'And I have wanted so much to ask you how you got on with the General?' murmured Randall.

'Never mind that now. You took everything out of the safe, and burned it?'

'Everything except the papers relating to Rumbold. Those I kept in case of accidents.'

'And you were going to hush the whole thing up? Let Rumbold get away with it?'

'You must remember that I am not a policeman, Superintendent. I am merely concerned with my family's good name.'

'However much I personally may sympathize with that point of view, it was wrong, Mr Matthews!'

'Well, that isn't going to worry me,' said Randall tranquilly.

'Where is that statement you said you had for me?' asked Hannasyde.

Randall looked at him with amused comprehension. 'My dear Superintendent! Oh, but this isn't worthy of you! Did you really think I was going to hand it you, all guileless and trusting?'

'Where is it?' repeated Hannasyde.

Randall finished what was left of his drink. 'It's in the post, of course, and will reach you at Scotland Yard tomorrow morning.'

Hannasyde smiled reluctantly. 'You think of everything, don't you?'

'Well, not quite,' said Randall modestly.

Hannasyde set down his glass, and rose. 'I think I'll go and sleep on it,' he said. 'You don't seem to have left me much else to do – except clear up the mess.'

'You wrong me, Superintendent: there's very little mess. Much less than you would have made.'

'Yes,' admitted Hannasyde. 'From your point of view that's true enough. I take it your name doesn't figure in Rumbold's statement?'

'Oh no!' said Randall with a sleepy smile. 'I don't come into the case at all, my dear Superintendent.'

284